THE
BRAWL

WALL STREET JOURNAL & *USA TODAY* BESTSELLING AUTHOR

DEVNEY PERRY

THE BRAWL

Copyright © 2022 by Devney Perry LLC

All rights reserved.

ISBN: 978-1-957376-23-3

This is a work of fiction. Names, characters, places and incidents are the product of the author's imagination or are used fictitiously. Any resemblance to actual events, locales or persons, living or dead, is coincidental.

Editing & Proofreading:

Elizabeth Nover, Razor Sharp Editing

Julie Deaton, Deaton Author Services

Judy Zweifel, Judy's Proofreading

Cover:

Sarah Hansen © Okay Creations

OTHER TITLES

Calamity Montana Series

The Bribe

The Bluff

The Brazen

The Bully

The Brawl

The Brood

The Edens Series

Christmas in Quincy - Prequel

Indigo Ridge

Juniper Hill

Garnet Flats

Jasper Vale

Crimson River

Sable Peak

Treasure State Wildcats Series

Coach

Blitz

Clifton Forge Series

Steel King

Riven Knight

Stone Princess

Noble Prince

Fallen Jester

Tin Queen

Jamison Valley Series

The Coppersmith Farmhouse

The Clover Chapel

The Lucky Heart

The Outpost

The Bitterroot Inn

The Candle Palace

Maysen Jar Series

The Birthday List

Letters to Molly

The Dandelion Diary

Lark Cove Series

Tattered

Timid

Tragic

Tinsel

Timeless

Runaway Series

Runaway Road

Wild Highway

Quarter Miles

Forsaken Trail

Dotted Lines

Holiday Brothers Series

The Naughty, The Nice and The Nanny

Three Bells, Two Bows and One Brother's Best Friend

A Partridge and a Pregnancy

Standalones

Ivy

Rifts and Refrains

A Little Too Wild

CHAPTER ONE

RONAN

THE MAN outside my office window glared at my car's license plate as he strolled down the sidewalk.

"Why do Montanans hate Californians?"

My brother had warned me about this when I'd told him I was moving to Montana. I'd waved it off, but maybe he had a point.

Gertrude, my new assistant, shrugged. "Hate is a strong word."

"Dislike," I corrected. In the past seven hours, I'd learned that Gertrude was a tad on the literal side. "Why do Montanans *dislike* Californians?"

"Mostly because Californians move to Montana and try to make Montana like California," she said.

I hummed. "Well, fear not. I have no desire to change Calamity."

This town was perfect, a relatively undiscovered jewel in southwest Montana, nestled in a mountain valley surrounded by indigo peaks. It was everything I'd hoped for as I ventured into this next chapter of my life.

Roughly two thousand people called Calamity home. A far cry from the hundreds of thousands in San Francisco. There would be no traffic jams. No crowded aisles at the grocery store. Police sirens wouldn't wail around the clock, and I doubted I'd turn on the local news to a report of gang violence. Did Calamity even have a local news channel?

Probably not. I made a mental note to snag a subscription to the newspaper.

But even though the town was small, there were enough residents in the area that minor trouble would undoubtedly arise, requiring the services of a lawyer. And, effective today, Thatcher Law was open for business.

There hadn't been a crush stampeding through the door when we'd opened at nine. We actually hadn't had anyone stop by today, but eventually, word would spread that there was a new lawyer in town—me. Then business would pick up. That was, if my future clientele could get over the fact that I hailed from California.

"I should probably update the registration on my car and get new license plates."

Gertrude nodded. "Sooner rather than later."

Literal, and brutally honest.

Gertrude and I were going to get along just fine.

I walked to the window that overlooked First Street, taking in the slice of downtown by my office. Nearly every building had a square roofline, the properties either butting up against one another or separated by a narrow alley. The place across the street had a faded, red brick exterior and had probably been built a hundred years ago. The building beside it had a graying barnwood façade.

In any other town, the Western element might have seemed cheap and forced. Here, it was as authentic as the big, blue sky.

Proving that I was equally authentic was going to be my challenge here, wasn't it? Showing Calamity that I wasn't some smarmy lawyer trying to bleed them dry with an outrageous hourly fee was top priority.

For the most part, the community seemed rather friendly. Granted, I'd only been here since Saturday. Three days wasn't long enough to pass final judgment. But when I'd come downtown yesterday to check out the office, catch up with Gertrude and make sure everything was ready for our first official day in business, people had offered me smiles and hellos.

Except on Sunday, when I'd popped into the gas station for a six-pack of beer. The attendant—an older gentleman with a gray beard braided beneath his chin—had taken one look at my driver's license and grumbled under his breath. And yesterday, when I'd picked up a medium, thin-crust pepperoni from Pizza Palace, the woman at the register had asked how long I was vacationing in Calamity. When I'd told her that I'd just moved here from California, her lip had curled.

Eventually, they'd realize I had no intention of leaving. As of Saturday, I was no longer a Californian. Still, I'd put a rush on the plates for the car. And a new driver's license. That ought to make it easier to distinguish me from random tourists, right?

"If you're trying to fit in, you might want to lose the tie," Gertrude said.

I turned from the glass, looking down at the gray silk tie I'd picked this morning because it matched my slacks. "What's wrong with my tie?"

"It's very . . . fancy."

Fancy? Good thing I'd left two of the three pieces of this suit in my closet. "I'm not really a Wrangler jeans and square-toed boots kind of guy, Gerty. Can I call you Gerty?"

Her lips pursed.

"We'll test it out this week." I grinned, tugging loose the half Windsor knot at my throat.

With the tie folded and stowed in my pocket, I opened the button at my collar, then uncuffed my white shirt at the wrists, rolling each sleeve up my forearm.

"So . . ." I clapped my hands. "What's next?"

Gertrude adjusted her fuchsia glasses, lifting them higher on her nose before clicking the mouse to wake up her computer. "I believe I've made it through your entire list with the exception of your shelves. I'm still working on unboxing books."

"Excellent. You've done a hell of a job getting this place set up. Thank you."

"It's what you're paying me to do. But you're welcome."

"Any chance you want to help me unpack my house?"

"No."

I chuckled. That was a hard no if I'd ever heard one.

I smoothed a hand over the cognac leather couch beside me. Matching chairs were staged in front of the window. A fiddle-leaf tree sat in the corner, a fresh bouquet of tulips on the rustic coffee table beside a few magazines.

The space was cozy and intimate, entirely different than the modern six-story firm I'd left in San Francisco. Gertrude's desk sat opposite the sitting area, positioned so that she could greet clients as they came inside. My office was beyond the sitting area. There was one bathroom. One kitchenette. One conference room with a long table and—empty—bookshelves.

The walls were lacking artwork but I was hoping to buy some local pieces. Reese Huxley Art across the street looked promising.

This office wasn't big. I didn't need much space, considering it would just be Gertrude and me for the foreseeable future. But it was comfortable and the owners of the building had recently remodeled this unit as well as the studio apartment on the second floor.

Next door was a retail shop clearly aimed at drawing in tourists. They sold everything from fishing poles to toys to *CALAMITY MONTANA* apparel. On our other side was an accounting firm, and with any luck, the CPA would kick some business my direction for clients needing a bit of legal work.

In an ideal world, I'd own this building rather than rent, but at the moment, there weren't any properties for sale in downtown Calamity. And a prime location had been my priority, not only to gain visibility in the community, but so that on slow days, I could stare out my gleaming office windows and people watch.

I'd moved to Calamity for a change of scenery. A slower pace. What better way to soak in the view than from right here on First?

"Can I help you with anything in your office?" Gertrude asked.

"Nah. I think I'm done for the day." I'd spent all morning setting up my desk and workstation. Then this afternoon, I'd returned the emails I'd been ignoring all weekend and paid a few bills.

My diplomas needed to be unboxed and hung on the wall, but that was on tomorrow's agenda—the only item until I got some clients. Maybe without a crippling workload I'd be able to breathe. To relax. To come to terms with everything that had happened this year.

The past three months had been nothing but chaos. Preparing for this move had consumed every available minute. Buying a house in Calamity. Selling a house in San Francisco. Jumping through the hoops to get my license to practice law in Montana. Saying farewell to the California firm where I'd worked for the past decade.

Moving had consumed my every waking minute, but that hectic pace had been my salvation. And hopefully Montana would become my sanctuary.

"It might get boring around here for a while," I told Gertrude, taking a seat on the couch. Firm yet comfortable. The leather was as smooth as butter—as it should be for the price tag.

"Do I need to be worried that you'll go out of business? Because I left a perfectly good job to come work for you."

I chuckled. "Your job is safe."

"Good. If I don't have anything to work on, do you mind if I read?"

"Nope." As long as she got her work done and was

gracious to clients, I didn't care what she did to pass the time from nine to five.

Gertrude had tackled most of the office setup these past three weeks. After I'd signed my five-year lease with the owners, I'd spent a week here interviewing candidates for her position. Hiring her had been an easy choice given her experience. And once she'd been hired, I'd handed over the reins—and my credit card—giving her a rundown of what I wanted for the space and letting her sort the details of furniture delivery and setup.

But now that it was done, now that I was here and getting settled, the pace would change.

Slow was not my preferred speed at work, but at least I didn't need clients to keep Thatcher Law afloat. I wanted clients. But I didn't *need* them.

Thanks to the huge case I'd won last year, my finances were solid. Dad had suggested I take my windfall and retire, but I enjoyed being a lawyer—Mom joked that I'd come out of the womb poised for an argument. Sitting around, by myself, I'd go stir-crazy. So my plan was to keep the caseload light. I'd work enough to pay the office's expenses and Gertrude's salary. Anything left would be a bonus.

I relaxed deeper into the couch, spreading my arms across the back and kicking an ankle over a knee. "How long have you lived in Calamity?"

"About thirty years. My husband grew up here. We met in college and moved here after getting married."

Gertrude was in her early fifties, though she looked closer to my thirty-five. Her brown hair showed no signs of errant grays. Her smooth, olive skin was likely the envy of many women.

"Do you know the other lawyers in town?" I asked.

"I do." She nodded. "Most are nice."

"Most. Not all?" I arched an eyebrow, wanting all of the dirty details about my competition. "Who don't you like?"

"Julian Tosh." Her brown eyes glinted with a hint of mischief behind those pink frames. "He's a miserable shit. He'll hate that you're here. And I, for one, hope we steal all of his clients."

"Oh, Gerty. You've got a ruthless side. I like it." I chuckled. "Tell me more about Calamity."

"What do you want to know?"

"What the tourists don't."

She leaned back in her chair, swiveling it away from her desk. "Well, we've got a couple famous people in town."

"Really? Who?" I'd make sure to steer clear. I'd dealt with enough famous people to last a lifetime.

"Lucy Ross, the country singer. Though she goes by Lucy Evans here since she's married to the sheriff."

"I'll confess that I don't listen to much country music."

Gertrude held up a finger. "Might want to change that along with your license plates."

"Noted." I grinned. "Who else?"

"Cal Stark."

"Cal, I've heard of. I'm a diehard 49ers fan, and every year he played with Tennessee, they kicked our asses. That, and I heard he's an asshole."

"He's not so bad. We've bumped into him a few times around town, and he's always been nice. Cal's wife, Nellie, is a sweetheart."

"Good to know." I glanced out the window just as a

woman walked by, slowing to read the gold lettering on the front door's glass.

Thatcher Law

I loved those gold letters.

When the woman spotted Gertrude behind the desk, she smiled and waved.

"Who's that?" I asked.

"Marcy. She's a waitress at the White Oak. And that"— Gertrude gestured to the man passing the window wearing a tan uniform—"is Grayson. He's one of the sheriff's deputies. Word around town is that he's about to propose to his girlfriend."

"Maybe they need an attorney to draw up a prenuptial agreement."

Gertrude snorted. "Don't hold your breath. Most people around here don't get prenups."

"Then maybe they'll want a last will and testament."

"Maybe."

There wasn't a lot of foot traffic downtown, but as one person passed by, followed by another, Gertrude rattled off their names and occupations along with little nuggets of information.

Turns out, there were still riches to be mined in Calamity, Montana.

When it came to gossip, Gertrude was pure gold.

It was close to five. I had just sat up, about to cut Gertrude loose for the day, when a swish of silky, chestnut-brown hair snared my gaze.

A stunning woman strolled past the glass, oblivious to the fact that my heart had momentarily stopped beating. A smile lit up her oval face as she waved to someone driving by.

Her cheeks were flushed the same shade of pale pink as her soft lips.

My breath caught.

Damn. She was gorgeous. Maybe the most beautiful woman I'd ever seen.

"That's Larke Hale," Gertrude said as I tracked Larke's every step, willing her to slow down so I could get a longer glimpse of her face. "She's a teacher at the school."

I stood from the couch just as Larke disappeared from my view. "Is she single?"

"Um . . . as far as I know."

Good enough for me. Before Gertrude could say another word, I rushed for the door. Chasing a woman wasn't part of the plan, yet I couldn't stop moving.

Sunshine streamed through the cloudless blue sky, but the early April air had a chill that bit into my skin. There weren't many cars parked on the street today, and most of the diagonal parking spaces were empty.

Larke was about twenty feet ahead of me, that pretty hair swishing across her shoulders as she walked. I hurried to catch up. She tucked a hand into the pocket of her black wool coat, pulling out a set of keys and hitting the fob. The lights on a white Toyota 4Runner flashed.

Another thirty seconds and she'd be gone. I'd lose her.

An idea sparked. So I reached into my own pocket, fishing out the twenty I'd gotten in change this morning from the coffee shop.

This was a ridiculous way to approach a woman. Stupid and tacky as hell. But it didn't stop me from clearing my throat. "Excuse me, miss?"

Larke slowed, turning to face me.

Absolutely fucking gorgeous. What I hadn't been able to see from the office were her eyes. A bold brown, like melted chocolate, framed with sooty lashes. They were wide and expressive, eyes that missed nothing and gave away too much.

Honest eyes.

With my career, honest eyes were a rarity. A treasure.

She blinked, like she was waiting for me to explain why I'd stopped her.

"I, uh . . . I think you dropped this." *Smooth, Thatcher. Real fucking smooth.*

Larke's gaze darted to the twenty in my hand. "No, I don't think so."

"You sure?"

"Positive."

"Huh." I made a show of glancing around the sidewalk, searching for another person. There wasn't one.

"I guess it's yours," she said.

"Guess so. I'm Ronan." I shoved the twenty into my pocket and extended a hand. "Ronan Thatcher."

"Larke Hale." Those long, delicate fingers slid against my palm, but her handshake was firm. Strong. She pulled away before I was ready to let her hand go.

"I just moved to Calamity. I was thinking of trying out the White Oak Café tonight. I don't suppose you'd want to—"

Larke's mouth flattened into a thin line before she narrowed those beautiful eyes, spun on a heel and walked away.

"Join me," I muttered as she opened the door to her Toyota and climbed inside.

She shot me a glare from over the steering wheel.

"Huh." I liked that glare. I liked it a lot. Women with fire were always the most fun to date. Though no one had ever rejected me quite so effectively.

The last time I'd been rejected had been, well . . . never. I couldn't think of a time when I'd asked a woman on a date and she'd said no.

Until Larke.

Odd, but I kind of liked that she was the first. Why? Not a clue.

So I grinned, raised a hand in a wave as she reversed out of her space, then strode back to the office, whistling a tune on my way.

I eyed the California license plate on my Corvette as I passed.

Tomorrow, I'd stop by the courthouse for a new registration.

Goodbye, California.

Hello, Calamity.

CHAPTER TWO

LARKE

PARKING IN FRONT of my sister's house was always surreal. The first time I'd come to Kerrigan and Pierce's place, I'd pinched myself. It wasn't exactly a mansion but it wasn't *not* a mansion.

They'd built this sprawling house in the countryside with acres of wooded land to give them privacy. The security system was state of the art and the gate at the long driveway would probably deter an armored tank.

Given Pierce's extreme wealth, my sister could have demanded a golden castle and he would have built it for her. But in true Kerrigan fashion, it was tasteful and classic. The wooden and stone exterior blended with the landscape. Inside, Kerrigan had designed each room to perfection. It was lavish, yet homey. Opulent while still being grounded in our Montana roots. The perfect blend of Pierce and Kerrigan, and a dream home for their three kids.

I glanced in the rearview as I parked the 4Runner,

smiling at my seven-year-old nephew, Elias. "I'll take your backpack in."

"Okay, thanks, Aunt Larke." He unbuckled his seat belt and opened the door, flying out of the car and racing for the front door.

It opened before he could touch the handle, Kerrigan standing in the threshold with her arms wide. She pulled Elias into a hug before he slipped past her, probably to get a snack.

I could use a snack myself after that long-ass day. With his backpack slung over my shoulder, I headed for the door, my footsteps heavy as I covered a yawn with my hand.

Kerrigan had a hug waiting for me too. "Long day?"

"Is it the last day of school yet?"

"Uh-oh. That bad?"

"It wasn't great." I handed over Elias's backpack, stuffed full of his latest papers and first-grade art projects. "He showed me all the stuff they worked on today. I miss elementary school."

"Next year."

I crossed my fingers on both hands. "God willing."

And if my future with the Calamity School District meant years of teaching high school, well . . . maybe my future wasn't with the Calamity School District.

Kerrigan waved me inside, leading the way to the giant playroom on the main level, where the kids were playing.

Where the light of my life, a beautiful sixteen-month-old little girl, was attempting to kick a big, green bouncy ball.

Wren spotted me and her face lit up. "Mama!"

"Hi, baby." I scooped her up as she toddled over, peppering her chubby cheek with kisses.

"Ball." She pointed to the ball.

"That is a ball. Did you have fun?"

"Ball."

I kissed her again. "I missed you today."

"She missed you too," Kerrigan said. "She was very snuggly this morning after you dropped her off."

I pressed a hand to her forehead, grateful that she didn't feel warm. Her brown eyes, the same color as mine, weren't as drowsy as they'd been this morning. "Thanks for watching her."

"It's the least I can do, considering it was my children who gave her the cold."

I propped Wren on my hip, then walked over to the couch where Constance was cuddled under a blanket watching a Disney cartoon. "Hi, sweetie."

"Hi, Auntie Larke." My four-year-old niece gave me a tiny smile as I kissed her hair.

"Are you feeling better?"

She nodded, her gaze shifting back to the TV.

"Is Gabriel asleep?" I asked Kerrigan, scanning the playroom for my almost-two-year-old nephew.

She nodded. "Yes, but I bet he'll wake up soon."

Elias came strolling into the playroom carrying a juice box in one hand and a plastic plate loaded with snacks in the other. He plopped on the couch beside Constance and started stuffing his face.

"Want something to drink?" Kerrigan asked.

"Anything with caffeine." I kissed Wren's soft brown hair, setting her down so she could play or watch TV with her cousins, then followed my older sister to the kitchen, where I took a seat at the massive island while she made us iced coffees from her cappuccino machine. "Hopefully we can go back to daycare tomorrow."

"If not, just call me. I'll watch her."

"Thanks. Mom said she could take her again too." It was Wednesday and Wren hadn't been to daycare once this week. But I was hoping tomorrow we might be back to our normal routine.

Though normal seemed to be ever changing these days. Being a single mother felt a lot like learning to juggle—with steak knives.

This morning, I'd brought Wren to stay with Kerrigan and, in turn, taken Elias with me into town, saving my sister the drive to Calamity.

"So what happened in your day?" she asked, taking the stool beside mine.

"High school is more brutal now than when I was actually in high school." I sighed. "I miss teaching fifth grade."

When I'd gone to pick Elias up this afternoon, I'd taken one step into the elementary school and instantly felt homesick.

"Any word on if you'll get your regular classroom back next year?" she asked.

I shook my head. "No. I think they're still trying to figure out how many kids they'll have."

For the past two years, the incoming kindergarten classes had been nearly twice the average size. Calamity was growing. It was becoming home to people looking to escape the city. Tourists who'd swing through the area on their way to explore Yellowstone National Park would fall in love with our quaint little town and decide to give small-town life a try.

There were some who hadn't liked the harsh winters and

had already left, but for the most part, our numbers were on the rise. New businesses. New buildings. New students, every one excited to be a Calamity Cowboy.

But the influx of kids had caused a few headaches for the school's administrators. Classrooms had been shuffled. So had teachers.

I'd assumed I was safe in my fifth-grade classroom. Oh, how wrong I'd been. When the district superintendent and the high school principal had both walked through my door, I should have known there'd be trouble.

This past fall, even with all the shuffling and reshuffling, they had still been short one high school English teacher. They'd begged a newly retired teacher to come back temporarily until they could fill the position, but she'd refused to teach high school.

Now I knew why.

Mrs. Baker was sitting comfortably in my fifth-grade classroom while I was in hell at the high school, dealing with teenagers who couldn't care less about creative writing and the Oxford comma.

"I'm so tired, Kerrigan." I took a long gulp of my coffee. "Every time I introduce an assignment, the kids complain. It's like pulling teeth to get them engaged in a classroom discussion. The seniors have two months left but most of them have already checked out. I miss smiling faces. I miss hearing *Good Morning, Ms. Hale* when they come into the classroom and getting a few hugs on the way out. I miss teaching anything other than English."

"Two more months to go," Kerrigan said.

"Two more months," I muttered. I hadn't been shy about telling the high school's principal that I missed the elementary school. She was a nice woman, also new to Calamity, and hopefully my not-so-subtle hints wouldn't go ignored. "It doesn't help that Asshole Abbott's classroom is right across the hall from mine. These kids are wearing my patience so thin that the next time he scowls at me, I might snap and attack him with a Bunsen burner."

Kerrigan put her hand on my arm. "Please don't go to jail."

I laughed. "Seriously? Why me?"

Not only was I in uncharted waters, swimming with hormonal teenagers, but I was forced to face my archnemesis daily.

Wilder Abbott had moved to Calamity years ago to take a job teaching high school science. From the day we'd first crossed paths in the teachers' lounge, he'd been nothing but a complete jerk.

He rarely made eye contact. If I asked him a question, he responded with a grunt-glare combo. I had no idea what I'd done to earn his scorn, other than say, "Hello. Welcome to Calamity."

But apparently my friendly nature had been too much for the jackass. Wilder was currently sitting in the top spot on my Shithead List. These days, I mostly tried to avoid him, which had been much, much easier when I was teaching in the elementary school.

"I hate men," I muttered as the image of a different man's face popped into my mind. "Want to hear something weird?"

"Always." Kerrigan leaned in closer.

"So yesterday, I stopped downtown after work before heading to Mom and Dad's to pick up Wren because I needed some cash from the bank and to buy a birthday card for Grandpa. I was walking back to my car and this guy stopped me. He had a twenty in his hand. He held it out and told me I dropped it. Which, of course, I hadn't."

"You never carry cash."

"Exactly." If I had cash, I spent it. So I rarely had cash. "I told him it wasn't mine. He pretended like it wasn't his. Then he tried to ask me out."

Kerrigan giggled. "Bold."

"If bold means cheesy."

"What did you do?"

I shrugged. "Turned around and walked away."

I was a thirty-five-year-old single mother. I had no time for lame pickup attempts, even if they were made by an insanely handsome man with a cool name.

Ronan Thatcher.

He was tall with broad shoulders and a muscular physique. His hair, a brown so dark it was nearly black, had been artfully styled. And when he'd smiled at me, show-casing the sharp corners of his jaw, the colors in his hazel eyes had danced.

Two years ago, I would have told him to use that twenty to buy me a drink. But a lot had changed in the past two years. The last thing I needed in my life was complications from a guy.

"Was he good looking?" Kerrigan asked.

Yes. Mostly definitely, yes. "Not bad."

"Then why don't you give him a chance?"

My daughter's cry from the other room saved me from Kerrigan's dating advice. I loved my sister, but she was so happy with Pierce that she couldn't understand why anyone, especially me, preferred to stay single.

We slid off our stools, rushing to the playroom, where Wren was on a rocking dragon, her arms raised in the air and a pout on her precious face. She'd gotten herself onto the dragon but couldn't climb off.

"Did you get stuck?" I walked over, lifting her up. "Should we go home?"

"No."

She had a few words nailed. *Mama. Ball. Hi. Bye-bye.* There were a few others in the list, along with her favorite.

No.

"Yes." I tickled her side, earning a smile and a peek at her eight teeth.

"No."

"Yes. Mama needs some sweatpants." With Wren propped on my hip, I collected her things. Then I said goodbye to Kerrigan and the kids, loaded my daughter into the car and aimed my tires toward town.

I yawned three times before I made it back to Calamity, then groaned when I realized I didn't have much in the fridge. I'd planned to go to the grocery store tonight, but at the moment, the idea of shopping—or cooking—made me want to cry.

The speed limit slowed as the highway became First Street. My father's car dealership was no longer alone out here on the edge of town. There was a new office complex being built beside the service entrance's parking lot. Beside that complex, the footings had been poured for a Dairy Queen. It was even going to have a drive-thru.

Half of the town was ecstatic about a fast-food stop. The other half was terrified it would bring too much change to

Calamity. As a french fry lover, I couldn't wait. Though the White Oak Café would always own my heart.

"Screw it." The grocery store could wait until tomorrow. I searched for a parking spot in front of the café. We'd have dinner, then I'd go home to a pair of sweatpants and a glass of wine.

Wren was kicking in her seat, smiling as I opened the back door.

"Come on, baby. Let's get a grilled cheese."

She let out a string of babble as I unbuckled her, grabbed her water bottle from the diaper bag and headed inside.

"Hey, Larke." Marcy greeted me at the hostess station, plucking a menu from a stack. "Just you two?"

"Always." Me and my girl. That was all I needed in life. Whether that life was here in Calamity. Or somewhere beyond the county line.

"Pick any spot you want," she said. "I'll bring over a high chair."

"Thanks." I scanned the restaurant, seeing a few familiar faces.

The three booths along the front glass windows were taken, as were most of the tables. The counter along the far wall was mostly empty, but squeezing Wren's high chair in between stools wasn't ideal. So I walked toward the back, finding a vacant table for two.

From the outside, the White Oak looked a lot like it had during my childhood. The signage was outdated and it had a rustic, greasy-spoon vibe. But years ago, the owners had remodeled the interior, giving it white tiled floors and a chalkboard-paint wall where they listed the daily specials.

"Here you go," Marcy said, setting down the chair for Wren. "Would you like something to drink?"

"I'll have a Diet Coke, please. And I might as well order. I'll have today's special and Wren will have a grilled cheese with french fries."

"You got it." Marcy nodded, then headed for the register.

When I had Wren seated, I slumped into my own chair, breathing for what felt like the first time all day.

"Want some toys?" I dug into my purse for the stackable cups I took with me everywhere.

"Cup." Wren tapped the table, my cue to stack them up, just how she liked them. She waited until they were in a pyramid before she swatted a hand and sent them flying. "Uh-oh."

"Uh-oh." I feigned a gasp, holding up my hands, just like she was. Then I went about our little game, restacking the cups still on the table before bending to pick up the two that had fallen to the floor. Except as I stretched to grab the pink cup, a large hand snagged it first. My gaze lifted, meeting a pair of striking hazel eyes.

Ronan.

Yesterday, when we'd met, I hadn't noticed all of the colors. Mostly they were caramel, like the color of Dad's favorite whiskey. But the sage and hunter-green striations jumped out at me tonight. There were a few gray flecks too.

"Here you go." Ronan waved the cup.

"Oh, um, thanks." I tore my gaze away, my cheeks warming as I took it from his hand. *They're just pretty eyes. No need to stare, Larke.*

"You're welcome." The corner of his mouth turned up as

he stood tall. Then he glanced to Wren. "Cute kid. Your daughter?"

"Yes. And thank you." I sat up straight, watching as Wren tipped her head way back to take him in. At least I wasn't the only one staring.

"What's her name?" he asked.

"Wren."

"Larke and Wren. I like it."

My daughter tilted her head sideways, like she wasn't sure what to make of him.

Well, that made two of us.

Like she was testing him, she batted the cups off the table, this time sending each and every one of them clattering to the floor.

Ronan chuckled, bending to retrieve them all. His navy slacks molded to the curve of his ass as he moved. His white shirt stretched across broad shoulders and muscular biceps. Like yesterday, the sleeves were rolled up, revealing tan, sinewed forearms.

My mouth went dry.

Over forearms.

What was wrong with me tonight? Once more, I had to tear my eyes away. This was clearly a sign that I hadn't had sex in far too long. Two years, actually.

"If I give these back to her, she'll just toss them on the floor again, won't she?" Ronan asked, grinning at Wren.

"Most likely."

He nodded, but instead of handing me the cups, he bent and stacked them in front of my daughter.

The moment the last one was on top, her hand flew through the air. So did the cups.

"Uh-oh," she crooned.

It earned her another deep, gravelly chuckle. Just like before, he picked them up from the floor and once more, stacked them for Wren.

Another swat of her little fist and away they went.

"This is my first trip to the White Oak," he said, bending and stretching and looking far, far too attractive for my own good. "I had the special."

"Their sandwiches are always great." Tonight's was a french dip.

"Maybe I could buy you one sometime." He stacked the cups for Wren, his gaze flicking to mine.

Two years ago, I would have let him buy me dinner. Without question. I would have gotten lost in the colors of those hazel eyes and made some decisions that would have most likely ended with me in tears, drowning my sorrows in ice cream and pizza.

But the Larke from two years ago wasn't the woman sitting at the White Oak tonight.

Sure, I missed sex. My vibrator wasn't the same as toe-curling, can't-get-enough-of-each-other, addictive sex. But my priority was Wren. So I gave him a kind smile, because he'd been kind to my daughter.

"Have a good night, Ronan."

He blinked, his forehead furrowing, as he studied me.

I concentrated on Wren. The cups went back into my purse. I held my breath, hoping that he would take the rejection gracefully. The last thing I needed tonight was a scene.

Ronan hovered beside the table for a moment while I braced for the worst. An angry comment. A criticism. In my experience, most hot guys were assholes, especially when their ego was bruised.

But instead of doing what I expected, he surprised me. Not many people surprised me these days.

Ronan smiled. A blinding smile of straight, white teeth and soft lips. If he had been handsome before, his smile made him irresistible now. Almost.

I'd perfected resisting men in the past two years.

"Good to see you again, Larke. Enjoy your dinner." He dipped his chin, like a bow, then winked at my daughter. "Nice to meet you, Wren."

Then Ronan strode through the restaurant, lifting a hand to wave at Marcy.

She waved back, her cheeks flushing.

Never, in all my years of coming to the White Oak, had I seen Marcy blush.

I tracked his every step to the front door.

He paused, looking back at my table, flashing me that smile again. It was brimming with confidence. With challenge.

I'd told him no. Twice.

Ronan seemed like a man who didn't often hear *no* from women. Given the glint in his eye, I had the sneaking suspicion I'd get another chance to say it again.

I wasn't into guys who couldn't take a hint.

So why did the idea of telling Ronan no seem like a lot of fun?

CHAPTER THREE

RONAN

"APPRECIATE YOU COMING IN." I shook hands with my new—and only—client. "I'll give you a call early next week. We should be able to knock this out in a few days."

"That would be fantastic. Welcome to Calamity." With a wave, he pushed through the door, leaving Gertrude and me alone in the reception area.

"He'd like to set up a new LLC," I told her. "I'll get the document drawn up, then we'll just have to file the info with the state."

"Okay. What can I do?"

"I'll have you do the filing and deal with the state's website."

"No problem." She nodded. "I haven't done that before, but I'll poke around and do some research."

"I haven't dealt much with Montana's system either, so we'll figure it out together."

Before coming here, Gertrude had been working at the Calamity hospital as an assistant to their general counsel.

She'd liked the hospital, but her former boss had been a bit of a micromanager, enough that she'd quietly started searching for a new job. So while we'd be dealing with cases and clientele here different than what she was used to, she was at least familiar with the basics. And what she didn't know, I'd teach her.

My career had started with work like this. Clients needing documentation for their small businesses. People sorting out personal affairs like divorces and estate issues. My firm had believed in giving young associates a wide variety of work to test their mettle and find their talents.

Torts had become my specialty. But I wasn't entirely unfamiliar with corporate and family law. I just needed to dust off the cobwebs.

"Thatcher Law's first client." I took a seat on the couch. "We should celebrate. I'll bring in champagne for us tomorrow. And to toast the end of our first week."

Albeit a boring week. Hell, setting up an LLC was boring. But that was the point of Calamity, right? A slower pace. A simple life.

Slow and simple were overrated. I was already going stir-crazy, and I'd been here less than a week. Had moving been a bad decision?

"Tell me more about Larke Hale." Without something to fill the hours at the office, I'd resorted to gossiping with Gertrude. I gave myself a mental pat on the back for waiting this long to ask her about Larke.

The beautiful, puzzling woman had been on my mind since bumping into her at the café last night.

"Why do you ask?" Gertrude's eyes narrowed.

"Well . . . because she blew me off. Twice."

Behind those fuchsia glasses, Gertrude's eyes smiled. "I take it that doesn't happen often."

"No, it doesn't." I rubbed my jaw, replaying last night's conversation for the hundredth time. "You said she was single, right?"

"As far as I know," Gertrude said. "But maybe she's started dating someone and I just haven't heard about it yet."

Maybe the reason Larke had dismissed me last night was because she was already with a man. But if that was the case, why not just tell me she had a boyfriend?

Or maybe she wasn't interested in me. Maybe she didn't find me attractive.

No. No fucking way.

Larke had tried to hide it, but she'd checked me out last night. Head to toe. And judging by the pink in her cheeks, she hadn't been disappointed. So why had she shot me down? Again?

"The Hale family has been a staple in Calamity for generations," Gertrude said. "I believe they can trace their lineage back to the mining days in this area."

"Interesting. So she probably has quite a bit of family in town."

"Quite a bit would be an understatement. Aunts, uncles, cousins. Her dad owns the car dealership. It's the largest of their family's businesses, though that will likely change soon."

"Why's that?" I asked.

"Larke's sister is Kerrigan Sullivan. She's married to Pierce Sullivan, and that man has more money than God."

I chuckled. "Rich, huh?"

"Another understatement. They've been investing pretty

heavily in Calamity. They own the brewery in town, plus a bunch of real estate in the area, especially along First. Rumor has it they're going to build a resort soon. A hotel with a spa. Real bougie."

"Kerrigan." I hummed. How did I know that name? "Wait. She owns The Refinery, right?" I'd stopped in just this morning to check out the fitness studio. Yoga and Pilates weren't really my thing. I preferred to run or lift, but I'd been curious, and I was making it my mission to stop by every business along First to meet people.

Kerrigan hadn't been at The Refinery, but the girl at the counter had mentioned her name when I'd asked who owned the studio.

"Yes, she does. Kerrigan owns that whole building," Gertrude said. "She started the fitness studio seven years ago, I think? I can't remember exactly when."

So Larke's family was a Calamity staple. Was that the reason she'd turned me down? Because I was an outsider. Even with the new Montana license plates I'd picked up yesterday at the county courthouse, I was a new face in town. A former Californian.

Fuck, this was bothering me. I'd been stewing over her for hours. Why had she said no? Was this a test or something?

Six months ago, I would have walked away. Moved on to a woman who preferred yes to no. Except something about Larke had me fascinated. And considering I had very little stimulating me professionally at the moment, I was up for a personal challenge.

I wanted a date with Larke. And damn it, I wasn't giving up. Not yet.

"What's the deal with her daughter? Wren?" Maybe Larke's hesitancy had nothing to do with me but with Wren's father. Was he still in the picture? Was Larke in love with him? There'd been no ring on her left hand. "Is Larke divorced?"

"I think we've talked about Larke enough for today." Gertrude turned to her monitor, her fingers poised over the keyboard.

"You are a shrewd woman, Gerty." I chuckled. "You wield gossip like a weapon."

"Only against you. Larke is a lovely woman."

Interesting. Gertrude was shifting to protection mode. I liked that. A lot.

Gertrude didn't trust me quite yet, did she? We didn't know each other well enough. But we'd get there eventually. Adjusting to this slow and simple pace was proving difficult, but deep down, it was for my own good. Calamity was home now, and I wasn't going anywhere. Gertrude and I just needed time.

"Yes, Larke is lovely," I said. "I'm asking out of curiosity, not malice."

Gertrude stayed tight-lipped as she studied my face.

I raised a hand. "I swear, my intentions are pure." Well, not entirely pure.

Larke had inspired very unpure, very erotic thoughts these past couple of nights.

"This will sound arrogant," I warned. "But women don't typically turn me down when I ask them out on a date. So now I'm intrigued. And if I learn more about her, maybe the next time I ask, she won't say no."

"You're right." Gertrude smirked. "That does sound arrogant. But I supposed most women do find you handsome."

"Ouch." I smacked a hand over my heart. "You say that like *you* don't find me handsome. Do you need your glasses checked? Maybe that prescription is getting a little outdated."

She rolled her eyes. "One of these days I'm going to come to the office and you'll be stuck in the doorway because your ego has grown so big you can't fit."

"Oh, Gerty. I think having you around will keep my ego in check."

She laughed. "We'll consider it part of my *other responsibilities as assigned*."

"Touché."

Gertrude blew out a long breath, her smile dimming. "No one really knows much about Wren's father. I'm sure her close family members know the details, but they haven't shared and neither has Larke. I suspect that was intentional."

I sat up straighter, my own grin fading. "She wasn't hurt, was she?"

"No, I don't think so. At least, I hope not."

"That makes two of us."

Gertrude sighed. "There were rumors floating around about her. Though there are always rumors. They ebb and flow. They surfaced when people started noticing she was pregnant. Then they died down for a bit, flaring up after the baby was born. Everyone was speculating."

"What were the rumors?" Part of me even hated to ask. To perpetuate the gossip. But my curiosity won out. I wanted to know what people were saying about Larke. About that adorable little girl who was her mother's mini, from the chestnut hair to those expressive brown eyes.

At this point, the more information the better, right? That way I could take care when talking to Larke. I didn't need to bring up a topic that would sting.

"People said she was seeing a man on the sly and got pregnant. Some people think he's from out of town and didn't want anything to do with her. Some people say she got a sperm donor. Others think the reason she's kept it a secret is because the man is married."

What the fuck? "That's a fairly serious accusation."

"For the record, I don't think that last one is true," Gertrude said. "Larke is a wonderful person. I don't think she'd have an affair with a married man."

Regardless, it wasn't my place to judge. If there was one lesson I'd learned from the disaster three months ago, it was that love was fucking complicated.

So I turned toward the window, watching as a few cars and trucks rolled down First. *Shit.* I felt slimy now. And I was annoyed on her behalf. These were people who'd likely known her since childhood and they were secretly accusing her of an affair.

Today's lesson learned—the Calamity rumor mill could be brutal.

"I doubt we'll have anyone else stop in today," I said, changing the subject. "Why don't you go ahead and duck out early. I'll lock up."

"Are you sure?"

"Yep. I won't be far behind you."

"That would be great. I've got to take a trip to the store and would love to get home a bit early to cook dinner."

Gertrude stood, then went about collecting her things while I retreated to my office. She called a goodbye before slipping out the door, leaving me alone with my thoughts.

They spun around Larke Hale.

When was the last time a woman had raided my mind so exhaustively? Never. Not even Cora could compete.

What was it about Larke that had me so . . . hooked? It wasn't just her beauty. Stunning as she was, there was more than just a physical attraction here. Which was ridiculous, right? I'd shared two incredibly short conversations with the woman.

Yet I kept picturing those honest eyes. I kept hearing her melodic voice. I kept wondering how her soft lips would taste.

"Fuck." I dragged a hand through my hair. I'd been staring blankly at my computer monitor long enough that the damn thing had gone to sleep.

Work would wait until tomorrow, so I took the keys from my desk drawer, then walked through the office, hitting the lights. With the front door locked, I headed for my car parked on the street.

My 1969 Chevrolet Corvette Stingray was my pride and joy. Its silver paint gleamed under the afternoon sky. This car wasn't entirely practical for Montana, but I had a truck in the garage at my house for the winter months. And until the first snow flurry, I'd be driving the Stingray.

That's what Dad would want. He'd loved this car too when he'd been the man behind the wheel.

This car had been a gift. An incredible gift. Not many men would just hand over the keys to a classic they'd spent decades saving to buy.

But Dad wasn't like most men.

He'd only driven the Corvette for five years before he'd given it to me. And in those five years, he'd driven it as often as possible. Maybe some would keep it hidden, a treasure tucked away in a garage. But Dad always said there was no point in having an amazing car if you didn't drive the damn thing.

Since Dad couldn't drive anymore, he hadn't wanted it to go to waste.

The fact that he'd given it to me instead of Noah, well . . .

Any doubts that Dad loved me had died that day.

As I slid into my seat and gripped the wheel, I closed my eyes for just a heartbeat, like always, and said a silent thanks to the angel who'd brought James Thatcher into my life. Then I turned the key in the ignition, soaking in the vibration and purr of the engine before shifting into reverse and pulling away from the office.

With its dramatic lines and sleek body, this car turned heads.

Larke wasn't all that different. She'd turned mine immediately. Maybe that was why I was so interested. Because Dad hadn't just taught me to appreciate fine cars. He'd taught me to appreciate a woman who turned heads too.

I rolled my window down, leaning an arm against the door as I rolled down First, barely going ten miles per hour. There was no rush to get home. I didn't have anything waiting for me except boxes to unpack and a cold ham sandwich for dinner. So I soaked in every detail, this street becoming more and more familiar with each passing day.

Amidst the older, Western-style properties, there were some newly restored buildings. Maybe those were the ones owned by Larke's sister. They gave Calamity a modern touch, with large windows and a fresh design.

The combination of old and new worked, appealing to those who wanted to visit a traditional Montana town but who didn't want to live without creature comforts. It was a unique blend of character and convenience. The trendy coffee shop had daily latte specials. Gertrude had mentioned earlier today that when they opened the Dairy Queen, she'd be getting her own membership at The Refinery to compensate for ice cream calories.

I relaxed deeper into my seat, picking up speed as I left downtown, following First toward the town's limits. About a mile from the office, I took the turnoff that wound past one neighborhood and into another. Mine.

According to my realtor, this was a newer subdivision, only having been started eighteen months ago. The three- and four-bedroom homes all had a unique style so that nothing looked cookie cutter. The homes were tailored for families, including a large park in the center of the development complete with a play structure and splash pad.

But the selling point for me had been the house itself. Construction had finished only a week before I'd come to Calamity on my house-hunting trip. The fresh paint and the open floor plan had won me over immediately.

Never in my life had I thought I'd buy a new house. I'd always gone for older homes with character. Quirks. But this move was all about change. So when my realtor had brought me to a brand-new house, I'd put in an offer for full asking price.

As a bonus, it took me less than ten minutes to get from

work to home. In San Francisco, my commute had been nearly an hour.

If I was feeling ambitious, I could walk downtown.

After navigating the quiet streets, I turned onto my cul-de-sac. Six homes total made up Paintbrush Circle. The streets in this neighborhood were all named after Montana flowers.

A man at the first house on the street was outside mowing his lawn. He waved as I passed. I waved back.

With how busy I'd been unpacking, I hadn't met any of my neighbors yet. The moving truck had arrived here twenty minutes after I'd rolled in on Saturday morning, and within six hours, they'd unloaded. Then I'd gotten to work putting the house to rights.

One day, I'd stop and introduce myself, but for now, I headed to my house at the end of the circle. Its brown paint was so dark it was nearly black, not unlike my hair color. Each of the houses had a deep shade in earthy tones that all coordinated, probably an intentional choice from the developer.

The home adjacent to mine was olive green. Judging by the size of the bushes and ornamental grasses, it had been here the longest. Its trees were double the size of the saplings in my yard.

I hit the garage door opener and eased into my three-car garage, parking the Corvette in the center bay beside my truck. The garage was stuffy, so I left the bay open. Then I headed inside, breathing in the scent of paint that still lingered in the air.

Since Saturday, I'd made a decent dent in unpacking. The only rooms left to unpack were my office and the kitchen. The movers had done most of the heavy lifting, situating furniture and leaving boxes in their designated rooms.

Tonight's plan was to tackle the kitchen so I could stop eating on paper plates. And I was desperate for my coffee maker. So I quickly stripped out of my slacks and shirt, changing into a pair of jeans and a gray T-shirt.

I'd worked through eight boxes when my stomach started growling. The dishwasher was running, rinsing a load of plates and silverware. The counter was stacked with sheets of tissue paper. I grabbed a stack of collapsed boxes, wanting to clear them away before I made my dinner.

With the boxes tossed in the back of my black Silverado, I was about to go in and make myself that ham sandwich when a white 4Runner pulled into the driveway of the house next door.

I knew who drove that Toyota.

"No way." I chuckled to myself.

Maybe I had met a neighbor after all.

What were the chances that Larke lived next door? I shook my head. *Damn.*

The lots here were wide, each house given space from the next. The driveways curved in so that garages didn't face the street, but other houses. Our lots were separated by a lush, green lawn, and her garage faced mine.

I stood beside my truck, watching as she unloaded Wren from the backseat. She set her daughter down, then came to the rear of the SUV, popping the hatch door.

Larke hefted out a diaper bag and her purse. Then she started looping grocery bags over her forearms. I was about to go over and help when she snagged the last and hit the button for the door to come closing down. "Come on, baby."

With Wren rushing to keep up, they disappeared inside the house. But she'd left the garage door open.

So I waited until she emerged again, Wren trailing not far behind. Larke walked out of the garage and down the driveway to the green garbage can waiting on the sidewalk.

Today was Thursday. Garbage day.

And I hadn't collected my empty can either.

I grinned, then strode outside.

The moment Larke spotted me, her eyes went wide. The sun caught the strands of gold and cinnamon in her hair. She was wearing a black jumpsuit with a denim jacket and a pair of black and pale blue sneakers. It shouldn't have been a sexy outfit. But it was. Everything about this woman was sexy.

Including the shock on her beautiful face.

God, I loved this little town and its little surprises.

"Hey, neighbor."

CHAPTER FOUR

LARKE

THIS WASN'T HAPPENING. Ronan was my new neighbor? Was this a joke?

I'd been dreading a neighbor. Any neighbor.

When I'd first moved here, this had been *my* cul-de-sac. My neighbors had been the construction crews hired by Pierce and Kerrigan to build this development. They'd worked house by house, filling the block with family homes. Their trucks and trailers had crowded the curbs, and the sound of thudding hammers and buzzing power tools had filled the air.

The noise hadn't bothered me, not when I'd just left for work each morning. By the time dinner rolled around each evening, the crews had been gone, leaving me alone on my cul-de-sac.

But slowly, house by finished house, I'd gotten neighbors. Two of the families who'd moved in were people I'd known for years. Like me, they'd wanted to upgrade homes and expand. The only drawback was their kids were older, beyond the age to play with Wren.

One of the houses had been sold to a family new to Calamity. Mrs. Edwards, a woman who'd known me since birth, lived in the other. She had a beef with my aunt, and apparently, that extended to me because she'd hardly spoken ten words to me since she'd moved here.

Five out of six houses had been taken. I'd considered myself lucky when the place next to mine had been completed last. I liked having this end of the street to myself.

Apparently, my luck had run out.

Kerrigan had mentioned not long ago that this house had been sold. But my sister wasn't involved much at this point. With the homes designed and built, she'd turned the listings over to her realtor and moved on to the next project.

Besides, I hadn't asked for details about my new neighbor. She hadn't offered them either. When it came to local gossip, Kerrigan knew my stance had changed. Dramatically. After the rumors that had flown around Calamity about me these past two years, well . . .

I was content to live in my bubble, forming my own opinions and taking everything I heard with a block—not a grain —of salt.

It was none of my business who was sleeping with who. Unless it was a relative, I didn't care who was getting divorced. I had no interest in the scuttlebutt from whatever had happened at Jane's bar the previous weekend.

I minded my own business, even doing my best to ignore the gossip at work. It wasn't easy, considering that the school's rumor mill made Calamity's look like child's play. But I'd gotten very good at muting the world.

Only maybe I'd gone too far.

As Ronan strode toward me, his long legs eating up the concrete with that confident swagger, I realized there were consequences to putting my head in the sand.

I definitely should have asked Kerrigan about my new neighbor.

Damn.

"This is a surprise." He grinned, stopping in front of me. He was so tall, a couple inches over six feet, that I had to crane my neck to keep his gaze.

"Sure is." I nodded, doing my best not to stare at the way his biceps strained his T-shirt.

So far, I'd only seen Ronan in slacks and starched shirts. Dressed up, he was deliciously handsome. But like this, wearing a pair of faded jeans and a plain shirt that molded to his broad chest and flat stomach, he was without a doubt the most gorgeous man I'd ever seen.

I couldn't have this sort of temptation next door.

This was bad. This was very bad.

"Ball!" Wren's voice carried through the air as a ball came rolling down the driveway. "Mama! Ball."

Before I could rush to catch it and stop it from going into the street, Ronan jogged around me, snagging the small pink soccer ball that my brother had given Wren last week.

Wren came toddling down the driveway, always going too fast for my comfort, but somehow, she kept her balance. She veered off her intended path when she spotted Ronan, her thumb instantly going into her mouth as she raced for my leg.

"Sorry. We're, um, working on the thumb sucking." I

braced as Wren collided with my leg, clinging to me as she stared up at Ronan.

"Why are you apologizing?"

Good question. I shrugged. "Apologizing seems to go hand in hand with motherhood."

Sorry, she's got a runny nose.

Sorry, she's loud.

Sorry, she's taking a nap so I'm going to be late.

And lately, the thumb sucking.

"My dad keeps reminding me that if I don't stop her from sucking her thumb soon, it's going to become a habit and be harder to break down the road. That it might lead to teeth problems."

Another crux of parenting. You got to worry that the smallest decision made today would have lifelong repercussions.

"Ah." Ronan nodded. "Well, not that you asked for my opinion, but she seems pretty little to me. I'd say let her suck her thumb. Maybe get her to stop before she goes to college. Or if the dentist says she's got teeth problems."

Odd how a stranger's permission to let my daughter suck her thumb suddenly made me feel better about it. Wren was little. And she didn't do it all the time. Just when she was nervous or shy.

I stroked Wren's soft hair as she stared up at him, her eyes wide.

He dropped to a crouch, holding out the ball to her.

She eyed him carefully, but slowly, the thumb came loose from her mouth. Then with a slobbery hand, she took the ball and ran for the grass.

"Seems like a good neighborhood," Ronan said as he stood, towering over me.

I'd always had a thing for tall men. *Damn it.*

"It is." I inched away from Ronan's magnetic tug. "My sister and brother-in-law built this development."

It was the only reason I'd been able to buy a house in this neighborhood. Living on a teacher's salary, as a single mother, it would have taken me years to save enough for the down payment required at a bank. But instead of taking out a loan, I had a contract directly with Pierce and Kerrigan.

"They did a nice job," he said, his gaze drifting to Wren as she played. A smile ghosted his lips as she tried to kick the ball and instead lost her footing and fell on her butt.

He seemed . . . enamored.

And God, it was attractive. The only men who'd ever adored Wren were her relatives.

A warmth spread through my chest at the same time a jolt of panic surged.

My job right now was to think about consequences and how they impacted Wren. Ronan had *consequence* written all over that insanely handsome face.

"I'd better get her inside," I said.

Wren was still sitting on the lawn, plucking blades of the short, spring grass. Her pants had to be soaked. The yard was soggy since it had rained most of last week and still hadn't been warm enough to dry out the ground.

"How about burgers?"

"Huh?"

"Burgers. I'll go into town. Pick up dinner for us."

This man was persistent, I'd give him that. And part of

me wanted to say yes. A part bigger than I was going to admit to myself. "No, thanks."

He tilted his head, his eyes narrowing. "Did I do something? Or do you keep rejecting me because I'm an outsider?"

"An outsider?"

"Yeah. You know, not from Calamity." He leaned in closer, looking around like he didn't want anyone else to hear. "I'm a Californian."

I giggled. I couldn't help it. The way he said it, the playfulness in his tone, I laughed. It had been a long, long time since a gorgeous man had made me laugh.

"Why would I care if you're a Californian?"

"Montanans don't like Californians."

"Who told you that?"

"A few people. My assistant. My brother, also a Californian, said it was a well-known fact."

"Some of the old curmudgeons in town don't love how Calamity is changing. They don't like that Californians, and plenty of people from other states, have brought along different lifestyles and opinions that may contradict their own. If they had it their way, this town would be exactly the same as it was thirty years ago. The same businesses. The same people."

And our town would be on death's doorstep.

"You don't feel that way?" he asked.

"No. I like that we're changing. I hope Calamity stays a small town. There's security that comes with the familiar. I like knowing my neighbors and not fretting if I accidentally leave my garage door open while I'm at work. I like knowing I can walk down First at night and not worry about being mugged. But I want my daughter to have opportunities I didn't as a kid. And that means we can't stay the same."

And the more I considered Wren's future, the more I wondered if it was in a different town.

"So you don't have an issue with Californians?" He smirked. "Then what is it about me that makes it so easy for you to say no?"

It wasn't easy. Every time he asked, my resolve weakened. "Did you really find a twenty on the sidewalk? The day we met."

"No." Ronan didn't hesitate. His hazel eyes sparkled as his smile widened. "I was desperate. It was the best I could come up with on the spur of the moment."

"It wasn't very subtle."

"Subtlety is overrated." He glanced over to Wren, like he was making sure she was okay.

That little look, and I had to stifle a groan. *Hell.* Why couldn't he have just ignored her like most single men? Pretend the daughter doesn't exist until they score with the mother?

Not that I'd had any scores.

I'd been on two dates since Wren was born, both with the same man. The first date, I'd kept conversation light. I'd let him kiss me as he'd walked me to my car and it had been . . . okay.

On the second date, I'd purposefully brought Wren's name into the conversation as often as possible, wanting to gauge his reaction. By the time the waitress had brought over the check, he'd been squirming in his chair.

No surprise, he'd never called me again.

"You come on very strong," I said.

"Yes. When I see something I want." The way his eyes locked with mine made my breath catch in my throat. "I make no apologies for coming on strong. That's just who I am, Larke."

Oh, damn it. That was so freaking sexy.

Heat spread through my veins. I swallowed hard, ignoring the fluttering in my lower belly. It was a good thing he'd already asked about dinner and that I'd already told him no. Because at the moment, I really wanted to change my answer to a yes.

"I'd better get her inside."

He chuckled, dragging a hand through his dark hair. It mussed the way he'd had it combed, making him look even more undone. "You're hell on a man's ego."

"Sounds like your problem, not mine." I fought a smile.

He laughed, shaking his head. "I'm a good neighbor."

"We'll see."

"I can give you references."

I held up a hand. "Not necessary."

"I'm handy too. Most people probably assume that since I'm a lawyer, I wouldn't know the first thing to do with a tool-box. But my father is a carpenter. He taught me a lot. I owned an older house in San Francisco. There were always repairs needed. I even built my own treehouse when I was fifteen."

"Considering you're standing here today and not dead from a broken neck, I guess the treehouse was a success," I teased.

"It's still in my parents' backyard."

"Well, if I ever need a treehouse, I'll know who to call."

"Is that you asking for my number? And here I was, thinking you weren't interested."

We were flirting. When was the last time I'd flirted? I'd forgotten how much fun it could be to flirt with a sexy, smart guy. I'd forgotten just how much I liked a deep, smooth voice.

A squeal from Wren had us both turning. She'd stood, both of her hands full of grass and dirt. And the seat of her pants was soaked.

"Is it because I'm your neighbor?" he asked. "Is that the reason you keep turning me down? Too close to home."

"Well, up until five minutes ago, I had no idea you were my neighbor." I'd seen the moving truck arrive on Saturday morning, parking in front of his place, but I'd been on my way out to go to Dad's birthday party at my parents' house.

And I'd purposefully avoided seeing who'd moved in next door, dragging out my blissful ignorance until we bumped into each other. Like today.

"I figured you'd know who was living next door," he said.

"No," I drawled. "How would I know?"

He shrugged. "Long-time Calamity resident. Teacher at the school. Lots of family in town. I guess I just assumed you would have asked about your new neighbor."

I stood a little straighter, my spine stiffening. "How did you know I was a teacher? And that I have family in town?"

"I asked about you."

My jaw clenched. Wrong answer. "You asked about me."

Asked who? What exactly had he heard? Apparently enough to know my last name. To know my occupation. So much for flirting. Ronan might as well have dumped a bucket of ice water over my head.

Maybe he'd thought I'd be an easy connection to people in this town. A way for an "outsider" to meet the locals and grow his law firm. Maybe he'd heard that in my younger days, I'd hit up Jane's every Saturday and, after a few drinks, go home with the hottest guy in the bar. Maybe he'd heard that I'd been sleeping with a married man for years until I'd accidentally gotten pregnant—sheer bullshit that always made my blood boil.

My molars ground together as I marched for my daughter, picking her up from the grass.

"Hey, I didn't mean to upset you." Ronan held up his hands. "I was just curious."

"I guess your curiosity has been sated, hasn't it? Because instead of asking me about my job or family, you've already got your answers." I huffed. "See you around, Ronan."

With that, I stalked across the lawn, taking Wren inside, grass clumps and all. I hit the garage door, closing out my new neighbor and his goddamn curiosity.

Why was I such a fool? I'd practically drooled over his good looks. I'd nearly swooned at the attention, both for me and my daughter.

Meanwhile, he'd probably heard the gossip that I was a whore. A sure thing. No wonder he kept asking me out. How convenient for him that I lived next door.

"Boys are dumb," I told Wren, carrying her to the bathroom.

"Dee." She held up her hands, the grass pieces falling all over the counter as I turned on the faucet.

"Dirt," I said, blowing out a deep breath. Then I picked up a blade, holding it up. "Grass."

She let out a string of babble before trying to shove a dirty hand into her mouth.

"Oh, no you don't." I picked her up, spinning her to the sink where I washed her hands.

Wren squirmed and fussed, mad that I'd destroyed all of her hard work. "No no no."

"Sorry, baby."

Wouldn't life be easier if adults could squirm and fuss? To lay our emotions bare instead of keeping them hidden inside? Maybe a good screaming tantrum would make me feel better. Or maybe what I needed was a glass of wine.

So I took Wren to her playpen in the living room, leaving her to her toys and the cartoons I turned on for background noise. Then I retreated to my bedroom to change into a pair of sweats and a tee.

I made myself a salad and Wren some pasta. Then after her bath, we made our way to her bedroom to read a book and cuddle in her rocking chair.

Her bedroom windows overlooked Ronan's house. From this spot, in the chair set right beside the glass, I could see into his garage.

One of Kerrigan's design stipulations for the development had been for the garages to be set sideways so they didn't face the street. In her opinion, curved driveways enhanced curb appeal. She wasn't wrong. But tonight, I really wished I didn't have a front-row seat to Ronan Thatcher's home.

He came through the door that led inside the house with a stack of flattened cardboard boxes under an arm. He tossed them into the back of a shiny black truck, then returned to the house.

Two years ago, I would have thrown the guy a bone. I wouldn't have cared one bit if he'd asked around about me, because I would have asked around about him too.

Too much had changed these past couple of years. Too much had changed since Hawaii.

So I kissed Wren's hair as she yawned.

Then I reached for the blinds, blocking out the setting sun.

And Ronan Thatcher.

CHAPTER FIVE

RONAN

ADMITTING defeat was like swallowing razor blades.

But Larke's message had come through loud and clear. Whether I liked it or not, the answer was a resounding *no*.

I'd spent the past five days sulking. Nursing my wounded pride. Replaying our conversations to see what I'd missed. There'd been a spark. She'd felt it too, hadn't she? Or had this been one-sided?

Why was it that every time she rejected me, I liked her more and more? Larke's elusiveness was as hypnotic as those breathtaking eyes.

"Fuck," I muttered, propping my elbows on the desk and letting my face fall into my hands. What the hell was wrong with me? Why couldn't I get her out of my head?

All weekend long I'd found myself glancing through my windows, hoping to catch a glimpse. It was embarrassing. I really needed blinds.

By Sunday evening, I'd been so pissed—at Larke, at myself—that I'd gone on a five-mile run to burn off some steam. Not even the exercise had helped get her off my mind. Neither had the shower afterward when I'd wrapped a fist around my aching cock, willing this desire to vanish.

I'd hoped that by coming to the office today, by getting away from the cul-de-sac, I'd get past this. Yet here I was, dwelling on the woman.

Forget about her.

Effective immediately, no more pining over my neighbor. I had more important things to worry about right now, like my business. So I shoved away from the desk and walked out of my office to check in with Gertrude. "Hi."

"Hi." She swiveled away from her desk, closing the paperback she'd been reading.

"Anyone call?"

"Not since you asked me that"—she glanced at the clock —"twelve minutes ago."

I huffed.

Maybe this fixation on Larke had nothing to do with the woman but with the fact that I was going out of my goddamn mind without enough work.

No, it was the woman.

But the boredom wasn't helping.

"You're especially irritable today," Gertrude said.

"You're especially direct today," I grumbled. "I'm bored, all right? I'm not used to sitting idle."

She frowned. "We've only been open a week. Give it time."

I frowned and walked toward the windows, staring out at First. Gertrude could think that business was the sole source of my frustration. Being this torn up by a woman was pathetic. Was this how ugly men felt?

Three times. Larke had rejected me three fucking times. All I was asking for was dinner. Maybe a drink and a chance to get to know her. Hell, at this point, I'd settle for the fucking time of day.

It wasn't like I was looking for a serious commitment. I certainly wasn't looking for love. Not now. Not after the epic disaster that had been my marriage. Not after I'd come to the conclusion that love was nothing but a damn lie we told ourselves so we wouldn't be alone.

Personally, I liked living alone. I had no qualms about a quiet house. But I liked women. I liked sex. I liked Larke.

Forget about her.

Maybe it wasn't me, but this town. Maybe moving here, where everything was so different, had been a mistake.

"Ronan," Gertrude said.

I spun away from the glass. "What?"

"You're glowering."

"Huh?"

"You're standing in the window, glowering. You'll scare clients away before they even walk through the door."

"Oh." I scowled and went to the couch, sinking down on the edge. "Any emails?"

She arched her eyebrows.

"I'll take that as a no."

"Why don't you get out of here? I'll stick around and call you if anyone calls or emails or walks in."

"Nah. I don't want to leave." Even if it was painfully slow.

The work for our first client, the man who'd come in to have us set up his LLC, was done. Friday, a woman had come in looking for an attorney to help her with her divorce.

Granted, it was an uncontested divorce, so it would take next to no effort, just a bit of coordination with the husband's lawyer and putting the documents in place for the judgment. But I'd been overjoyed to help because any work was better than nothing. And maybe if I could keep my mind occupied, it would stop wandering to Larke.

Except today had been brutally quiet. We'd had no activity. None.

Maybe I'd gone too small in picking Calamity. I could have chosen one of the larger Montana towns, like Bozeman or Missoula. A place where gossip didn't run quite as rampant.

Fuck. That had been my downfall, hadn't it? When I'd mentioned that I'd asked about her.

I could have sworn Larke had been close to a yes too. Until I'd fucked it all up.

"Ronan, you're glowering again," Gertrude muttered, glancing over the edge of her book.

"No, I'm not." Yes, I was. I felt the crease between my eyebrows.

Gertrude pursed her lips, her stare flat.

It was a look I'd seen countless times on Cora's face. I hated that damn look.

Great. Not only was I dwelling on Larke, but now I was thinking about Cora. *For fuck's sake.*

I shoved to my feet and stalked to my office so I wouldn't glower in Gertrude's presence. Then I collapsed in my chair, swiping the baseball from my desk. It fit perfectly in my palm, the stitching as familiar as my own skin.

My brother had given me this ball years ago as a birthday gift. When I'd been a twelve-year-old kid who'd had dreams of the major leagues—I was good but not great. It had taken me a few years to realize baseball would only be a pastime, not a career.

But Noah had believed in my dreams almost more than myself. He'd told Mom he wanted to buy me his own gift that year, so at six, he'd raided his piggy bank for some cash. Then she'd taken him to the store and he'd picked out this baseball.

I'd kept it close ever since, taking it to college and law school. It had sat on every one of my desks, including this one.

I leaned back in my chair, so deep that I had to kick my feet up. Then I tossed the ball toward the ceiling. It came falling back into my hand.

Throw after throw, I let the ball soar, bumping the ceiling with a thud before it dropped.

"Ahem." Gertrude cleared her throat, forcing me upright so fast that I nearly fell over.

"Is someone here?"

She crossed her arms over her chest as she stood in the threshold. "Stop that."

"Stop what?"

"The bouncing. It's annoying."

"You realize I'm your boss, right?"

"Yes. Your point?"

Apparently, I didn't have one. "I'm bored."

"No kidding," she said dryly. "Want a book? I brought two."

"What kind of book?"

The grin she gave me was sheer evil. "Romance."

"Bring it in," I said, calling her bluff.

That smirk of hers fell just a bit before she recovered, leaving momentarily for her desk and returning with a book. There was a couple in a clinch on the cover, the woman's gown bared over her shoulders and the man's torso bare.

I'd never read a romance novel before, but if it would get Gertrude off my ass, then I'd give it a try. It wasn't like I had anything else to do.

"Looks great," I said, opening it to the first page.

"Ronan." Gertrude waited until I met her gaze. "Go home."

I set the book aside, pinching the bridge of my nose. "I don't have anything to do at home either."

While I'd stewed and sulked about Larke all weekend, I'd finished unpacking. So all that waited for me was the television, which oddly seemed less appealing than the romance novel at this point.

"I'm struggling, Gerty," I confessed. "Was your old job this boring?"

"No, but I also don't expect this job to be boring. You've already had two clients. Assuming both leave here happy, they'll refer others your way."

Word of mouth. That would make or break my business. Just like it had broken my shot with Larke.

At the moment, I didn't trust my chances.

"What if we placed some ads in the local newspapers? We could put some out in Bozeman too." It was only two hours away. At the moment, driving two hours—one way—seemed like a great way to kill some time.

"Would you like me to find out how much it would cost?" Gertrude asked.

"Yes, please."

She nodded, about to leave when she turned back. "You'll get used to the slower pace."

"Yeah," I muttered. Did I even want to get used to it? I was a man who'd spent his adult life in perpetual motion. This was just too much standing still. Too much time to think.

It was a lot easier to ignore the past, my mistakes, when I'd been stressed to the point of exhaustion.

"Maybe I should become a pilot." The idea came out of nowhere, but I didn't hate it.

Gertrude blinked. "What?"

"I could take flying lessons in my free time."

"Do you like to fly?"

I shrugged. "Not especially."

"Be honest. Is this move to Calamity a midlife crisis? Because I'll just warn you, I already suffered through that with my husband, and I won't do it again."

"I'm thirty-five. That's not midlife."

She crossed the room, snagged her paperback, then left me alone, this time closing the door behind her.

Was this a midlife crisis? Maybe I was destined to die young. I swept up my phone, calling one of the few people who'd be straight with me.

Noah answered on the first ring. "Hey."

"I'm bored."

He chuckled. "Small-town life not all it's cracked up to be?"

"Was this a mistake?"

"Don't know. Maybe give it a month or two before you throw in the towel."

"Yeah," I muttered. "How are you?"

"Good. Busy."

"I'd kill to be busy." To be so consumed with work that I wouldn't be fixated on my neighbor.

"I'd kill for a vacation," he muttered. "I was thinking about booking a trip. Somewhere tropical. It's been a while since I spent a week on a beach. Booze. Women. Paradise."

"Wait. I thought you were dating that girl, what was her name? Jenny?"

"Nah. We were just fucking. I dropped her a few weeks ago."

"Ah." Time to steer the conversation back to work.

I loved Noah but I wasn't in the mood for a recap of his latest sexual escapades. He was good looking—he was my brother, after all. And Noah was currently embracing his life as a young, single, budding attorney with disposable income and a panty-dropping smile.

"What are you working on?" I asked. "Let me live vicariously through you."

"Well, I just got assigned to a defamation case. Your specialty. Though it's not a big case. Nothing like you'd take."

"How are you feeling about it?"

"Not sure yet," he said. "But I might hit you up for some advice after I get into the details."

"I'm here." Always. For my half brother, I'd do just about anything.

Mom joked that the day she and Dad had brought Noah home from the hospital was the day I'd developed a second shadow.

When we were kids, he'd copied me in nearly all things, from my haircut to my clothes. My hobbies had been his hobbies. When he'd called to tell me he was considering law school, none of us had been surprised.

Maybe the six-year age difference was the reason, but the imitation had never bothered me. Noah was mine. He'd claimed me as I'd claimed him. Just like Dad had claimed me, even though Noah was his only biological child.

We were brothers, no matter how much blood we shared.

"I ran into Bobbie at the gym this morning," Noah said. "We talked about coming to visit you this summer."

"Yes." Not only would I gladly take the distraction, but I missed familiar faces. "Just pick a date. It's not like I have anything else happening."

Noah chuckled. "I'd better get back to work."

"Braggart," I muttered with a smile. "Bye."

"See ya."

The moment the call was over, I pulled up Bobbie's name.

"Hey," he answered. "How's Montana?"

"Meh. How are you?"

"Busy."

Everyone was fucking busy. Jealousy was a nasty bitch. "I just got off the phone with Noah."

"Yeah, we're coming to see you this summer."

"The sooner the better."

"Aww. Miss me already? Want me to send you a selfie later so you can use it as your phone's wallpaper?"

I chuckled. "Just no dick pics."

Bobbie and I had met during our first year at undergrad, and we'd stayed tight ever since. He'd taken a different path with his career, preferring criminal cases over civil court. He worked for the district attorney's office, and considering his dedication to punishing the filth of San Francisco, I suspected he'd be wearing a judge's robes someday soon. The man worked nonstop.

A knock came at my office door, so I shifted the phone from my mouth. "Yeah?"

Gertrude opened it just enough to wave me out. "There's someone here to see you."

A client.

Thank fuck.

"I'd better let you go," I told Bobbie. "Do me a favor and hang with Noah every now and then? I'm worried he doesn't have enough good influences around now that I'm in Montana, okay?"

He chuckled. "I'll do my best, Thatch."

"See ya." I ended the call and stood, smoothing down the front of my shirt, then strode out of the office.

Gertrude was standing beside her desk, eyes locked on our client.

No, not a client.

A kid.

A teenager.

The girl paced the waiting area, her arms crossed over her chest and her eyes locked on the floor. A backpack, straining at the seams, was looped over both her shoulders. Her coat was a deep purple, the same color as her scuffed and faded tennis shoes.

Maybe the girl wanted a job. Or a donation for a fundraiser. Or to be emancipated. That could be fun.

"Hi there." I walked over, hand extended. "I'm Ronan Thatcher."

The girl stopped pacing, her eyes locking on my hand first, then lifting to my face. "You're a lawyer?"

"Last time I checked." I left my hand out for another moment, waiting for her to shake it. But apparently she had no intention of uncrossing her arms, so I dropped my arm to my side. "Can I help you with something?"

"How much do you cost?"

"Well, that depends on what you want. Typically, I bill my clients hourly."

"What's your hourly rate?"

This girl, with her black hair and green eyes, had headache written all over her young face.

"Look, Miss . . ." I waited.

And got nothing.

No name. Just silence. "What's your name?" I spoke the words slowly, accentuating every syllable.

"Oh, um, it's Ember Scott."

"Ember." I gave her a tight smile. "Are you writing a report or something? Trying to decide if you want to be a lawyer when you grow up? I'd love to help you, but I'm very busy and—"

"No, he's not." Gertrude returned to her chair, giving me a knowing glare. Either I answered this girl's questions or she'd make my life hell.

"Helpful, Gerty. Thanks," I grumbled, waving my hand in the air. "Fine. Ask your questions, Miss Scott."

Ember looked between me and Gertrude, then swallowed hard. "What's your hourly rate?"

"Two hundred and fifty dollars."

Her eyes bugged out as her jaw hit the floor.

Hell, that was a discount. When I'd worked in California, I'd charged five hundred per hour. But considering I didn't exactly need the money and living expenses in Montana were significantly less than they'd been in San Francisco, I'd decided to cut the Calamity community a deal.

"Anything else?" I asked Ember.

Her mouth was still hanging open.

"Okay, well. Nice to meet you, Ember." I didn't bother with a farewell handshake. But before I could retreat to my office, two hands, stronger than I'd expected, clamped around my elbow and held me in place.

"I need to sue someone."

I loosened my arm from her grip, planting my fists on my sides. "How old are you?"

"Eighteen."

"A little young to start suing people, don't you think?"

"It's important." She drew in a long breath, then stood taller, her shoulders pinned back like she was about to give me a rehearsed pitch. "I'd like to sue my teacher. She's out to ruin my life."

Yes, I was definitely getting a headache. "Ember, look. You're in high school. Kids your age are prone to theatrics and exaggeration. I'm not going to sue your teacher. This sounds like something you need to take up with the principal."

"I already did!" Ember's voice rose to a near shriek, loud enough to make me wince.

"Who's your teacher, honey?" Gertrude asked.

Ember's chin began to quiver. "Larke Hale."

CHAPTER SIX

RONAN

"LARKE HALE," I repeated. Surely I hadn't heard her right. "Larke Hale is the teacher you want to sue?"

"Yes." Ember drew in a long inhale, blinking away the sheen of tears in her eyes as she composed herself. "She purposefully gave me a bad grade because she's trying to destroy my life."

Again with the melodramatics. Any other kid, I would have sent her on her way. But now that she'd mentioned Larke's name, I was interested.

"Why don't we sit and talk in my office?" I shifted to the side, waving a hand for the open door.

Ember marched past me, the zippers on her backpack rattling with every step, like they were shouting for some relief against the sheer volume of stuff she'd crammed into that bag.

"Do you know her?" I asked Gertrude, keeping my voice low.

"No. This is, um . . . has this ever happened to you before?"

Had a teenager stormed into my office to sue her teacher? "Nope. Would you mind bringing in some water?"

"Not at all." She nodded, then hurried to the small kitchenette across the hall from the conference room while I strode into my office, rounding the desk to take my chair.

"So, Ember. You must be a senior this year."

"Yes." She was sitting on the very edge of her chair. It was one of two across from my desk. Her backpack was still strapped over her shoulders.

"This might take a few minutes. You can set your backpack down."

"Oh." She jerked, like she hadn't even realized she was still wearing it. Then she stood, shrugging it off and setting it on the floor. But when she sat, she was back to the edge of the chair again, her posture rigid.

Gertrude walked in with two cans of sparkling water, handing one to me and the other to Ember. "Just let me know if you need anything else."

"Thanks," I said, popping the top and taking a fizzy drink.

Ember just held the can in her lap, glancing all around my office.

I waited as she seemed to memorize every detail, from my diplomas to the fake pothos plant on the top tier of my bookshelf to the baseball resting beside my computer's mouse.

Were all high school kids this observant? Doubtful. Then again, most high school kids didn't want to hire lawyers to sue their teachers.

"How about you start at the beginning? Give me some background." I plucked a pen from a jar on my desk and pulled a notepad out of my drawer.

Ember nodded, clutching that can of water tighter. "Ms. Hale has hated me from the first day of school."

Hate seemed like a strong word, but given the fact that Larke had rejected me three times, I could see why a teenager would jump to the extreme. "Why do you say that?"

"Because she just does. I can tell. She talks to the other kids more because they've all known her for longer."

"And she doesn't know you?"

"I just moved here this year."

Another outsider. Ember and I had something in common. "Where from?"

"Minneapolis."

"Ah. Well, I just moved here too. I'm from California. Apparently some Montanans have a thing against Californians. Maybe there's a stigma with Minnesotans too?"

Ember blinked.

"Or not," I mumbled. "Okay, keep going. Ms. Hale doesn't talk to you much."

"Never. Well, not never. You know what I mean. She doesn't talk to me like she does the other kids. Some of them even call her Larke. And she doesn't care."

"What do you call her?"

"Ms. Hale."

I leaned forward, my elbows on the desk. "When you say she talks to the other kids, what do they talk about?"

"Sports and stuff. Clubs. People they know from around town."

Considering Ember was new, she wouldn't have a tie to the Calamity community. "And you're not in sports or clubs?"

"No."

"All right. Has Ms. Hale ever said anything mean to you? Is that why you think she hates you?"

"She hasn't *said* anything mean. She just . . . doesn't like me. I can tell."

Yeah, well, Larke didn't like me either. *Join the club, kid.* "Do you have an example of a time when you could tell she didn't like you? I'm just trying to get an idea of your relationship."

"Okay, um, yeah." Ember's forehead furrowed as she thought about it for a long moment, searching her memory. The silence dragged. Which was answer enough to my question.

If Larke had actually wronged this kid, Ember would have been able to rattle off example after example.

"You know, let's not worry about that right now," I said. "Let's talk about this bad grade. Tell me about the assignment."

"It was a creative writing paper. We have three papers this year and they make up seventy-five percent of our grade."

"What makes up the other twenty-five?"

"Quizzes, book reports and homework," she said.

"And how are you doing on that front?"

"I have one hundred and ten percent. I turned in some extra credit."

"Kudos." I made a few notes about her scores, then

leaned back in my chair. "Give me more specifics about the paper in question."

"It was a dumb assignment." She rolled her eyes. "We were supposed to write a story about a superhero."

"Not a fan of superheroes? Aren't you kids into Marvel and Spider-Man and stuff these days?"

"No." Disgust filled her expression. That and a blatant *duh*. "I don't watch fluffy stuff."

"I wouldn't exactly call the Avengers *fluffy*."

Ember opened her mouth, probably to argue, but I held up a hand.

"Never mind. Let's move on. Tell me more about the assignment."

"It had to be eight to eleven pages and at least two thousand words."

I jotted down the requirements on the notepad. "How much did you write?"

"Eight pages. Two thousand, eight hundred and thirty-six words."

"Well done."

"Yes, it was well done." She scoffed. "But it's subjective and this was her chance to destroy me."

"Destroy. Right." I wasn't cut out to deal with teenagers. The attitude was stifling. How did Larke handle a classroom of them, each and every day? "What was your story about?"

"Bellerophon."

"Who?"

"The Greek warrior who rode Pegasus and killed the Chimera." Another unspoken *duh* got tacked onto that statement.

"Forgive me, it's been a while since I've brushed up on

my Greek mythology." I took a long drink of my water, already dreading my next question. "So tell me, how is a paper about Bellerophon considered creative writing?"

Ember's eyes flared.

Yep. I'd found the sore spot. My guess is that this was why Larke had given her a bad grade.

"Because I wrote a different ending. I changed it so that he didn't defeat the Chimera but died trying and it was Pegasus who actually killed the monster but no one was there to watch so people assumed Bellerophon sacrificed his life instead."

"Uh . . . great?" But was that really a creative writing assignment if she'd just changed the ending to someone else's story? "What grade did Ms. Hale give you?"

"A C plus. Seventy-seven percent."

"That's not bad."

Ember reared back like I'd slapped her. "Yes. It is."

"Yeah, you're right." I held up my hands. "That's horrible."

"It took my average to a B plus."

"And I'm guessing that's bad too?"

"Obviously." *Duh. Duh. Duh.*

Fuck, I had a headache. I'd always excelled at school, but I'd had a few B plus grades and hadn't taken them this seriously. Hell, even Noah, a kid who'd been twice as dedicated to his studies as me, had never bemoaned a B plus.

"It's the worst possible thing that could ever happen to me," Ember snapped.

Oh, if only this kid knew more about the horrors of the world. It was just a grade. "Why is it the worst possible thing that could ever happen to you?"

"Because it means I won't graduate with a four point. And that's basically like taking a grenade to my future."

"Scholarship?"

"Yes. I need to be perfect."

Interesting word choice. *I need to be perfect.* Not her grades. Her.

"Have you talked to Ms. Hale?" Sure, Larke had brushed me aside, but I had a feeling that she cared for her students. I doubted that she would intentionally kill this girl's chances at a college scholarship over a creating writing paper.

"I've tried. But like I said, she hates me." Ember scowled at an invisible spot on my desk.

I used the break in conversation to try and get a read on this kid. Her jeans had holes in both knees. The distressed look was popular but these holes didn't exactly look intentional. They looked like she'd earned them honestly.

She wasn't wearing much makeup besides a little mascara to accentuate her eyes. A few of the partners at my firm in San Francisco had teenaged girls. When they'd come into the office, they'd been caked with makeup and dripping in designer apparel.

Not Ember. She was unassuming. Normal. Her coat was frayed at the sleeves' hems. Its muted color seemed much like the jeans, caused by wash and wear.

She didn't come from money, did she? That fit with her wanting to know about my hourly rate. And her desperation for a good grade to get a scholarship.

"What did Ms. Hale say when you talked to her about the C plus?"

"She said I didn't do the assignment correctly. That I was

supposed to write an original story." Ember's chin dropped, defeated. "My story was original."

The truth, the belief, in those words made my heart squeeze. "The concept is definitely unique. Did you ask Ms. Hale for a chance to try again?"

"Yes. She said no."

Damn. "And what did the principal say?"

"That grades were given by the teachers. And that Ms. Hale was the only person who could change it."

I was her last resort, wasn't I? And I was about to destroy her hope. "Lawsuits are expensive. More expensive than taking out a student loan and paying some interest."

She shook her head furiously. "I need perfect grades. I deserve more than a C plus. She *has* to change it. We have to *make* her change it."

"I don't know if that's possible," I said, trying to be as gentle as possible.

"No." Ember's voice cracked as her eyes flooded. She looked on the verge of having a full-blown meltdown in my office.

Stretching across the desk, I waved for her to hand over her can of water. When she did, I popped the top and passed it back. "Take a drink. Take a breath."

She gulped, as ordered, then filled her lungs after she swallowed.

"Better?"

Ember nodded. "Do you take on pro bono cases?"

"Sometimes."

A spark of hope glittered in her green eyes. "Will you take mine?"

I sighed. "What do your parents think about all of this?"

Ember dropped her gaze to her lap and stayed quiet.

Another silence that was answer enough.

She'd get no support from her parents. Not that she needed it. She was eighteen. But they probably wouldn't be willing to help her cover the cost. And if they were against this, I had no desire to get between a child and her parents.

"Look, kid. I get it. You're upset over this grade. I'm not trying to discount your feelings here, but take it from someone who's spent a long time in the world of higher education. Student loans aren't the end of the world. And you don't need to be perfect."

Even full of unshed tears, Ember's eyes blazed. "Yes, I do. Larke Hale is a monster. She has to be stopped."

It took every ounce of strength not to laugh. Mostly because this kid was dead serious. Had I been that dramatic as a teen?

"I wish I could help you." I gave her a sad smile, feeling a pinch as her expression fell. "Your chances of winning this aren't good."

Once upon a time, my mentor had taught me that being honest with your clients was half the battle. Guiding their expectations.

"But it's possible," Ember said.

"I mean . . . maybe?"

She thought about it for a moment, then sat taller. Hopefully that meant she'd accept this was a dead end.

I stood from my chair, extending a hand. "Good luck—"

"I'll just have to represent myself."

"Um, what?"

"That can happen, right? People can act as their own lawyer?"

"Yeah. It's definitely not a great idea."

She gave me a flat stare. "Of course you'd say that. You're a lawyer. Without clients, you don't get paid."

"And I don't get paid for pro bono jobs either."

"I am not going to let this go." Ember raised her chin.

Shit. There was determination in her gaze. And sheer stubbornness. "This will be enough of a mess without a high schooler attempting to navigate the legal system."

"Can you at least tell me what to do? How this works?"

"No, I—"

"Please." She held up a hand, cutting me off. Then she set her water on the desk and dove for her backpack, the zipper loosening with a whirr, then paper rustling. When she sat straight, she held out a wad of cash. "Here's one hundred and seven dollars. Can you just give me thirty minutes?"

"Put that away." I frowned at the money, then let out a growl. "Fine."

The air rushed from her lungs as she breathed, "Thanks."

"If you go through with this, Ms. Hale will be served with a complaint. It explains how the defendant—that's Larke—caused the plaintiff—that's you—damages. Then you also state what you're asking for in relief. That would be like money."

"Or a better grade."

"Or a better grade." I shrugged. "Though I've never heard of a student suing a teacher for a better grade before. That said, I suppose anything is possible."

"And then the jury will decide who's right or wrong."

"This will hit small claims court. There's no jury." And

though she could have a lawyer as long as both parties are represented by one, she really didn't need an attorney. "You'll present your case in front of a judge and the judge will decide."

"Oh." Something about that she didn't like. "But people will hear about this, right?"

"I guess." Given this town's affinity for gossip, chances were it would definitely be discussed.

"Good." Ember gave a single nod. "If I can't get a better grade, then at least I can ruin her reputation."

"Wow. That's, uh, rather . . . vindictive." Yet considering we were even having this conversation, it fit Ember's motive for revenge.

"I'm going to fight this." There was an edge to her voice. Steel.

Yeah, she'd fight the grade. And in doing so, she'd create an epic clusterfuck, dragging Larke into the middle of it all.

Where were Ember's parents? Why weren't they with her? Or better yet, why hadn't they told her this was a fool's errand?

The chances that a judge would side with Ember were slim at best. But there might be some people in town who'd believe this girl. Who'd make Larke out to be a villain.

But what if there was a way to keep the disaster contained? What if I could convince Ember this was a waste of her time? It might give me a migraine but it would save Larke one hell of a headache.

Fuck my life. This interest in Larke Hale was going to be my downfall.

"I'll need your paper."

"W-what?" Ember's face lit up. "You're going to help me?"

I held out a hand, snapping my fingers. "Your paper?"

Ember burst into action, hauling her backpack to her lap. She opened the main compartment and it practically exploded. A sweatshirt fell to the floor, followed by a textbook. Then came fruit. Two apples and a banana. The produce was followed by a sandwich wrapped in clear cellophane.

"Did you skip lunch or something?"

She paused, glancing up as her cheeks flamed. "Um . . ."

That was all I got for an answer as she kept digging through her bag. Binder. Composition notebook. Pens, pencils and highlighters. Until finally, she pulled out a blue folder that had seen better days. Its edges were worn and the inside pocket ripped. But the paper she pulled out was mostly crisp, just a few minor wrinkles from being read. And graded.

Ember handed it across my desk.

Eight pages. Two thousand, eight hundred and thirty-six words.

With a bright red C+ written in the upper right-hand corner.

Maybe we could solve this with a bit of mediation. Keep the court out of it entirely.

"Give me a chance to read this over. Can you come back tomorrow after school?" I asked, scanning the first page and the notes written in the margin.

Larke had beautiful handwriting. Neat and clean. I liked her handwriting. Of course I did. *Christ.*

"So you'll really help me?" Ember asked, her voice wobbling.

I looked up from the paper just as a lone tear streaked down her cheek. A lone tear so full of relief and hope it made the hairs on the back of my neck stand on end.

Hold up. What was I missing here? I'd spent years studying people, both friend and foe. The instincts I'd honed were screaming. There was more to this than a mediocre grade. But what?

There was only one way to find out.

"Tomorrow, kid." I nodded. "We'll talk tomorrow."

Her entire frame sagged, like she hadn't heard those words in a long, long time. "Thank you."

"You're welcome." I stood, giving her a small smile, then waited as she shoved her things back into her bag.

It had to weigh over twenty pounds. Ember couldn't have been more than five two. She probably weighed just over a hundred pounds. And that pack was so heavy that when she strapped it on her shoulders, it took her a moment to find her balance and adjust to the added load.

"Do you have a ride or car?" I asked, escorting her to the front.

"No, I, uh, walked. It's not far."

"Okay." I pushed the door open for her, letting her step outside. "Tomorrow."

She gave me a nod. "Tomorrow."

When she was out of sight, I stepped inside. Gertrude's gaze waited.

"Well?"

I lifted a shoulder. "I guess you can mark Ember Scott down as our third client."

"This seems like the kind of thing people are going to talk about. And not the good kind of talk," Gertrude said. "Are you sure you know what you're doing, helping this kid?"

With the door open to my office during that meeting, she'd heard every word.

"No," I admitted. "But I think I'll take your advice. Head home." Maybe go for a run and see if I could make sense of that meeting with Ember.

Being new to town, the last thing I wanted was a controversial lawsuit attached to my name. A high school teenager suing her teacher was destined to cause a stir. But there was something at play here. I just had to find out what.

So I gathered my things, including the Bellerophon paper, and headed for my car.

The cul-de-sac was quiet as I rolled down the street. It wasn't quite five and people were probably still at work. I parked in the garage and climbed out of the Stingray. But as I turned to shut the door, I froze.

My gaze had automatically gone next door, searching. I'd lived here for days, and seeking her out had already become a habit.

Larke came walking into the bedroom that faced my garage. She had a laundry basket in her arms. All weekend, the blinds had been drawn in that room. But today, she must have wanted to let light in. Maybe she hadn't expected me home so early.

She did a double take when she spotted me, her steps slowing.

Damn, but she was beautiful. No wonder I couldn't forget about her. No wonder I'd been so relentless about getting her attention. From the stupid twenty-dollar-bill pickup line to approaching her at the White Oak.

It took effort not to walk to her house. To tell her about Ember and get her side of the story. But first, I had some research to do. So I lifted a hand to wave, not surprised when she dropped the laundry basket and disappeared from the room.

Fuck.

Well, like it or not, I was definitely about to get Larke's attention.

CHAPTER SEVEN

LARKE

MY LUNCH BAG was tucked under one arm. The stack of papers I'd taken with me to the teachers' lounge was under the other. One hand held an open can of Diet Coke and the other gripped a bottle of water for my afternoon classes.

I was perfectly balanced.

Or would have been, until I passed Asshole Abbott's classroom just as he marched through the door, his bulky arm slamming into my shoulder.

"Ah!" I yelped as my bottle of water and lunch bag went flying. Somehow, I managed to save my pop from splashing on my clothes but the papers scattered to the floor. "Freaking great."

I crouched to pick up the papers.

Abbott grunted, his familiar scowl fixed in place as he bent to pick up the water and bag. The moment I stood, he thrust them into my arms and walked away.

No apology for bumping into me. Shocking. I guess I

should just count myself lucky that he'd bothered to pick anything up off the floor.

"Asshole." My lip curled as I headed for my own classroom.

My day had been . . . strange. A run-in with Wilder was par for the course. The kids had been acting off since first period, snickering and whispering to each other in every one of my classes this morning.

Something was going on, but I hadn't wanted to ask. When it came to high school drama, it was just as awful as it had been when I'd been a teen, and the less I knew the better.

Was it summer yet? According to the countdown on my whiteboard, there were forty days to go. That seemed like a lifetime.

I trudged to my classroom and stowed my lunch bag. Then I took a seat at my desk, finishing both my Diet Coke and the papers I'd been grading just as the bell for fifth period echoed through the building.

The sound of kids talking and laughing and rushing through the hallways filled the silence. But the noise disappeared as quickly as it had appeared when the bell sounded again, save for one lone pair of footsteps that pounded across the floor as a kid streaked past my door, racing for his next class.

I sighed, reaching for the stack of book reports in the basket on my desk. Fifth was my prep period and since I hadn't felt like working at home last night, I was catching up on the reports my sophomores had turned in yesterday.

Maybe another high school English teacher would have pushed *Macbeth* or *Lord of the Flies* or *Animal Farm*, but those books had been miserable for me to read, and I just hadn't been able to force my students to suffer. Or maybe I was saving myself the pain of reading twenty-five reports on books I hadn't enjoyed.

For all of my classes, I'd chosen a single required read: *To Kill a Mockingbird*. Beyond that, the students were responsible for reading nine books of their own over the course of the school year—a book a month—then providing me with a two-page report on each.

The report on the top of the stack was on a John Grisham novel. It was a book I'd read myself. The student had chosen it because she wanted to be a lawyer. Her conclusion, at the end of the paper, was that it sounded like a lot more fun to become an author than an attorney.

Part of me wanted to make a copy of her summary and leave it in Ronan's mailbox, just to tease him a little. It was tempting, much like the man himself.

Yesterday, when I'd seen him in his garage, he'd waved at me. He'd looked so lonely. So apologetic. And I'd almost caved. I'd almost invited him over for that dinner he'd kept asking for.

Had I been too quick to judge last week? I'd thought about it constantly over the weekend. I'd put myself in his shoes, trying to fit in a new place. Calamity was probably a lonely town for an *outsider*, as he'd deemed himself. We weren't without our fair share of cliques.

Meanwhile, on any given night, I could have dinner with a number of family members. I could call a dozen friends to hang out. I'd been born into this tight-knit community, so I didn't have to ask about others. For the most part, I already knew.

Even if I had dinner with Ronan, it didn't mean we had to date, right? We could just be . . . neighbors.

I had overreacted last week, hadn't I? The gossip thing was a touchy subject. But he'd just been curious. Maybe I was a bit curious too.

I shook thoughts of Ronan away, focusing on the reports in front of me until the next bell rang, and this time, my classroom flooded with students, everyone rushing to take their seats. The whispering I'd dealt with all morning had apparently bled into the afternoon periods too because nearly all of the kids had formed little huddles. A few glanced my direction before they started giggling.

It was almost like they were laughing at me. Okay, what the hell was going on? If it was about me, did I really want to know?

Probably not.

The bell rang again and when the chatter didn't stop, I clapped my hands together twice. "Let's get started."

"Ms. Hale." A boy in the front row shot his hand into the air.

"Yes, Beckham."

"Can I have a hall pass?"

"You were just in the hall." I shook my head but opened my desk drawer for the hall pass, taking it to his desk. "Five minutes. Not a second more."

"I swear. I'll be right back." He practically leapt out of his seat, racing for the door.

Another hand shot in the air. "Ms. Hale."

"Rainey." I nodded to the girl who'd read the John Grisham book. "What's up?"

"Have you ever gone to court?"

"Court," I repeated. "Like the courthouse? Yes."

"For what?" another student asked.

"To get the registration for my car."

"I had to do that last week," Marie said from the row of desks closest to the windows.

Matt, sitting in front of Marie, glanced over his shoulder with an eye roll. "Not all of us have our license yet, Marie."

"Or we have our license but we don't have a rich dad to buy us a car," Rainey muttered.

Marie sneered at her classmates while a new wave of snickering filled the air.

Sophomores. *Heaven help me.* They were the hardest.

The freshmen weren't much better, though there were a few who were still innocent and sweet. My junior class was my saving grace, mostly because they were so intent on their studies, nearly every kid starting to think about college. The seniors had been solid early in the year, but at this point, with only forty days until graduation, they'd all checked out.

This wasn't the first time I'd taught Matt or Rainey or Beckham—he'd always needed extra bathroom breaks in fifth grade too. But there were others, like Marie, who were new to Calamity and still trying to fit in with the kids who'd been here since birth.

Ronan's face popped into my mind, and with it a twinge of guilt.

"Let's focus," I told the kids, and myself. "Please take out your grammar books."

That won me a chorus of groans.

"Yes, I know. It's everyone's favorite." I rounded my desk, taking my teacher's version of the book. "Page one hundred and nineteen."

The hour was excruciating. The kids never did focus and when I turned them loose to work on an assignment, the whispering returned. A few kept giving me strange looks, like they knew a secret I didn't. Or they were trying to figure out if I'd heard whatever it was that they'd heard.

I tuned it all out, working through their book reports and handing them out by the end of class.

"By Friday, you need to go through your reports and make corrections to grammar and spelling," I said, just as the bell rang.

The thunder of their exit was replaced with the trampling of the freshmen, who were just as unfocused. By the time the last bell rang for the day, I felt as if I'd run ten miles. And I still had more grading to finish.

Wren was at daycare and part of me wanted to blow it off like yesterday, to go home a little early and grade papers tonight after she was in bed. But I forced myself to sit at my desk and work through a pile of worksheets so that when I went home, I could disconnect.

"Knock, knock." Emily Cain, the high school's principal, walked in as I was packing up. "Hey, Larke."

"Hey." I smiled, standing to greet her.

Emily was also newer to Calamity. She'd only been at the high school for two years but everyone adored her. Her predecessor had been a complete jerk, rude and abrasive. He'd been the principal to hire Asshole Abbott, which seemed fitting since they both had personalities as soft as sandpaper.

While Emily, on the other hand, was open and honest. This year had been hard, but at least I had a great boss. Her kind eyes always seemed to draw out the truth. She was just the type of person you confided in. Probably good in her line of work. I suspected she was good at drawing out student confessions, even from the troublemakers.

"How's it going?" I asked.

"I need a nap." She laughed. "It's been a long year."

"Amen. I'm not cut out for high school."

"You're going to leave me next year, aren't you?"

"Maybe." I gave her an exaggerated frown. "I really miss fifth grade."

And though I was hoping to get back to the elementary school, there was a chance I'd be gone entirely. That I'd be the new person in a new town for a change.

The idea of moving made me equally nervous and excited. I was torn, split straight down the center, like I was standing on a cliff and something was either going to shove me over the edge or haul me back to familiar ground.

"Got a minute?" Emily asked.

"Sure. What's up?"

The look she gave me had my stomach twisting. Knowing this school, knowing Calamity, I was sure it had everything to do with whatever the kids had been buzzing about today. "Oh, no. What happened?"

"One of my student aides stopped by my office before she left. There's a rumor floating around the school."

"About me?" Dumb question. Of course it was about me. Otherwise, Emily wouldn't be in my classroom.

"Unfortunately." Emily held up her hands. "And I want to preface this with it's just a rumor. But if it was me, I'd want to know."

"Okay," I drawled, my pulse racing.

"Apparently, there's a rumor that you're about to be sued."

My jaw dropped. My heart stopped. "What?"

Oh, God. This wasn't happening. I clutched the edge of my desk to keep my balance.

A lawsuit. Something I'd feared for two years.

I scrambled to recall everything I'd learned from my Google searches about custody agreements, about rescinding parental rights. But that had been during my pregnancy and the details were fuzzy.

How was this happening? How had other people heard about this before me?

"I don't understand. He said he didn't want her." But if he was suing me, then I guess he'd changed his mind.

"Huh?" Emily asked. "Who doesn't want her?"

Wren. "Wait, what are you talking about?"

"My student aide is a senior. She has a few classes with Ember Scott. You gave Ember a C plus on a paper recently."

"Yes." I nodded.

Ember was in my senior class. For the most part, she was quiet. She only spoke if I called on her, and given how she'd state the answer while staring at her desk, I didn't call on her often because the spotlight seemed to make her uncomfortable.

When she walked into the room, she went straight to her desk and didn't interact much with the other kids. The same was true for when she left. But Ember was smart. Her work was always top level, though she'd missed the mark with her creative writing paper.

"I stand by that grade, even though she's not happy about it. I asked for an original storyline, and she took an existing story and simply changed the ending. She came to talk to me about it last week, demanding I change the grade. But I won't. It was a C plus paper."

The most I'd ever heard Ember say had been when she'd approached me after school, pleading her case for that A. Given the way she'd tensed, my explanation and a firm *no* hadn't been what she'd wanted to hear.

Since then, she'd barely looked at me, no matter how many times I'd tried to make eye contact.

"She took it to Vicky too," I told Emily. Vicky was the assistant principal, another addition to the administration along with Emily.

"Vicky gave me the scoop," Emily said. "You know we support you."

"Thank you." That support wasn't always guaranteed. Neither was a heads-up about school rumors. "Wait. Is *Ember* suing me?"

"Apparently. Ember told my aide she was going to fight this. She's even hired a lawyer."

My jaw dropped again. "Is that— Can she even do that?"

"I don't know." Emily shook her head. "I've never had this happen before."

"But she's hired a lawyer? Who?"

"Also something I don't know." Emily gave me a sad smile. "Sorry. I came in here with very little to share. I know next to nothing because it's just a rumor. And maybe it's nothing."

Or maybe it was something.

And maybe the lawyer Ember had hired wasn't such a mystery after all.

My hands balled into fists. "Thank you for telling me."

"You're welcome." Emily put her hand on my arm, giving it a gentle squeeze, then left me alone.

If Ember's lawyer was Ronan, if he'd agreed to come after me for a fair grade, I was going to lose my ever-loving mind. To think I'd been feeling guilty for rejecting him. I'd almost let that man into my home.

"That son of a bitch."

Yes, I was jumping to conclusions, but I knew the other three lawyers in town. Other than Julian Tosh, who was a complete and total prick, they were good people. And Julian was so arrogant I doubted he'd even entertain the idea of working for a teenager.

Were Ember's parents involved? I hadn't a clue who they were or where they lived. If they were so concerned, then why hadn't they come to me?

It took a solid five minutes for the red coating my vision to clear. Then I moved in a flurry, collecting my things and shutting the lights off in the room before I marched to the parking lot and drove across town to daycare, my hands strangling the steering wheel.

Not even Wren's smile could erase my anger, though it eased a bit. My daughter gave me something else to concentrate on for the rest of the evening while I bided my time. While I waited for my neighbor to get home.

The blinds in her room stayed open. I lost count of the times I looked out the living room windows, searching for a shiny silver Corvette to rumble down the street.

Finally, well after Wren's bedtime, headlights flashed as he rolled up his driveway.

With the baby monitor in my hand, I stormed outside

and across the lawn, not needing a coat because, despite the chill, I was a raging inferno.

Ronan climbed out of his car, slamming the door before he stood tall, his shoulders pinned. Then he turned, totally unfazed to find me storming across his driveway.

I stomped into his garage, stopping in front of him and crossing my arms over my chest. "Ember Scott."

Just a name. That's all I gave him.

But it was enough.

Not a flicker of confusion marred that handsome face. No, the only emotion in his expression was guilt. The bastard.

"This is ridiculous." I tossed a hand in the air. He was officially on my Shithead List. "I am doing my job. That grade is a fair grade, goddamn it."

He held up his hands. "Larke—"

"Is this because I don't want to date you?"

"Let me explain—"

"No," I snapped. "You're despicable."

"Would you just listen—"

"Talk to my lawyer." I spun, about to walk away, but he caught my elbow, turning me back to him.

"Please, let me explain." Ronan's voice was gentle, desperate, as he inched closer. His grip on my arm loosened, but he didn't drop his hand. His fingertips trailed, featherlight, across my skin, the touch sending a jolt of electricity through my veins.

My breath hitched. I lifted my gaze, locking with his hazel eyes. A hint of cologne filled my nose, masculine and clean. Wood with a hint of citrus.

"Please." His deep voice sent a shiver down my spine.

That plea didn't have anything to do with his explanation about Ember, did it?

Why wasn't I leaving? I should move. I should walk away. But I couldn't unglue my feet. I couldn't tear away from those eyes.

"Larke."

God, I liked how he said my name.

Ronan's hand lifted like he was going to touch my face. Like he wanted to thread his fingers through my hair. Or maybe that was my want, not his.

A whimper. Not from me or Ronan, but from the baby monitor I'd forgotten I was carrying. The haze snapped. Wren's noise broke the spell.

It was like someone had snapped their fingers in my face, jolting me free. I took a step away, then another.

Ronan's hand was still lifted, frozen in midair. "Larke."

I didn't trust myself to stay in this garage, so I whirled around, nearly running back to the house.

I would have let him kiss me. Oh, God. If he had leaned in, I would have let him kiss me. Had he wanted to kiss me? What was that? Maybe this was just his tactic to catch me off balance. To use a lapse in my control against me.

Maybe this was all a game.

And goddamn it, I was so fucking sick of being played.

My hands were shaking as I rushed to the kitchen, swiping my phone from where I'd left it on the counter earlier. My whole body was coming apart. I was confused. Angry. Hot. The sparks from Ronan's touch still tingled on my arm.

But I pulled up my sister's name, pacing in front of the island as I waited for her to answer my call.

"Hey," she said.

"I need a lawyer." My voice was as shaky as my hands.

"Oh my God," she gasped. "He's coming after her?"

"No." I sagged, my feet stopping as I closed my eyes. At least I wasn't the only one to jump to that conclusion. "Some student might be suing me for giving her a bad grade. And apparently she's using the new lawyer in town, who also happens to be my next-door neighbor."

"Hold on. What?"

I caught Kerrigan up to speed, every ounce of energy drained by the time I was done.

"This is absurd," she said.

"Yep." I barked a dry laugh.

"Okay, I'm hanging up so I can tell Pierce. Call you in a minute."

"Thanks." I sighed, ending the call.

I couldn't afford Pierce's lawyer. Hell, I couldn't afford any lawyer. But at this point, I didn't have much of a choice.

With my phone clutched in a hand, I padded through the house, shutting off the lights and making my way toward Wren's room.

She hadn't made another noise and was sleeping soundly, her pink lips pursed and her eyes fluttering.

And as far as lawsuits went, I guess I'd rather go to court for a grade than for custody of my daughter.

The blinds were still open. Ronan's garage door was closed. His house was quiet. Dark. Lonely.

The sympathy I'd had for him earlier had evaporated.

I stood taller, steeling my spine.

Ember had earned a C plus. I didn't have much to my name, but I had my integrity. And I would not be intimidated into changing my decision by a bratty teenager or the new lawyer in town, no matter how attractive he might be.

If Ronan Thatcher wanted to battle this out, fine.

If Ember Scott wanted to brawl for a better grade, great.

It would be my utmost pleasure to beat them both.

CHAPTER EIGHT

RONAN

EMBER STARED at the document in front of her on the desk. "This is it?"

"That's it."

"Oh. I was expecting it to be longer."

"Nope."

"Are you sure there isn't more to add?"

This kid was killing me. "Yes. I'm sure."

The official complaint against Larke was relatively simple. It outlined the issue, as well as Ember's request to have her grade changed. No monetary compensation. Just a B instead of a C plus.

It would have been better to file for monetary damages, but since Ember didn't have a scholarship that she'd lost because of this grade and because she couldn't prove Larke was out to cost her said imaginary scholarship, there wasn't much else to request.

So, we were sticking with the grade change.

The judge was going to have my damn hide for wasting court resources. This was a fucking joke.

Yet I'd drafted the complaint anyway, and even though it was only three pages, including standard information like names and other personal details, it had taken me all damn day. Every word typed had been painful.

Especially after that interaction with Larke in my garage last week.

"Now what?" Ember asked, setting the document on my desk.

I leaned back in my chair, taking in her clothes. They were the same as Tuesday's outfit. Yesterday's clothes were the same as Monday's, which happened to be the same as Friday's. So far, I'd counted three outfits. Just the three, for a teenage girl.

Maybe they were her favorites.

Or maybe they were all she had.

"This will get filed with the court," I told her. "Then they'll decide how to handle it."

I'd dragged this out for as long as possible in an attempt to get a better read on Ember. But she was a mystery, even though she'd stopped by the office every day since her initial visit.

She was antsy to get this moving, but I'd lied, telling her I had other cases to handle before hers. Part of me had hoped if I waited long enough, she'd forget it. That this lawsuit was an impulse and someone—her parents or a friend—would talk her out of it. But she was just as determined as she'd been in the beginning.

So here we were, staring at an official complaint that I would take to the courthouse in the morning. Or, if I could come up with an excuse, I'd do it Monday and buy myself a few more days.

"How long does it take for the court to review it?" she asked.

I lifted a shoulder. "Totally depends on what else is happening. A week. A month. Six months."

Hell, if I was lucky, this would happen after she'd graduated and maybe realized that a C plus wasn't the end of the fucking world.

Ember's eyes widened. "Six months? But I need this changed, like, now."

"We're at the mercy of the court for timing."

She shrank in that chair, worrying her bottom lip between her teeth.

"Let's play a game of hypotheticals. Let's say your grade doesn't change." I'd been warning her for a week that a permanent C plus was the most likely outcome, but she had this uncanny ability to either ignore what I was saying or just refuse to hear it. Maybe she thought I was a damn idiot.

For taking this case, maybe I was.

"My grade has to change."

"But what if it doesn't?" Why was this so critical? Every time I'd asked, she'd avoided the answer. And given the way she sat straighter, raising her chin without looking at me, today would be no different.

"When will Ms. Hale get served?"

I sighed. "Is this even about the grade? Or just getting revenge?"

"I deserve a better grade."

Stubborn girl. "I don't know when they will serve Ms. Hale."

"Will it be at school?" There was hope in Ember's voice, like she was going for absolute humiliation here.

"I don't know."

It grated on my nerves and pissed me the fuck off how vindictive this kid was toward Larke, but I did my best to hide it. If Ember realized I was on both her side and Larke's side, she'd storm out of this office, and I'd never see her again.

Ember picked up the complaint again, scanning the first page.

"Remember, there is a good chance this won't work. The judge will likely support the school and not interfere."

Also something that seemed to fall on deaf ears. "It's not five o'clock. Can we file this today?"

Yes. "No."

"Why?"

"Because."

Ember's eyes narrowed as she held the document closer to her chest, like she was afraid I'd take it away from her.

Her desperation wasn't as glaringly obvious as it had been that first day she'd come to the office, but it was there, along with the repeat clothes and the backpack that always seemed to be carrying too much.

"Why don't you keep that draft? I'll reprint the official copy that goes to the courthouse."

She nodded, reaching for her backpack.

I hadn't been able to come up with an excuse for her to open her bag yesterday, but I'd been trying all week, anything to get her to show me what she had stuffed inside.

On Tuesday, she'd had two bananas and a carton of chocolate milk. Monday, she'd had white milk with an apple and another sandwich.

Today, as she worked to stow the complaint, she hauled out her purple coat along with two oranges and a box of apple juice. Then came something wrapped in a series of brown napkins. Ember set it on her knee as she pulled out a folder. One of the napkins shifted, revealing a cheeseburger.

What the actual fuck? Why was she carrying around a cheeseburger?

My gut twisted.

But I pretended to be oblivious as Ember put the document away and began restuffing her bag. Tonight after work, I'd stop by the grocery store and get some snacks for the office, trail mix and protein bars. The next time she came here, if she was hungry, I'd have something she could eat. Maybe I'd hit the White Oak too and buy a handful of cookies. It wasn't like I was in a hurry to go home anyway.

"Should I come back tomorrow?" she asked.

"Probably a good idea to check in daily at this point," I lied. There was no point, but she didn't need to know that.

"Okay." She stood, hefting that bag over her shoulders.

I followed Ember out, holding the door for her, and when she was gone, I faced Gertrude. "Did you find out anything about her family?"

"No." She shook her head. "No one seems to know about her or her parents."

"Damn." I dragged a hand through my hair. Maybe the food was because Ember had just skipped lunch. Maybe it was for an animal. Maybe she wore those clothes constantly because everything else she owned was uncomfortable.

Maybe my boredom was making me see things that weren't there.

"Good news," Gertrude said. "While you were meeting

with Ember, I got two phone calls. One is a woman wanting you to review an estate plan. The other is a man who'd like you to set up a corporation for his family's farm."

"That's great." So why wasn't I the slightest bit excited?

Two additional clients brought my total count to eight, after a few other inquiries earlier in the week. An estate plan and incorporation would be easy, predictable tasks. Exactly what I'd hoped to find in Calamity.

Except all I could think about was Ember Scott.

And Larke Hale.

"Would you mind locking up tonight?" I asked Gertrude, needing to get out of the office. To go for a drive and think about how I was going to handle this lawsuit between Ember and Larke.

"Not at all," she said. "See you tomorrow."

After collecting my wallet and keys, I left the building, getting in my car and spending an hour cruising along the highway. There were more deer and cows than other vehicles, another change from the city I didn't mind. The drive was nothing but blue sky, rambling fields and towering mountains. Spring in Montana was hard to beat with the green meadows that filled the valley between the ranges surrounding Calamity.

Any other day, I would have appreciated the scenery. Today, I was too stuck in my head.

It took the entire hour of driving to come to a conclusion: I didn't know what the fuck to do.

Not something I admitted often, to others or myself, but as I finally headed home, turning into the cul-de-sac, I couldn't deny that I was totally out of my element when it came to Ember Scott.

I needed help.

So I parked the Stingray in the garage, and instead of going inside my house, I tucked the keys and my phone into a pocket, then strode across the driveway to Larke's.

This was a mistake. Ember was my client. Even if we hadn't signed a contract, and I was working for free, I'd agreed to stand on her side of the line, with Larke on the other.

Except who else was going to help her? Child and Family Services wasn't an option because Ember was eighteen. The sheriff's department would want evidence, not some stupid hunch. And it wasn't like I could approach Ember's parents and blatantly accuse them of neglect when, again, I had no proof.

Larke was Ember's teacher. Who else did I know who saw the kid every day?

Ethically, I should stay far, far away from Larke, even if this lawsuit was a pile of steaming bullshit. But did I turn around? No, I kept on walking.

Fuck. I was risking my license for this. Yet I couldn't seem to stop.

Gerty was going to be so pissed if I lost my practice and she had to find a new job. Hopefully a huge-ass severance check would appease her.

With my shoulders squared and a fortifying breath burning my lungs, I stepped onto Larke's stoop, stopping before the welcome mat and pressing the doorbell. Would she even answer the door? *Guess I'll find out.* My pulse raced as I waited, hoping she wouldn't ignore me tonight.

Faint footsteps came from beyond the door before the lock flipped. Then there she was, making my heart skip a beat like always. Damn, this woman. What the hell was she doing to me?

I cleared my throat. I should have planned what to say. For a man who was fairly good at speaking, one look at her and I was lost for words. "I, uh . . . hi."

Larke arched her eyebrows, crossing her arms over her chest. She was wearing a loose sweatshirt that draped wide at her throat. It revealed the hollow at the base of her throat, her delicate collarbones and flawless, smooth skin. That skin was made for my tongue. I wanted to taste every inch of her. A lock of chestnut hair had fallen out of her messy knot, the strands following the long line of her neck.

It was sexy but I loved her hair down, cascading over her shoulders. Free of any tie and waiting for my hands to tangle in those tresses.

"Did you need something?"

Get a grip, Thatcher. "Sorry to bother you."

"You say, 'Sorry to bother you,' yet here you are." She rolled her eyes, stepping back to shut the door, but I held out a hand.

"Please. Just one minute."

She frowned but didn't slam the door in my face. That was something, right? "I cannot speak to you without my attorney present."

Well, shit. Good for her. If she were my client, I would have told her the same thing. "Call him. Or her."

"What?"

"Call your attorney. Or FaceTime. Because I need to talk to you. Tonight. And if he or she needs to be present, then call."

"Um, no."

"I'm not leaving." I mirrored her stance, crossing my arms over my chest and giving her a defiant stare. If I had to stand out here all night, so be it.

Larke's nostrils flared as she glared up at me.

"You're beautiful, even when you're irritated." The words slipped out without any warning. *Christ.*

But Larke's composure slipped, just a fraction, and she dropped her gaze to her bare feet.

It was a window and it wasn't wide open, but I took a leap headfirst anyway. "I'm not helping Ember Scott because you didn't want to date me. This isn't some scheme of vengeance."

"Then why?" She leveled me with a stare. There was pain in her eyes. Pain I'd caused because I hadn't talked to her in the first place.

"Every time she's in my office, she's wearing the same clothes. Or the same variation of a few outfits."

"So?"

"So don't teenage girls sort of go crazy about clothes?"

"Not all of them."

"Okay, fine. Maybe Ember is different. But how often do you see her in different clothes? Or something, anything, new?"

A crease formed between her eyebrows as she thought about it. Or maybe that tiny line was because she realized she was talking to the enemy. She uncrossed her arms, digging out her phone from the back pocket of her jeans, then tapped the screen before holding it up between us as the ringtone sounded on speaker.

"Aiden Archer," a deep voice rumbled on the other end of the call.

"Hi, Aiden. It's Larke Hale. Sorry for calling so late."

"No worries. What's up?"

Larke aimed her gaze my way as she spoke. "Ronan Thatcher is paying me a visit. He's standing right here."

"Ah. Well, Mr. Thatcher, my client has nothing to say to you, so I suggest you head to your own house. Maybe brush up on what happens to attorneys who grossly violate ethical boundaries."

Lawyers. What a pain in the ass. Not that he was wrong. "I need to talk to Larke about Ember."

"For what purpose?" Aiden asked. "We're under the impression that you'll be filing a civil case on behalf of your client because of a grade Larke issued. And I'm sure you understand that if that's the situation, we won't be discussing it via FaceTime."

Yeah, this was a horrible idea. "There's something wrong with this kid." I held Larke's gaze, silently pleading for her to listen.

"Because she wears the same clothes," Larke said, either to me or Aiden, I wasn't sure. "Those are probably her favorite outfits."

"I don't think so. My gut says that's all she's got. Unless you can tell me different. You've seen her every day for months. I've only known her for a little over a week."

Larke's eyebrows came together again. She didn't say anything, but I could tell she was replaying the school year.

"Mr. Thatcher—" Aiden started.

"She always has food in her backpack." I cut him off and again aimed this conversation at Larke.

"What food? Like a snack? So what? I pack Wren afternoon snacks every day."

"Milk cartons. Fruit with a peel, like apples or oranges or a banana. School food."

"Is there a point to this?" Aiden asked.

"Yes." I nodded. "Today, she had a cheeseburger."

"So what." Aiden huffed, but Larke's eyes widened.

"So, what was for lunch today at school?"

"Cheeseburgers," Larke murmured.

"Why is she taking food from school home and not just eating it *at school?*"

The color drained from Larke's face.

"I don't know what is going on with Ember, but something isn't right. The clothes. The food. This crazed need for perfect grades. It's not normal. And maybe I just don't know the first thing about teenagers, but the reason I even entertained this lawsuit in the first place wasn't because I think you were wrong in giving her that grade. But because it seems like she's screaming for help. Desperation is leaking out of her pores. She is in a panic about this grade, like if it doesn't get changed, it's the end of her life."

"That's teenagers," Aiden said. "They get dramatic. I have two of them and the sky is always falling."

Maybe he was right. Maybe I'd made something out of nothing because Gertrude had hit the nail on the head and I was having a midlife crisis. But if there was something happening with Ember, if she was in danger or being neglected and I'd done nothing, I wouldn't be able to live with myself.

"I don't know," I confessed, stepping closer, lowering my voice, just a little. "I just . . . I need help."

Larke's expression softened, her frame relaxing. She

stepped closer, just an inch, but enough that I could haul her into my arms.

I didn't, but it took restraint. "I'm sorry about the lawsuit."

"Are you really going through with it?"

"I'm afraid that if I don't file the complaint, this kid will disappear."

On the other end of the call, Aiden scoffed. For a moment, I'd forgotten he was still there. "There are other ways to help a troubled teenager than by suing an innocent teacher."

"Yeah." I sighed, waiting for Larke to say something, anything. But she dropped her gaze again.

Her toes were painted the palest of pinks. Pretty. Feminine. Perfect.

"Mr. Thatcher, this conversation has gone on long enough," Aiden said. "Please leave my client alone. If you go through with filing the complaint, we can continue this in front of a judge. And if you continue harassing my client, I'll be happy to file a grievance with the Office of Disciplinary Counsel."

Damn. Yep, I was kissing my license goodbye. But I waited anyway, hoping Larke would wave me inside, but she kept her chin tucked. I'd been dismissed.

"Thank you for listening." I turned, heading for home. I was halfway across the lawn between our houses when her door clicked shut behind me. "Shit."

It could have gone worse. It could have gone better, but it could have gone worse. She'd listened, sort of. I'd pissed off her lawyer, and I was crossing enough boundaries that I should be carrying a passport.

Yet all I could think about was that cheeseburger.

The doubts about Ember were swirling. Had I just made up this thing with her clothes and the food? Was she just an emotional, spoiled teenager who was pissed about a grade?

Larke saw Ember every single day. So did the other teachers. Calamity didn't have that big of a school system, so it wasn't like kids didn't get noticed. If something was wrong in Ember's home life, someone else would have spotted the signs, right?

I was nearly across the lawn when I paused to glance over my shoulder, taking in her olive-green house and the few lights still on inside, glowing brighter and brighter by the minute as the sky darkened.

It was a Thursday. The garbage truck had come this morning, and Larke's trash can was still out. So I turned back, walking toward the street to roll her empty container up to her garage. Then I walked to my own, about to haul it up the driveway when I heard my name.

"Ronan." Larke walked down her driveway, then turned on the sidewalk, meeting me in the middle between our homes. She pointed behind her to the garbage can. "Thanks."

"Welcome."

"You really think something is wrong with Ember?"

"I do." I nodded. "And if I don't file the complaint, she'll do it herself." At least this way, I'd still be involved.

Larke had the baby monitor in her hand. She checked the black and white screen once before standing a bit taller and saying the last thing I expected her to say.

"Then you should file the complaint."

CHAPTER NINE

LARKE

RONAN BLINKED. "SERIOUSLY?"

"It's not every day you tell your neighbor to sue you." That was a weird sentence. I shook my head. "What a strange night."

But this lawsuit wouldn't just buy him more time with Ember. It would give me a chance too. A chance to take notice of a girl I clearly hadn't given enough of my attention.

"You sure about this?"

I shrugged. "If I told you not to do it, would you listen?"

"Yes." No hesitation. The sincerity in his eyes was as dangerous as the electricity between us.

So I dropped my gaze, because getting lost in those hazel irises was much too tempting.

"What's your lawyer going to say about this?"

I lifted a shoulder. "Oh, I'm sure Aiden won't be happy, but he's also not concerned about a victory here."

The corner of Ronan's mouth turned up. "If it makes you

feel better, I'm not really concerned with your chances of winning either."

"Probably not something you should tell me, Mr. Thatcher."

Ronan chuckled. "Do me a favor, don't tell your attorney I said that."

"No promises," I teased.

Aiden Archer was a local lawyer whose reputation was unmatched. The only problem was that he didn't live in Calamity. He was from a neighboring town, but thankfully, when I'd called, he'd agreed to take my case and travel over when needed.

Pierce had discussed this case with his own lawyers, but since those licensed to practice in Montana were more familiar with corporate law than civil suits, he'd encouraged me to stick with Aiden.

And yes, Aiden wasn't going to love that I was having this conversation, but when I'd heard the clatter of my garbage can being rolled up my driveway and looked out the window to see Ronan, well . . . Aiden would have to deal with it.

"I stand by the grade I gave Ember." I refused to be bullied into changing my mind.

"I read her paper. It was good."

"It was well written. But it wasn't the assignment."

Ronan nodded. "I agree with you."

"Oh." I'd been prepared to launch into my argument about her work and how it hadn't followed my instructions, but apparently explaining was unnecessary.

"My hunch is that a judge is going to toss this out and tell

Ember she has to deal with the school administration," he said.

"They're supporting me on this."

"As they should."

With the previous principal, that support probably would have wavered, especially under public scrutiny. And this would definitely be the talk of Calamity. But I trusted Emily Cain to have my back. That, and I'd sent her every other paper from my class. Yesterday, she'd read them all and had told me that my C plus had been generous.

Plus Emily was concerned about the precedent this could set. If this blew up, if a judge made me change Ember's grade, then not only would they lose me as an English teacher—I'd already drafted my resignation letter—but they'd also open the door for students to sue their teachers time and time again.

But I wasn't going into this unprepared. That's why I'd hired Aiden. I wasn't even sure what was in the realm of possibility at this point. Did the court system even have this kind of authority over a grade? I guess I'd find out.

At this point, it wasn't really about the lawsuit. "Do you really think there's something going on with Ember?"

"Yeah, I do." Ronan nodded. "It's just a feeling but . . . I'd rather be wrong, look like a fool and risk my license, than be right and have done nothing."

Well, damn. I was beginning to like Ronan Thatcher. "It's hard to despise you right now."

Ronan chuckled. "Sorry?"

"You should be." I fought a smile. "I'll ask around about Ember."

"Thanks, Larke."

Every time he said my name I wanted to hear it again. So before I could get myself in trouble, before he inched closer, before I let him, I backed away. "Good night."

"Night." I was three steps away when he called my name.

"Larke, hold up." He closed the distance between us with a couple of long strides. He stopped close. Too close. Not close enough. "When I file this complaint at the courthouse, do me a favor."

"Okay."

He lifted his hand, like he was about to touch my face. But instead, he dropped his fingers to my neck, touching a lock of hair that had fallen out of my bun.

Tingles zinged across my skin. Ronan had such a beautiful mouth. I'd never thought a man's mouth could be beautiful, but Ronan's lips had this soft pout. Not too full. Not too thin. Not too wide or narrow. The perfect mouth. I couldn't look away as he spoke.

"Don't forget."

"Forget what?" My voice was breathy.

"That you don't despise me."

That voice was like sin, wrapping around me and chasing away the cold. He leaned in, barely an inch, but it was a fight to keep my heels on the ground and not rise up to meet him. To kiss that mouth.

"I am sorry," he murmured. "For what it's worth."

God, I wanted to believe him. I wanted to believe every word.

"Good night." He dropped his hand and turned, leaving me on the sidewalk as his long strides carried him toward his open garage.

I watched every single step until a breeze snapped me out of my stupor. I blinked, tearing my gaze from his broad shoulders and that firm, sculpted ass, then hurried into my house.

Wren hadn't slept well last night. Wanting to check on her one last time, I flipped off the lights as I moved toward her room, tiptoeing through the door. Then I inched toward the windows, the blinds open barely a crack, but it was enough to see Ronan's garage. He hadn't closed the door. So I waited, my heart thumping, until he came out a few minutes later, wearing a fitted T-shirt that molded to his shoulders and arms. His shorts were loose but they didn't hide the bulk in his thighs.

It would be dark soon but given the gray tennis shoes, he must be going for a run. He stood in his driveway, bending to stretch his hamstrings for a moment. Then, with his earbuds in place, he jogged down the street and out of sight.

As soon as he was gone, I could breathe again.

Why, of all the men in Calamity, did I have to be so attracted to Ronan? This would be so much easier if he were the shallow, rude man I'd thought he was last week. But this concern for Ember was endearing. Sweet.

Had I judged him wrong? Or was tonight's visit a trick?

When had I gotten so jaded?

Hawaii. After Hawaii.

I turned away from the window and toward the crib and my sleeping daughter. No matter what, she was the priority. No matter what, her happiness was all that mattered.

It was easier this way, wasn't it? Just Wren and me. There was no worry that a man would break my heart. Or hers.

Grabbing the pink throw blanket from the back of the rocking chair at my side, I took it to the floor beside Wren's crib, lying down on the soft carpet and snuggling beneath the throw.

Five minutes. My bed was calling, but I'd lie here beside my daughter for five minutes, like I used to when she was new. In the days when I wasn't sure what I was doing. The days when I survived hour by hour. The days when I doubted every thought, every decision.

Where was Ember's mother? Why hadn't I gotten a visit or a phone call after that C plus? Had Ronan met Ember's parents?

If it was Wren upset over a grade, I would have waded in. No question. Maybe the reason Ember's parents weren't in the mix was because she had shitty parents.

Tomorrow. I'd start asking questions tomorrow. Questions I probably should have asked months ago.

All I knew was that if Wren was in trouble, I'd want a man like Ronan keeping watch. If Carter ever came to steal her from me, maybe Ronan would be the guy to help me fight.

For two years, I'd been living with the fear of losing her. Strange how just the idea of Ronan's help had settled some of those worries.

Strange how his face was the last thing I pictured as I drifted off to sleep.

———

"MAMA."

I jerked awake, shooting upright. My head started swimming as pain shot through my neck. "Ugh."

Why did my shoulders and spine ache? Oh, right. The floor. I'd slept on the damn floor. Not ideal, but at least I had a cute face to greet me this morning.

Wren was standing in her crib, her hands gripping the railing as she bounced with her knees. Her hair was wild and her cheeks rosy. "Mama."

"Hi." I scooted closer to the crib, resting my forehead on one of its spindles. Then I reached in to tickle her leg. "How's my girl?"

"Mama buh beeee. Up."

"Okay. Up." I stood, stretching my aching back for a second, then reached in to heft her out and kiss her cheek. "Good morning. Should we change your diaper and get dressed?"

"Ooh no no."

"You're right. We won't put a bow in your hair today." I blew a raspberry on her neck, making her giggle, then I changed her diaper and dressed her in a cute green onesie with a pair of stretchy jeans. With her ready for the day, I trudged to my bedroom, where I set Wren on the floor with a couple of toys so I could take a shower and get ready for work.

Our morning was rushed because I'd slept on the floor and hadn't thought to set an alarm, but by some miracle, we walked out the door right on time.

I hit the button for the garage, buckling Wren into her seat as it lifted. And as I eased out of the driveway, my gaze went right to Ronan's house.

No matter how many times I told myself not to look for him, I did.

Every day. Even when I'd been angry.

We made it to daycare on time, and after dropping off Wren, I hurried to school, walking into the classroom fifteen minutes before the morning bell rang.

"Morning." Emily walked into the classroom.

I smiled, but it fell the moment another looming figure strode into the room. "Asshole Abbott," I muttered under a breath.

"What was that?" Emily asked.

"Happy Friday." My voice was too bright. "What's up?"

"Any news?"

"No. Still waiting for a complaint to be filed." I was keeping my mouth shut about Ronan's visit last night. Not only because I probably shouldn't have talked to him, but also because I didn't want him to get in trouble.

His heart seemed like it was in the right place.

"Well, I've been thinking. Maybe it's time we put a few added precautions in place."

"Okay," I drawled, glancing to Wilder, who was scowling at a spot on the floor. Better the linoleum than me.

"Wilder has prep first period," Emily said. "I'd like him to sit in on your classes with Ember. Come up with any excuse you'd like to tell the students. Then we'll have him review anything she hands in as well for a second opinion on any graded work."

My heart sank. Yes, it would be good to cover my ass. I'd already started documenting each class with her, noting any interaction—or lack thereof. But to have Wilder in here, like a babysitter, made me want to scream. "Good idea."

Wilder grunted, then spun around and strode across the hall for his classroom. If he'd hated me before this charade, he was really going to loathe me now that he was sacrificing his prep period.

Emily gave me a kind smile. "I'm sorry this is happening."

"Me too."

"I'll let you get ready for class."

My nerves spiked ten minutes later as kids streamed into the room, taking their seats. In the middle of the chaos, Wilder dragged in a chair, positioning it in the back corner. I held my breath as Ember walked in, her chin ducked like it had been for the past week. Or longer, if I thought back.

First period was my seniors, and as they chatted and teased one another, I took my seat, glancing at Ember as she sat at her desk.

She didn't engage with anyone. Had she ever talked to her classmates?

I couldn't remember seeing her doing anything but sitting there, staring at the surface of her desk. *Huh.*

But she had friends, right? She had to have friends. Who were they? I'd just assumed she didn't have any in this class. Or that she was shy. A handful of the boys in this class were on the football team. They were boisterous on their quiet days. But I'd known them since fifth grade and they were entertaining, so I let them be loud.

Except they drowned out Ember. Or was that just an excuse because I hadn't done a good job as her teacher?

The rumors about the lawsuit had died down. At least, the whispering wasn't as glaringly obvious. Everyone, including myself, was waiting to see what happened. And even though I'd hired Aiden Archer, there wasn't anything for me to do until there was an actual complaint filed.

Would Ronan do it today?

My stomach churned. It had been hard to see Ember this past week. It had been a challenge to pretend I wasn't angry. To ignore the rumors and fake that I hadn't heard them, or that I was above them.

But for all of my frustration with the girl, mostly I'd been pissed at Ronan. For not telling her how foolish this was. For not putting a stop to this before it had started.

After last night, everything seemed different.

Ember's backpack was straining at the zippers. She was wearing a pair of jeans and a simple gray T-shirt. I couldn't recall seeing her in different shoes than the plum, knock-off Converses she was wearing. She had a jacket about that color too, didn't she? The other kids would wear hoodies and sweatshirts on cold days, but Ember had that coat.

"Ms. Hale, *IforgotmynotebookcanIgotomylockerrealfast?*" a boy in the front row word-vomited, already standing from his chair.

What? "Yes." I waved him away, then smiled, aiming it in Ember's direction. "Good morning."

She didn't even look up.

Damn.

"Mr. Abbott, what are you doing here?" a student asked, making the entire classroom twist in their desks.

Wilder had brought a notebook along. He was doodling something inside, probably a caricature of my face with devil's horns and a forked tail. At the mention of his name, he glanced up from the page, about to answer the question when I spoke up first.

"He's just listening in to brush up on his grammar." I fought a smirk when his jaw clenched. "Okay, it's Friday, so that means reading and book reports."

It was something I'd done all year, giving them Fridays to simply read. I wanted them to read one book a month, so I gave them dedicated reading time.

For each book, I expected a two-page book report giving me a summary of the story's plot as well as what they liked and didn't like. They could read whatever books they wanted, and along with the book report, we'd sit down and visit about it when they handed in their report.

"Has anyone finished a book since last week?"

Three kids raised their hands, so one at a time, I called them up to discuss what they'd read. Then I let everyone read while I prepped for my next class, waiting until the bell rang. Wilder must have gotten bored writing in his notebook because he'd traded it for his phone.

Ember was reading *The Midnight Library*. On the book's spine was a white sticker from the school's library.

I grabbed the notebook where I listed books the kids were reading. I'd asked them to tell me what they were picking up, just in case I had extra reading time to give it a try myself—which didn't happen often, considering my reading time was scarce at best.

The last book Ember had reported reading was a thriller. Clearly, she'd moved on and hadn't spoken a word to me.

She hated me, didn't she? When she looked back on her high school career, she'd say my name with a sneer.

My insides twisted. Why did that bother me so much? I'd had students not like me before. But this felt . . . personal.

Part of me wanted to call her up, talk to her about the book. About her paper. About the lawsuit. Fix this.

But I knew that would only be asking for trouble. That, and Aiden had told me to limit interaction. The plan was to document every conversation and hopefully continue with life as normal, even after a complaint was filed. He didn't want me stepping down as her teacher, because he was afraid it would make me look guilty. If Emily had Ember removed from my class, well . . . that was the administration's call to make. Maybe Wilder's presence would be enough until the mess was sorted.

So I left Ember alone, waiting until the bell sounded. "Have a good weekend."

"Bye, Ms. Hale." A few kids came over, giving me a fist bump as they walked out the door.

Ember didn't so much as glance in my direction as she left.

Neither did Wilder.

The next class swept in and the rest of my morning vanished while my worries about Ember only seemed to grow louder.

She had great grades. She looked clean, even if she wore the same clothes on repeat. She was petite but didn't look unhealthy. There were no signs of a girl being abused or living on the streets.

But Ronan had planted this seed and it was growing like a damn weed. So when the lunch hour came around, instead of heading to the teachers' lounge like normal, I snuck into the cafeteria, glad that my noon break coincided with the seniors' lunch hour.

Slipping into a back corner beside a supply closet, I scanned the long tables for Ember.

She was sitting alone, reading. Her backpack took up the bench space beside her and it seemed to have more space in it now, like she'd dropped off some stuff in her locker.

Maybe she just liked to carry around all of her textbooks and binders. Maybe she was taking everything home at night and that's why Ronan had noticed her bag.

I watched, feeling like a creep, as she ate her lunch unhurried. She didn't scarf her food and her tray wasn't heaped full. But there also wasn't anything left on it when she took it to the dishwashing station. She ate every bite.

That didn't mean much. I ate my whole lunch too.

Seconds away from giving up, I pushed off the wall where I'd been leaning. My stomach had been growling for five minutes, reminding me that I had a peanut butter and jelly sandwich waiting.

But before I could rush to the teachers' lounge, Ember left the dishwashing station. Instead of going outside with everyone else, she walked into the lunch line. Nearly every senior had left already to mill around until it was time for their next class. The juniors, who had the latest lunch period, were piling into the cafeteria.

And Ember joined them, blending into the crowd seamlessly while she loaded up another tray.

Milk. Chicken strips. Two apples. She took it back to her seat, wrapping the chicken in extra napkins and stowing everything in her backpack. Then she left, no one the wiser to her extra meal.

Well, shit.

If I hadn't been watching, I wouldn't have thought twice. It was too busy, too noisy. Ember could have passed for a junior or a senior. And this year, because of a state grant, every student got a free breakfast and lunch. No applications or paperwork necessary. No need to key in their lunch codes either.

Ember was definitely sneaking food. Why?

"Ugh." A headache bloomed as I walked out of the cafeteria, making my way to the teachers' lounge.

The best way to find out about Ember Scott was the route I hated the most.

Gossip. Something as prolific at Calamity High as teenage hormones.

I strode into the lounge, hoping to catch a few of the other teachers. Except luck was not on my side today. The only person eating at one of the small tables was Asshole Abbott.

Shit. I hated him, but he'd given up his prep period to observe my class. That, and he had Ember in his class too. Maybe it was time to smooth things over a bit. So I walked to the table, muttering, "Hi."

He glanced up from his lunch, leftover stir fry, and the moment his dark eyes glanced my way, his expression blanked. "Yes?"

"You have Ember Scott in your class too, right?"

Wilder focused on eating, his attention fixed on his meal, as he gave me a slight nod.

Was this guy allergic to eye contact?

"Have you noticed anything strange going on with her?"

"You mean like how she's planning on suing you for a bad grade?"

I rolled my eyes. *Jerk.* "No, like if she wears the same clothes all the time or is acting off."

"Isn't she in your class? If you're curious about what she's wearing, don't you see her every day?"

This was pointless. Epically pointless. "Do you know who her friends are?"

"She seems to get along with about everyone. Well, except you."

My nostrils flared. "Have you ever spoken to her parents?"

"Have you?"

"No. I haven't."

He shoveled another bite into his mouth, his jaw flexing as he chewed. "Maybe you should."

I opened my mouth, but I didn't have anything to say. Asshole Abbott was right. Not that I'd ever admit that out loud.

Without another word, I walked to the fridge, snagging my lunch, then headed for my classroom to log into the school's database to get her home phone number.

There was no father listed, just a mother. Ashley Scott.

No one answered when I called the number. It was a local number, without an answering machine, and there was no cell phone listed. I jotted down the number on a sticky note to try again tonight, then scarfed my sandwich before doing some prep for my afternoon classes.

The minute the last bell rang for the day, I loaded up my stuff and headed downtown for Thatcher Law.

There was no one at the front desk when I walked through the door, inhaling the faint scent of Ronan's woodsy cologne that lingered in the air.

"Hey." Ronan appeared in the doorway of what must be his office, leaning against the threshold, looking as sexy as ever.

His white shirtsleeves were rolled up his sinewed forearms. His gray slacks draped to a pair of polished black shoes. But it was the heat in his gaze that made my breath hitch.

Ronan looked me up and down, taking his time as his gaze raked over my body, head to toe. It was obvious. Lazy. Bold. When he finally met my eyes, he just grinned, knowing exactly what he'd been doing. "No apologies."

God, I liked that. A man who didn't hide his desire. A man who knew exactly what he wanted—me.

"What's up?" he asked.

"You were right. About Ember. Something is going on with her."

He looked to the ceiling. "She believes me. Miracles happen."

I fought a smile. "You're going to be insufferable, aren't you?"

"Definitely. I'm not the kind of man who misses opportunities to say *I told you so*."

I couldn't help but laugh. I rolled my eyes for good measure. "You might be the cockiest man I've ever met in my life."

That grin of his widened to a full-blown, breathtaking smile. "Charming, isn't it?"

Yes, oddly enough. It was.

CHAPTER TEN

RONAN

EVERY CELL in my being wanted to cross the room and seal my mouth over Larke's. Fuck, but she was beautiful when she laughed and threw a load of sass my way. But I stayed put, not wanting to screw up the progress I'd made last night by following an impulse.

"I am expecting Ember to stop by this afternoon," I told her.

"Oh." She glanced behind her to the door.

"She typically comes around three thirty or four. However long it takes her to leave the school and walk here."

Larke nodded. "Where's Gerty?"

"You know Gerty?"

"Everyone knows Gerty."

"Why doesn't that surprise me?" I chuckled. "She went to the grocery store to pick up some trail mix and granola bars. Figured I'd leave some of them out for Ember to take."

Larke's eyes softened. "I tried calling her house but no one answered. And her mother doesn't have a cell number listed in the school system. I didn't see information for a father."

Probably because there wasn't one in the picture. "Ember only gave me her house number too."

Which was just another oddity to this entire situation. What teenager didn't have a phone? What adult?

"I assumed she just didn't want me talking to her parents. Or I guess just her mother," I said. "Maybe the mom doesn't approve of this lawsuit idea. Ember is eighteen, so I couldn't really push it."

"There's not much more I can do either," she said. "I'll keep calling."

I rubbed a hand over my jaw, feeling the scrape of stubble against my palm. "Is it weird that the school doesn't have the mom's cell number?"

"Yes. And I wish I had noticed sooner. I used to call parents when I was teaching fifth grade so I always had numbers handy. But this year, for the high schoolers, I've mostly just emailed."

"Have you emailed Ember's mom?"

"Just the regular group notifications about upcoming assignments. I can't think of a time when she replied. Most don't."

I hummed. "Do you have her address?"

"Yes. It's a trailer park on the edge of town."

Then maybe the only way to talk to Ember's mother was by making a house call. "When she comes in today, I'll tell her I didn't get a chance to file the complaint. I was planning on taking it down Monday. But I could try and stall until Tuesday."

"All right." Larke nodded.

"Gertrude said Ember's family is new to town. No one really knows about them."

"That's probably true. I can ask around. My parents or my brother might know who they are." Larke sighed, like the last thing in the world she wanted was to resort to gossip for information. But if Ember wasn't talking, we didn't have a lot of other options. "I'd better get out of here."

"Wait." The temptation to be closer, for just a moment, was crippling, so I pushed off the threshold and closed the gap. I walked close enough that she had to tilt her head back to keep eye contact. The lift of her chin, the way it angled her mouth, made my cock twitch. It would be so easy to kiss her. "Are you okay?"

She blinked, like that was the last question she'd expected me to ask. "Sure."

"You're a horrible liar."

Her shoulders slumped. "I just . . . I feel guilty."

"For the grade?"

"No. If something is wrong with her, if she's in trouble, then I've seen her every day for months and missed it."

"Sometimes we miss what's right in front of us." I was a living, breathing example of that fact. I'd missed the signs with Cora until it had been far too late. And that guilt had been eating at me for three months.

"I should have noticed." Larke gave me a sad smile. "See you later."

"Larke." I reached for her elbow, stopping her before she could escape. Except one touch and whatever I'd been about to say died on my tongue.

She smelled incredible. That scent had been faint the times we'd talked outside, but here, cozy in my office, her fragrance swirled around us. It was like lavender, soothing and rich, mixed with the freshest of spring rains. I drew in a long breath, then another.

I inched closer.

Larke's chocolate eyes dropped to my mouth.

Whatever hold I'd had on my control snapped.

I crushed my lips to hers, and fuck me, I was in so much trouble. A current zapped through my veins. Her mouth was soft and it fit mine just right. I licked the seam of her lips, tasting a hint of cherry lip gloss, as sweet as honey.

We molded together perfectly, like this was the millionth kiss, not the first.

Her hands slid up my torso, sliding against the starched fabric of my shirt.

My arms banded around her, hauling her against my chest and erasing that sliver of space between us.

Larke whimpered as I dragged my tongue over the seam of her lips again, but she still didn't open for me. So I licked her again, nipping at that full bottom lip until she gasped. I took the opening, sweeping inside.

One stroke of my tongue against hers and my body came alive. Desire, as hot as white flames, seared my bones. A lightning strike.

It rocked me on my heels, forcing me to break away.

Larke's eyes fluttered open, then widened, the shock of what had just happened written across her gorgeous face. Her hand lifted to her mouth, her fingertips brushing across her lips like she was trying to make sense of this too.

My heart galloped. "I, um . . ." I shook my head. Fuck. What was that? Was I really risking my license for a kiss?

A kiss to change a life.

That thought should have terrified me. Hell, it should have had me racing back to California as fast as the Stingray would go. Except something felt different beneath my feet. Like at this moment, my body had realized exactly where I was supposed to be before my head could keep up.

The door opened behind Larke.

I jerked, snapping back to reality as a flash of panic sobered me instantly. "Ember."

Except it wasn't the kid. It was Gertrude, walking into the office, arms loaded with three grocery totes.

"Oh, hi, Larke." Gertrude smiled, breezing past us for her desk, where she plopped down the bags and shrugged off her purse.

Meanwhile, Larke shifted quickly, giving Gertrude her back while she wiped her lips dry. Erasing me.

Now I needed to kiss her again. Except I couldn't, so I shot her a frown.

Larke shot me the same right back.

I shoved. She shoved.

This was a woman who wasn't afraid to dig in her heels. It was refreshing. Intriguing. Hot.

Larke's frown didn't last long before she turned it into a beautiful smile, not for me, but for my assistant. "Hey, Gerty."

"What brings you in today?" Gertrude asked. "Ember Scott?"

"Yep." Larke nodded.

I'd told Gertrude about my discussion last night with Larke and how we both wanted to help Ember if something was wrong.

"Ronan says she's likely to be here soon, so I'd better take off." Larke took a step toward the door, lifting a hand to wave. "Bye."

Gertrude waved back as Larke slipped out the door.

She left without much of a look in my direction, like that kiss hadn't just happened.

I rubbed my palm over my mouth, still feeling Larke's lips. Fuck it. "Be right back," I told Gertrude, then bolted for the door.

This time when I chased Larke down First, I didn't have a twenty-dollar bill in my hand.

"Larke," I called as she reached her 4Runner.

"Yeah?" She turned, keys in hand, and stopped beside her car's door.

I stepped off the curb, glancing around to make sure there was no sign of Ember. But the sidewalks were fairly empty still, something Gertrude had assured me would change the closer we got to summer and the more the tourists flocked.

A lock of hair caught the breeze and blew across Larke's face.

We both reached for it, but I beat her to it, tucking it behind her ear. "Fuck, but I want to kiss you again."

"Probably shouldn't say that to the woman you're about to sue."

I grinned. "Probably not."

"That was, um . . ." She inched back, shaking her head like she was still trying to make sense of it too. "I'll look into Ember and see if I can get ahold of her mother. We should probably just draw the line there for now, don't you think?"

No. Hell no.

But I kept that to myself.

Every time Larke spoke, I wanted to learn more about her. About her life in Calamity. About her daughter. About everything.

"You intrigue me."

"Why?" She shrugged. "I'm just a teacher and a mom. There's nothing special about me."

"I disagree."

"Well, you don't know me well enough to argue."

"How about we change that? Dinner. Tomorrow."

She shook her head. "I'm going to my sister's tomorrow."

"Then Sunday."

"Sunday my parents are having a barbeque." The corners of her mouth turned up, like she enjoyed always turning me down.

Either I was getting used to it. Or I was enjoying it too.

If she was busy all weekend, that was fine. A different idea popped into my mind, not that I'd share those details. But after that kiss, there was no way I was walking away.

"All right." I took a step away.

She gave me a strange look, like she'd expected me to press. Maybe she was disappointed when I didn't. A man could hope.

"Bye." I winked, then retreated to the office.

Gertrude waited, smug. "Oh, you like her."

"Oh, I like her."

Not something I'd thought I'd say this quickly into my life in Calamity. But Larke was a breath of fresh air. Witty and smart. Unexpected.

Gertrude steepled her fingers in front of her chin. "Have you heard the story about Calamity's name? It was originally founded as Panner City."

"Uh, no." I gave her a sideways glance. "Why?"

"Most people think we're named after Calamity Jane. She did live around this area as a child, but it's not how the town got its name."

I pointed out the window toward Calamity Jane's on the opposite side of the street. "But the bar is named after her?"

"The bar is owned by a woman named Jane Fulson. Hence Jane's."

"Ah. Clever." The place looked like it hadn't changed much in the past fifty years. All it was missing was a pair of swinging saloon doors.

"This was a settlement during the Montana gold rush in the 1860s," Gertrude said. "Home to nearly three thousand miners until a series of disasters struck. The mine collapsed in Anders Gulch. A flood washed out most of the claims and panning sites after a heavy spring rain. Then a fire spread through town, followed by a cattle stampede through the settlement."

"Calamity in Calamity," I said. "Interesting story."

"True stories usually are."

"Why are you telling me this?"

She gave me a sad smile. "Calamity has had enough disasters. Don't let Larke or Ember be the next."

"I'll do whatever I can." I nodded and went into my office.

———

EMBER CAME TEN MINUTES LATER, her cheeks flushed from the walk and her backpack as bulging as ever. When Gertrude came in with snacks, I pretended to have skipped lunch, then told Ember she might as well take the extras home because I wouldn't eat it all myself.

Somehow she fit two bags of trail mix and a granola bar in her bag before leaving.

Gertrude and I spent the next hour talking about the other items needing to be done on Monday. We weren't swamped, but another three clients had called this week.

According to Gerty's daily rumor report, word was spreading that there was a new attorney in town and he—me —wasn't an asshole. A compliment if I'd ever heard one.

She left first, heading home for the weekend, while I stayed to shut off the lights and lock up. Instead of climbing in the Stingray, parked in its usual spot, I strolled along the sidewalks toward the White Oak, where I placed an order for pickup, then killed time by wandering along First.

The weather was changing, the air crisp but warming with each passing spring day. The scent of lilacs infused the air. As I passed Jane's bar, country music drifted through the open door along with the smell of burgers and beer. A couple at the art gallery were in the front window, changing out the pieces on display. The few people I passed all offered smiles and hellos.

Calamity was sinking into my skin, day by day. But it was Larke that had me ensnared.

That kiss . . .

I wanted another. And another. And another.

I wanted her, until this craving faded. Until this desire burned out.

I made my way back to the White Oak, picking up my dinner. They'd packaged it in Styrofoam containers and white plastic sacks. With them in hand, I retreated to the Stingray and drove home. Except I didn't park in my drive.

I parked in Larke's.

She answered the door with Wren on a hip, the little girl's cheeks splotchy and her thumb in her mouth. "Um, hi."

"Hi." My gaze raked over her body, appreciating every inch.

She'd changed out of the jeans and blouse she'd been wearing earlier and into a pair of teal leggings with a white tee. The strap of a black lacy bra peeked out at one shoulder. Her hair was up in a bun, hiding from me.

"What are you doing?" She peered past me to the Stingray in front of her garage door.

I lifted the white bags in my hand. "Dinner."

She might be busy this weekend, but she hadn't said a thing about tonight, had she?

"Ronan, I—"

"Mrs. Edwards told me it was customary to invite new neighbors over for dinner. A chance to get to know one another."

"Mrs. Edwards?" With her free hand, Larke pointed to the house on the other side of mine. "*That* Mrs. Edwards? The crotchety woman who has barely spoken to me in all the time that we've lived here?"

"Yeah. She's a dear. We had dinner last Sunday. Goose casserole with a cornflake topping. It was a first for me. Not my favorite, but it wasn't bad."

Larke's mouth parted.

I took her momentary surprise as my opening, forcing my way past her and into the house. "I realized my mistake today."

"Excuse me?"

I walked through the entryway, glancing around to get the layout. The design of the house was different than mine. No surprise, considering the exteriors were quite different too. But I spotted the dining room table and carried the bags over, setting them down.

Then I turned. Larke stood a foot away.

Close. But not close enough.

I took her elbow and tugged her to me until she was just inches away. "You smell like lavender."

She glanced at her daughter, whose head was resting on Larke's shoulder. "It's Wren's baby lotion. I like it so I just use it for both of us."

I hummed. "Good decision."

"What mistake are you talking about?"

"I asked you on a date."

"And I said no."

"Numerous times." I lifted a hand to thread my fingertips into the hair by her temple. "Just as soft as I expected."

She frowned, adjusting Wren, but she didn't step away. "Do you have this much trouble staying on topic in court?"

I chuckled before winking at Wren. Then I turned to the table, lifting out the takeout containers, one by one, and setting them on the table. "Plates?"

"What mistake are you talking about?"

"I asked you out." I pulled out a chair for her to sit, but she stayed on her feet.

"And you're just now realizing that was a mistake? My rejections weren't enough?"

I grinned at the smirk on her face. God, she was fun to

banter with. So much fun, I just might have to make it part of my regular routine. "The mistake was that I asked."

Her eyes narrowed. "What do you mean?"

"I'm not asking anymore. If I want a date"—I swung my hand out to the food on the table— "I'll take it from now on."

She scoffed. "You might be the most stubborn and persistent man I've ever met in my life."

"Aww." I puffed up my chest. "Thank you."

Larke rolled her eyes, but there was a ghost of a smile on her lips.

CHAPTER ELEVEN

LARKE

WHY WAS my house such a mess?

My mother had this ability to keep her home clean and tidy at all times. Even with three kids and a husband, she'd never had cluttered counters or a messy dining room table. Why couldn't I take after her instead of Dad, who just tossed things in every direction? Maybe he did that because she picked up after him.

"Sorry, it's Friday," I told Ronan as I grabbed the stack of mail from the table. I tucked it under an arm and swept up the diaper bag with my free hand. Then I carried Wren to the living room, dodging toys that littered the floor.

Her favorite game at the moment was picking up something to throw over the playpen's mesh wall, then saying, "Uh-oh." But Wren was not in the mood for games tonight. The moment her feet touched the floor, she started to cry, her arms lifting in the air. "Mama. Up. Up."

"Just one minute, baby," I said, running to the kitchen.

The sink was full of dirty dishes because this morning I

hadn't emptied the clean dishwasher. The counters were cluttered with stuff I hadn't put away—groceries for the pantry and two Amazon packages.

Next to the kitchen was the laundry room. I'd managed to haul our dirty clothes in there, but they hadn't made it into the washer yet. Sorted piles covered every inch of the tiled floor. Not something I wanted Ronan to see, so I rushed to the door to pull it closed, hiding one disaster from sight.

If only I could close more doors.

Wren wailed in the living room, calling for me over and over. "Mama! Mama!"

"I'm coming," I called, hurrying to stow some of her bottles and at least clear a small sliver of countertop.

"Mama!" she cried, that noise shooting straight to my heart.

The mess would have to wait.

I hurried to the fridge, taking out a gallon of milk to make her a cup to have with dinner. I'd just twisted off the top when her crying stopped. I froze, listening and waiting. When she didn't make a sound, I walked to the living room, still carrying the milk jug, to find Wren in Ronan's arms.

My heart skipped.

Her big brown eyes were locked with his as the two stared at each other.

From the look on her face, she wasn't sure what to make of him. Wren was the same around my father and brother. It took her a while to warm up to men. Maybe because she didn't have a father at home.

Ronan just held her as she assessed him, giving her time.

But before she could decide if she liked him or not, she

spotted me, reaching across his chest and stretching out her arms. "Mama."

Ronan moved in the direction of Wren's arms, closing the distance between us. "Sorry. I tried."

"She just doesn't know you," I said. Neither did I. Yet I'd let him kiss me anyway.

It had just been a kiss. But even hours later, I was still so . . . flustered.

My head had been in a fog, and I wasn't sure which way was north or south, left or right.

"Is that milk for Wren? Or me?" he asked, still holding her on an arm because mine was full.

Right. There was a jug in my grip. "Oh, um. It's for Wren. Unless you want milk too."

"I like milk."

"All right." I spun for the kitchen, hurrying to take out two glasses and a sippy cup.

"Mama," Wren said, an order to Ronan to follow.

"Okay, firefly. To the kitchen we go."

Firefly. My heart tumbled.

That was, without a doubt, the cutest nickname for a child I'd ever heard in my life. That he'd given it to my daughter made my chest hurt. A good or bad ache, I wasn't sure.

"Nice place." Ronan's shoes clicked on my hardwood floors. "The layout is entirely different than mine."

"All of the houses on the cul-de-sac have a different floor plan." My hands were shaking as I poured Wren's milk. I fumbled with the lid to her cup, dropping it once and not threading it right. It took me two tries before I finally managed to screw it on.

Why was I so nervous? This was just a simple dinner. I should be grateful and relaxed that I didn't have to cook. But the jitters wouldn't stop.

Ronan and Wren came to stand beside the island.

My daughter was still checking him out, trying to make sense of Ronan Thatcher.

You and me both, baby girl.

"My house is a mess," I said, pouring a glass of milk for Ronan and me.

"So."

"So, I normally don't have people over on Fridays because by this point, the clutter has just built and built. Saturday mornings everything gets put back to rights."

"I don't care if you have a messy house on Fridays, Larke. Or Mondays. Or Wednesdays. Tidy Tuesdays on the other hand . . ."

A smile chased away some of the nerves as I returned the milk to the fridge.

"My mom always made us clean on Tuesdays," he said. "She called them Tidy Tuesdays. My sophomore year in college, I invited her to my apartment on a Tuesday. I was living with a buddy of mine and he was a slob. I knew it would drive Mom nuts but I couldn't resist."

I giggled. "That's horrible."

"Mom's a savage. She ordered us both to start cleaning or else she wouldn't buy us dinner that night. I got dinner that night. My roommate . . . she left him behind."

"Good for her."

"Where are the plates and forks?" he asked.

"I'll get them if you want to head into the dining room."

He nodded, toting Wren out of the kitchen like he'd carried her in there a hundred times.

Wow, this was strange. Was this a date? Did I want it to be a date?

Ronan was moving at light speed and my mind was sprinting to catch up. Part of me was still stuck in his office, drowning in a kiss.

Focus, Larke. I shook my head, then carried the glasses into the dining room.

He'd put Wren in her high chair but was trying to figure out the buckle.

"You don't have to buckle her. She'll be fine." I set her milk down, bending to kiss her hair as she snatched the sippy cup and stuck it in her mouth.

I traded our glasses of milk for the rest of the clutter on the table, hauling it to the laundry room, where I tossed it on the floor to deal with later. Then I grabbed plates, utensils and napkins and returned. Ronan was in a seat, opening three takeout containers I recognized from the White Oak.

The scent of bacon and potatoes filled my nose.

BLT wraps. I loved the BLT wraps from the White Oak. And he'd gotten potato salad, not fries, because no matter how quickly you took food home in takeout containers, fries always got soft. He'd even brought Wren's favorite grilled cheese.

"See see," Wren said, pointing to her meal.

"What does *see see* mean?" Ronan asked.

I plucked the applesauce pouch from beside her sandwich and twisted off the top.

"Ah." He nodded, watching as Wren practically inhaled the pouch.

Wren's eyelashes were wet. Before Ronan had shown up, she'd been crying while I'd set her down to change clothes.

I brushed a thumb across her soft cheek, then took her grilled cheese and tore it into small pieces on her tray. "She had a long day at daycare and missed her nap."

"I missed my nap too," he told her with a pout.

Wren stared at him, sucking on her applesauce.

Ronan stuck out his tongue, fast, like a lizard tasting the air.

Wren didn't so much as blink.

"Just like your mother, aren't you?" He shook his head, taking a bite of his wrap.

She watched him as he chewed, her beautiful eyes missing nothing.

He looked at her, then turned away. Looked at her again, turning away quickly, trying to tease her into a laugh.

Nothing.

My daughter was stingy with her affection. I'd always loved that about her, probably because she gave it to me without restraint. But seeing her give Ronan a hard time was priceless.

I smiled, diving into my own food.

Wren might not be giggling, but as she traded the applesauce for some grilled cheese, the sadness in her eyes began to fade. It was the happiest she'd been since I'd picked her up at daycare earlier.

"She has your eyes." Ronan made a funny face for her, puffing up his cheeks. She just ate another bite. "And clearly does not find me amusing either."

Oh, I thought he was amusing. And magnetic. And petrifying.

He did the lizard tongue thing again.

If Wren could roll her eyes, she would have given him a doozy.

"Still nothing." He hummed, taking a moment. Then he twisted in his chair, giving her his fullest attention as he smiled and gave her a wink.

A tiny crack crept into Wren's defenses. Her smile started small, then grew and grew until she flashed him not only the grilled cheese in her mouth, but her teeth.

Ronan's smile, genuine and victorious, widened.

My ovaries exploded.

I was so, so screwed.

"Do you know how to fist bump?" He held out his knuckles to Wren.

She took a chubby fist and smacked it against his.

"Nice." He chuckled as she blushed, ducking her chin like she was shy. "I knew I'd win you over."

He was one of the only, and it hadn't taken long. I wasn't sure what to make of that, so I didn't try. We were just neighbors getting to know each other. And if Wren ever needed anything, it was good to know she wasn't scared of the man living next door.

"Tell me something," Ronan said.

"Like what?"

He shrugged. "Something Gertrude wouldn't know."

"How much did she tell you about me?"

"Not much." He gave me a soft smile. "I only asked about you because I was interested. I saw you on the sidewalk and just had to talk to you. Then you shot me down, and I was, well . . . baffled. That doesn't happen often."

"Probably good for you."

"Probably." Ronan nodded. "Regardless, I didn't mean to upset you."

"I know." I sighed. "I overreacted. Honestly, I probably would have asked too. I'm just really tired of people talking about me."

Ronan's gaze softened. "Sorry."

"Don't be. It's the curse of small-town life."

"Then tell me something only the people closest to you know. Like . . . who's your favorite student?"

"Teachers don't pick favorites," I lied. We *so* had favorites.

"And lawyers don't like to argue." He smirked, his hazel eyes dancing as he leaned in closer. "Also, your poker face needs work."

"I don't play a lot of poker."

"Good. You'd be broke in ten minutes."

I laughed, my smile pinching my cheeks. This was . . . fun. Just like flirting with him had been fun. The last time I'd truly enjoyed time with a guy had been in Hawaii. And at that memory, a sour taste spread through my mouth, so I forked a bite of potato salad.

"Hey." Ronan stretched his hand across the table, his fingertips brushing mine. "What just happened?"

"Nothing." I waved it off, pulling my hand free.

He turned to Wren. "Does she lie to you all the time too? Probably not. Lucky girl."

"Mo." Wren tapped her fingers together, signing she wanted more.

So I tore up more sandwich for her, willing thoughts of the past away because tonight, I just wanted to be here. With Ronan.

"My favorite student this year is Evelynn Long. I had her in my fifth-grade class and now she's a freshman. She's this shy, quiet girl who hangs back at the end of class so that she can give me a hug when no one else is watching."

"Cute." Ronan smiled. "No one hugs me at work. Maybe Gertrude would if I gave her a raise."

I snorted. "You don't know Gerty well, do you?"

"Think she'll say no to the hugs?"

"Most definitely. My mom is a hugger. We were shopping together at the hardware store once and ran into Gerty. Mom moved in for a hug and before she could get within a foot, Gerty held up her hand and said she didn't like hugs."

"Why does that not surprise me?" He held out his fist to Wren again for a fist bump. "Will you hug me, Wren?"

"No. No. No." She shook her head so fast that the little pigtails I'd put in this morning swished.

"Ouch." He feigned an injury, then tickled her side until she giggled.

Wren was smitten. This man had enchanted her entirely over a grilled cheese sandwich.

"My favorite student ever is Barrett Johnston," I told him. "I had him in fifth grade, my first year of teaching. It took me a while after college to get a full-time position. It's been different this year with the influx of students, but at the time, openings in Calamity didn't come up very often."

"Makes sense." Ronan nodded. "People probably don't move away from Calamity often."

"Not really. Unless they are taking other jobs."

Like a fourth-grade position at an elementary school in Bozeman.

"I was just subbing at the time," I said. "But then another

teacher got divorced and moved away so I took her class. It was midyear, not long after Christmas break. My first day, I was so nervous, until Barrett walked in that morning. He stopped in front of my desk, looked me up and down, then said, 'Who the fuck are you?' "

Ronan threw his head back and laughed, a rich, deep laugh that came with a blinding white smile.

Then Wren started laughing too.

And that twist in my chest came back tenfold. Oh God, what was happening?

"Barrett sounds like my kind of kid," Ronan said.

"He's a special one. Every week, all the way through his senior year, he'd stop by to see me. And when he comes home from college, he comes to the school to visit."

Ronan took another bite of his wrap, making me realize that I hadn't really eaten, so I focused on my own meal.

"What do you normally do on a Friday night?" he asked when we were finished, collecting the empty containers and shoving them into the plastic sacks.

"Pick up. Play with Wren. Snuggle on the couch and watch cartoons. By Friday, we're both pretty wiped." I relaxed in my chair, not wanting to leave the dining room yet because leaving meant dishes and bath time for Wren. "Why'd you pick Calamity?"

"For the past six summers, I've come here to go on a guided fly-fishing trip on the Missouri. My brother and a few buddies always come along. We've stayed here a few times on our way to Yellowstone."

"Another tourist converted."

He chuckled, swinging an arm over the back of the chair beside his, looking entirely content to stay and talk too.

"There are some things I miss about San Francisco. The ocean. My favorite Thai restaurant. My brother and parents."

"You're close to your family?"

He nodded. "Yeah. We're more than family. We're friends. I miss them."

My heart squeezed as I glanced at Wren. We were years from discussions about her future, but I wasn't sure what I'd do if she lived far away. Move to wherever she was, probably. "What do your parents think about you living in Montana?"

"*Unsure* would be the right word. They're excited to visit this fall. Mom is a photographer, so the summers are her busiest time of year. Weddings mostly. Her schedule is hectic but she loves it so she says it never feels like work."

There were days at the school when I felt the same. Then others when I wanted to pull my hair out. "And your dad? You said he was a carpenter."

"He's retired now. He had his own company and sold it. It's, uh, been a tough couple of years for him. He's going blind."

"Oh," I gasped. "I'm so sorry."

"So am I." Ronan gave me a sad smile. "He's technically my stepdad. I never knew my biological father. But as far as I'm concerned, Dad loved me so much that his DNA imprinted on mine."

A hand came to my heart. God, I loved that. I wanted that for Wren.

"He married my mom when I was four," Ronan said. "A couple years later, they had my younger brother. He's a lawyer in the city too. And not to brag, but I'm his hero."

I smiled at that arrogant grin on his face. It was insanely

attractive. Mostly because the more I got to know Ronan, the more I realized that he wasn't really that arrogant. It was an act. Okay, maybe not entirely. He was confident, and it only added to the magnetism.

"Hopefully he'll come visit me this summer."

"I'm sure they miss you too."

"I'm very missable." He held his hand out to Wren for a fist bump. It was like he wanted to keep giving her attention so she didn't forget he was her new friend. Adorable. This man was ridiculously adorable.

"Mom is a bit irked that I moved," he told me. "Mostly because she is a self-proclaimed helicopter mom, always in my business. But she knows it was time for me to make a big change."

A big change. Not a change, a *big* change. A move from California to Montana was a big change, but something about the way he said it had me sitting straighter. Big. Like there was a mountain of a story behind that three-letter word.

"Why a *big* change?"

Ronan dropped his gaze to the table. His thumb on his left hand touched the base of his ring finger, and his shoulders stiffened. "My ex-wife."

"Oh." I hadn't realized he'd been married. I hadn't asked, but I'd just assumed he'd been single. Why, I wasn't sure. Maybe wishful thinking, because the idea of Ronan with another woman irritated me.

He didn't continue, so I figured that was the end of his explanation. But then he looked up, drew in a long breath and dropped a bomb on my dining room table.

"She tried to murder me."

CHAPTER TWELVE

RONAN

LARKE'S JAW DROPPED. "WHAT?"

What the hell was I thinking? This was not first-date conversation. Why had I just said that?

"I haven't told many people about it." I sighed, not entirely sure where my filter was tonight. Gone, apparently.

"You don't have to tell me. I understand if you want to keep it private."

Most women would probably be salivating over a juicy story. Not Larke. The look in her eyes spoke volumes. It was my choice. She wouldn't push.

Which made her the right person to tell. Before Gertrude. Before anyone else in Calamity dug up a news article from the incident. I wanted Larke to know the truth. "I'd like to."

"Okay. Let me get Wren cleaned up." She stood, picking up her daughter from the high chair and carrying her to the kitchen sink.

I collected the takeout containers, then followed, putting

everything in the trash while she wiped Wren's face and washed her hands. With Wren babbling and kicking her legs, we retreated to the living room, dodging toys on the floor as I took a seat on one end of Larke's couch while she sat on the other.

"Ball." Wren squirmed to get down, then toddled to a pink ball, picking it up and bringing it over to me. "Ball."

"Can you throw it?" I held it out for her to grab. She gave me that wonderfully serious stare of hers before plucking it from my palm. Then she wound up and chucked it across the room.

Larke gave Wren a little clap while the girl beamed.

"Nice throw." I held out my hand for a high five.

Wren gave me knuckles instead.

I hadn't spent a lot of time with toddlers. A few of my cousins had kids but I only saw them at the occasional family reunion. But there was something about Wren. She had a spark, like her mother. A firefly.

Larke reached beside her for the TV remote, turning it on as Wren zoomed to pick up her ball, tossing it in the air again. But when she noticed the cartoons, she plopped down on her butt, picking up a ring she banged around a few times before sticking it in her mouth.

"It was three months ago," I said, picking up the conversation from the table.

"Oh." Larke shifted, curling her legs into the couch to face me. "That's . . . recent."

"We've been divorced for five years. But we kept in touch. Mostly, Cora would call me whenever she needed help at the house."

"That handiness you were telling me about." There was

a slight tease to Larke's tone, like she could sense that what I was about to tell her was fucking heavy and she was trying to lighten the air. I appreciated it more than she'd ever know.

I preferred easy conversation. Banter with friends. Teasing family. I rarely turned away from a healthy debate about politics or religion or sports. But when it came to handling the real-life disasters, well . . . I was better when they were a client's problems, not my own.

"The house was partially remodeled when we bought it," I told Larke. "The rest, I did myself while we were married. After the divorce, Cora bought out my share with some inheritance money. I should have insisted we sell it."

"Why do you say that?" Larke asked.

"Because then I wouldn't have had that tie. When I first started working as a lawyer, I had so little free time. I busted my ass to prove myself to the partners, so those hours when I could step away from the firm and dive into a house project were precious. I felt this sense of loyalty, and it kept me going back."

"To the house? Or to her?" Larke asked.

"Both," I said. "I'm not great at admitting defeat. Being able to stay friends with my ex-wife was a way for me to say I hadn't failed miserably at my marriage. But as time went on, I went back more for the house than for Cora. Saying that makes me seem like an asshole, but it's the truth."

Above anything else, with Larke, I wanted to be honest about this so she'd know exactly who I was.

"I don't think so," she said. "That was your home."

"I loved that house. It was hard for me to let it go, but the divorce was my idea, not Cora's. We were both unhappy, but she wanted to pretend life was perfect. It was exhausting. And I just couldn't do it anymore."

To this day, I still felt guilty for walking away. Even though it had been the right decision for myself, I'd likely always carry that blame.

"Anyway, we got past the divorce. Kept in touch. Tried to keep our relationship amicable. When she called me three months ago because something was wrong with the kitchen sink, I didn't think much about it. Just told her I'd help. So I went over after work one night to check it out."

I'd been late getting there. My plan had been to go around six, but by the time I'd left the office, run home to change out of my suit and grab some tools, it had been almost nine by the time I'd finally made it to Cora's.

"I walked in and could tell the second I crossed the threshold something was wrong."

"How?" Larke asked.

"The place was trashed. There was stuff everywhere, from dirty clothes to dishes to beer bottles."

"Replace beer bottles with toys and you've just described this house."

I smiled, grateful once more for the levity. "This was different. This wasn't just clutter, this was filth. I'll never forget the smell. Like rotten food and stale vomit."

Larke cringed. "Gross."

"She was in the kitchen when I got there, smoking a cigarette. Cora didn't smoke."

"How long had it been since you'd gone over?"

"Five months, give or take. The last time I'd stopped over had been in the summer. One of the doors hadn't wanted to close so I'd needed to fix a hinge."

"And it hadn't been a mess?"

I shook my head. "No. It had been clean. Just like always."

Or I'd simply overlooked the signs that Cora had been on a downward spiral. She'd always been good at hiding her feelings.

"I asked her what was going on. Why she was smoking. Why the house was a disaster. She answered by taking out a folder full of pictures she'd taken. Pictures of me."

Larke sat straighter. "Like from your marriage?"

"Like after our divorce. Pictures she could only have taken if she'd been following me around."

"Why? If you were divorced, why would she follow you?"

"To know who I was sleeping with."

Larke gaped. "What?"

"Every picture was of me and a woman."

Hundreds and hundreds of pictures. Cora had strewn them across the island. Staring at them had been like a punch to the gut. The betrayal had been a slap across the face.

"After the divorce, I dated on and off," I told Larke. "Nothing serious and it wasn't often, but every single woman I'd seen during those five years had been photographed. Every date. Every second date." Every morning that I'd waved farewell to the woman I'd invited into my bed the night before.

"Oh my God." Larke's eyes were as wide as saucers and I hadn't even gotten to the gory part. "That's . . . I don't even know what to say."

"It was a shock, to say the least." I leaned forward, dropping my elbows to my knees. "The night I went over was just a couple of weeks after I'd won the biggest case of my life. It was a defamation case I'd been working on for two years. Quite a few of Cora's photos were of me and my client."

"She thought you were sleeping with your client," Larke guessed.

"Yep. I wasn't. That's a line I wouldn't cross. But Cora was convinced, probably because of how much time my client and I had spent together. She's an actress, so our meetings were often outside the office. It was very hush-hush. She didn't want people to know she'd hired my firm. It was important to keep it that way until the trial started. We knew it would be a media circus and wanted to avoid it for as long as possible."

Most of the time, our team would meet with her virtually. But there'd been times before the trial when we'd needed to prepare her for what was happening, how to testify and how to answer questions. The best way to coach her had been in person. And I'd been the lead, so I'd taken that responsibility.

Larke's forehead furrowed, like she was trying to figure out which celebrity. But she didn't ask. She respected that boundary. Not many would.

"From the outside, I can see how Cora would have thought it was an affair. Hell, the media speculated we had something going on too." Which was likely because of a smear campaign orchestrated by my client's ex-husband and his publicity team.

My client was a successful actress but had stepped back from Hollywood after her marriage. Her ex was a professional tennis player, and together, they'd been toxic. During their marriage, they'd said some rather horrific things to each other. There wasn't a truly innocent party in the mix.

But after their divorce, she'd hoped to put it behind her and move on. Their mansion in the Bay Area had been listed for sale. The tabloids had blasted news of their divorce on magazine covers around the world.

She'd stayed silent, chalking it up to two people who never should have tied the knot.

Except then her ex had posted a series of slanderous tweets on Twitter. He hadn't named her specifically, but his intention had been clear. He'd outed her for an eating disorder as well as an affair. He'd fabricated a drug and alcohol addiction too.

With her reputation on the line, she'd had no choice but to file a lawsuit.

Two years of preparation, of court delays, and we'd been able to take it in front of judge and jury, ending in a landslide victory in our favor. My fee would pad my bank account for my lifetime.

"The night before I went to Cora's, a few of us had gone out to dinner to celebrate. Cora had a picture of me talking to my client. We'd been leaning together because the room we'd reserved had been loud. The only way Cora could have taken it was if she'd been inside the restaurant. But from the angle, it looked intimate. And unknown to almost everyone, my client had just gotten engaged."

"So she saw you and your client close. She was wearing an engagement ring and thought you were getting remarried."

I nodded. "Cora confronted me. I told her it was none of her damn business and that she was delusional. But she didn't believe me. She started screaming and hitting me. I told her I was leaving, to call someone else when she needed help at the house. That's when she picked up a knife and charged me with it. She was aiming for my heart. I deflected it but she still managed to leave a gash."

Larke gasped.

Even now, months later, it still felt strange telling this story. The only times it seemed real were in the mornings, when I stood in front of the sink with a towel wrapped around my waist, and the scar—raised and pink—stared at me through the bathroom mirror.

I reached for the button beneath my throat, loosening it along with the five beneath. Then I tugged the fabric aside, revealing the seven-inch slash across my pectoral.

"Ronan." Larke's hand lifted to her mouth as she stared at the angry line.

"Cora was high. Cocaine. I should have noticed when I came inside, but I didn't."

"Did she have a drug problem?"

"Not when we were married." I rebuttoned my shirt, leaving the top two undone. "According to her mother, Cora had been acting off since the divorce. It continued to get worse and worse, though no one suspected drugs. They all thought she was battling anxiety and depression. And I'd been too busy to notice."

Larke's expression softened. "I don't think you can take the blame. You weren't married. You weren't living together. How could you have known?"

"We'd been together a long time. Since junior year of undergrad."

"That still doesn't make you responsible."

"Yeah, but I knew Cora. I knew she was a jealous person. Always had been. There had been signs. If I had been paying attention, I would have seen them."

The texts late at night, asking what I was doing. The calls early mornings, inviting me to meet for coffee. They'd almost always coincided with a date. Then there'd been the hugs that lingered too long. The kisses planted on my mouth that had made me uncomfortable. But I'd dismissed it all as habits between former spouses.

"I should have helped her." Instead, I'd been too busy living my own life. Enjoying my freedom. After the divorce was finalized, I'd been able to breathe for the first time in years. And I'd realized that I hadn't loved Cora the way a man should love a woman.

With his whole damn heart.

Hell, at this point, I doubted I was made for that kind of love.

"Where is Cora now?" Larke asked.

"A treatment program. In prison." Speaking those words hurt. And they were just as surreal as the rest of the story.

"I'm sorry," Larke said.

"Me too. I should have helped her."

"Maybe you did."

I wasn't sure prison was a help to anyone, but I could hope. "Maybe."

"That's why you came to Calamity."

"Yeah." My big change. "Thanks for listening."

"Thanks for telling me." She glanced at Wren, who had lain down on the floor, her thumb in her mouth. "I'd better get her in the bathtub."

"Sure." That was probably my cue to go home. Instead,

as she stood from the couch, collecting her daughter, I went to the table and cleared the milk glasses from dinner.

Splashing and running water sounded from the hallway when I got to the kitchen. The dishwasher was full of clean dishes, so I emptied it, hunting through cupboards and drawers until most everything was put away. Then I wiped down the countertops and took the trash to the bin outside.

Anything to delay my exit.

Larke emerged from the hall with Wren when I came back inside. She glanced around the kitchen. "You cleaned. You didn't have to do that."

"I didn't want to leave. Not yet." Maybe that was showing too many cards, but with the past raw and open, I wasn't ready to go home and be alone.

"Baba." Wren pointed to the fridge.

"Okay." Larke bent, setting Wren down.

The minute her toes touched the floor, Wren started to whimper and chase her mother. "Up. Up."

"I can't carry you and make your bottle." Larke opened the fridge for the gallon of milk.

"Come here, firefly." I dropped to a crouch, waving her over.

Wren stared at me, like I was a stranger and hadn't been here all night. Good to know that a break and bath time had set us back a bit. But I just waited until, one cautious step at a time, she came over and was close enough to pick up.

"Unicorn jammies. I have some of these at home too. Crazy, right?" I tickled her tummy, earning a smile. When I glanced at Larke, she was pouring a bottle with a smile on her face too.

It had been a long time since I'd worked so hard to make two females smile.

"We're going to watch TV and snuggle," Larke said as she screwed on the lid to a bottle.

Damn. I still wasn't ready to go. "I'll get out of your hair."

Larke walked over, handing the bottle to Wren. But she didn't steal her daughter from my arm. She just stared up at me with those captivating eyes, hooking me deeper and deeper. "Or . . . you can stay. Just no hogging the couch."

Hell yeah. "No promises."

CHAPTER THIRTEEN

LARKE

RONAN WAS A TORNADO, twisting me in circles.

From confusion to hate to lust to admiration to this budding crush. He'd left me reeling. And somehow, I liked his crazed, reckless spinning.

I liked Ronan.

Focusing on the television was pointless. I'd chosen *The Incredibles* on Disney because it was as entertaining for me as it was Wren.

Ronan chuckled at one of the jokes, drawing my attention.

I'd lost track of how many times I'd glanced his way from the corner of my eye. But this time, unlike my other chaste looks, his gaze was waiting.

Holy mother, he was hot. I couldn't have dreamed of a more handsome man. And his confidence, that cavalier attitude, was incredibly sexy.

We stared, unabashedly, like two people trying to read each other's thoughts.

Could he tell what I was thinking? Could he see my heart beat faster? Did he know how much I wanted another kiss?

There was as much desire in his hazel eyes as I felt thrumming through my veins.

Oh God. What was happening? It was getting dark outside and the glow from the setting sun was fading. The stubble on Ronan's sharp jaw was more pronounced in the shadowed light. His lips looked fuller, softer. The sliver of skin beneath his throat where he'd left a couple buttons undone was nothing but a tease, tormenting me to see what he looked like without the shirt entirely.

Wren's head fell heavy against my arm. Her eyes were closed. Her bottle was empty, barely held in her little grip. "I'd better put her to bed."

Ronan hummed, a rich, smooth note that gave me goose bumps.

Before I did something stupid, like beg him to stay, I stood from the couch and made my way toward the hallway.

My primary suite and Wren's room were on the main floor. Upstairs were two other bedrooms, a bonus space and an office I rarely used. The air was cooler as I descended the hall and it had nothing to do with the house's heating system. Whenever I was around Ronan, a fire blazed beneath my skin.

"What am I doing?" I murmured when I reached her room.

How long had it been since I'd felt this kind of attraction to a man? *Never*. Not even Hawaii.

My heart was pounding, so loud I feared it would wake Wren as I padded into her bedroom, stepping over the clothes she'd been wearing earlier. I'd been in such a hurry to get her in the bath and rush back to Ronan I hadn't bothered putting them in the hamper.

"Good night, baby." I kissed her forehead and laid her in her crib, standing by the railing for a long moment as she rolled to her tummy. Then when she was settled, I flipped on the sound machine and her nightlight before easing out of the room.

A wave of nerves hit as I lingered beside her closed door.

Wren had been a lovely buffer tonight. With her around, the tension between Ronan and me had been on simmer. Now that she was asleep, safe in her room, how far would this go? How far did I want it to go?

The answer to that question scared the hell out of me.

My knees were wobbly as I passed my bedroom door. Every breath lodged in my throat, my lungs too tight.

Maybe it would be best if I found the living room empty. If Ronan had slipped away and gone to his own house. A property line felt like a very practical and necessary boundary at the moment. Yet I sighed in relief when I found him in the same spot on the couch, relaxed, like that seat, which normally sat empty, had just been waiting for him.

"Why did you tell me about Cora?" I asked, staying on the opposite side of the room. If Wren wasn't a buffer, maybe the toys on the floor could be one instead.

"Because I wanted you to know." Ronan leaned forward, dropping his elbows to his knees. "Not many people do. I guess . . . it was important to me that you know the whole story. Before this continues."

How did he know exactly what to say? It was almost like he knew I had trust issues when it came to men. That I needed whole truths. Raw honesty. So he'd laid his past on the line along with his guilt. That way, I knew exactly what I was getting into.

"Thank you," I whispered.

"I'm going to kiss you again." Tonight. Tomorrow. Like he'd kiss me any damn time he pleased.

A shiver rolled down my spine. "Why did you kiss me earlier?"

"Because I had to."

Desire curled in my belly, and damn these toys, why was he so far away?

Ronan unfolded from the couch, his movements graceful and unhurried. He crossed the living room like a predator stalking his prey, not one glance to the floor, yet sidestepping every obstacle with ease. Then he stopped in front of me, his chest just inches from my own.

I stared at his sternum, nervous to meet his gaze. Maybe because I knew if I looked in his eyes, I'd see an invitation.

And I'd accept it.

So I stared at the buttons on his crisp white shirt.

"On Monday, I'll have to remind you, won't I?" His hand lifted, his fingers finding their way into my hair. With a quick tug, gone was my hair tie.

"Huh?" My mind was not working. Not with the heady scent of his woodsy cologne clouding my brain.

"That you don't despise me."

Because come Monday, the entire town would probably know that Ember Scott was suing me. Everyone would expect me to hate Ronan. "People will choose sides."

"I don't expect many on mine."

"You might be surprised," I muttered.

It wouldn't be support in masses, but he wouldn't be standing alone. Those who didn't like my family would side with Ronan just to spite the Hales.

"I've been thinking about that kiss all night." The rasp in his voice only made the desire in my lower belly coil tighter.

"Me too."

"Larke," he murmured my name as he bent, his mouth dropping to the corner of my own. His fingers threaded through my hair, shaking it out. Sparks cascaded down my scalp, over my shoulders and straight to my core.

My breath hitched as his lips lingered, barely touching.

Then he was gone, standing tall, his hands falling to his sides. His Adam's apple bobbed as he swallowed hard. "Good night."

I blinked. *What? Good night?*

In the moment it took me to realize what he'd said, he was gone, walking for the entryway.

Letting him leave was the smart decision. Except the message didn't make it to my feet. I chased after him, nearly tripping on the pink ball Wren had been tossing earlier. "Ronan."

He froze, just ten feet from the door. The muscles in his shoulders bunched as his hands fisted at his sides. "If I don't leave now, I'll stay."

I gulped. "What if I want you to stay?"

A pained groan escaped his throat as his head fell forward.

What was I saying? This was reckless. Impulsive. Foolish. This was bound to end in catastrophe, except the idea of him walking out the door made me want to scream.

Tonight, I wanted the tornado. I wanted wild, chaotic

passion. I wanted him to kiss me again just to see if what I'd felt at the office was a figment of my imagination.

Ronan turned, slowly straightening as he faced me. His jaw was clenched, his frame locked. God, I wanted to see him lose control. I wanted to watch that restraint shatter.

"You sure this is a good idea?"

"No," I whispered. But I wanted him anyway. So I closed the gap between us, placing my hands on his broad chest.

He was so tall that I had to lift up on my toes to kiss the underside of his jaw.

Ronan growled, the sound shooting straight between my legs. Then, just like I'd hoped, his control snapped. His arms banded around me as he hauled me against his hard body, his mouth crushing mine.

Yes. I moaned as his tongue swept inside.

He fluttered his tongue against mine before he pulled back to slant his mouth the other direction. He delved. He tortured. He nipped and sucked, like he was claiming my lips as his own.

It was, without a doubt, the best kiss of my life.

Alarms rattled in the back of my mind, warning me that tomorrow might bring disaster. But I silenced the fears, not caring if this was awkward in the morning. I'd deal with it then.

So I kissed him back, leaving it all out there, giving him everything I had. It was hot and wet. Fevered and rough.

Ronan's hands roamed my body, from my shoulders to my ribs to my ass. Every inch he touched ignited until my body burned. He thrust a bulky thigh between my legs, and it took a moment for me to realize why until he pressed it against my center, adding delicious friction to the kiss. Shamelessly, I rode his thigh, grinding against his hard body, until I was panting and aching for a release.

"Fuck." He tore his lips away, using a hand to wipe them dry.

"Yes." I needed to be fucked. Stepping away on shaking legs, I snatched his hand and dragged him through the house, down the hallway and to my bedroom, closing us inside the moment we crossed the threshold.

The throb between my legs felt like a bomb primed to explode.

Ronan reached for the hem of my shirt, hauling it over my head and tossing it aside so it could join the other clothes littering the carpet.

Our mouths crashed together, picking up exactly where we'd left off in the entryway. My fingers fumbled with the buttons on his shirt, flipping them free, one by one. Then I wrenched the cotton free from the waistband of his slacks, my tongue never untangling from his, as I shoved it off his shoulders.

Ronan's hand came to my breast, cupping it and the lace bralette I'd pulled on after work. He kneaded and massaged, his fingers finding my pebbled nipple and pinching hard enough that I yelped.

He chuckled against my mouth, his smile widening.

So I bit his lower lip, earning a hiss as he pulled away.

"You like to play dirty, babe?"

I lifted on my toes, nipping at the same place I'd just bit. "Filthy."

"Filthy." That word sounded like sex in his voice. The promise in his gaze was just as sensual.

His torso was a work of art, sculpted with honed muscle. Dark hair dusted his chest. My fingertips trailed across his washboard abs, bouncing between the dips and rises. I brushed his ribs before dropping to the V at his hips, then moved to his belt. I unbuckled it with hard tugs, all while he watched me.

Ronan was letting me take the lead. For now. The approval in his gaze made my breath hitch. His attention was rapt as his tongue darted out to lick his lower lip.

When his belt was undone, he toed off his shoes, his eyes never leaving mine. Then he swatted my hands away to unfasten the clasp on his pants before shoving them down his legs. His black boxer briefs strained across his arousal, and my mouth went dry.

"You're . . ."

He quirked an eyebrow, taking my hand to slide it beneath the waistband. Then, with his hand guiding mine, he fit my palm over his cock.

Oh. My. God. He was like steel. Thick and long. I stroked, wanting to feel him from root to tip.

"Fuck." He rocked his hips into my fist, his eyes closing for a second as he tipped his head to the ceiling.

I was about to drop to my knees and take him in my mouth when he pulled my hand free. Then I was flying through the air. In a flash, Ronan lifted me off my feet and tossed me on the bed, coming down on top of me to capture my mouth.

His erection thrust against my core, the material of his boxers and my leggings keeping me from getting the friction I needed. His tongue did a lazy swirl against mine before he lifted up, standing from the edge of the bed.

My leggings and panties went with him.

That cocky smirk stretched across his mouth as he shoved his boxers to the floor.

His cock bobbed before he fisted it, giving it a hard stroke. Oh sweet lord. I wouldn't be able to look at his house and not picture him naked. Never again. When I thought of Ronan, it would be like this.

Hard and naked, bathed in shadows and staring at me.

He reached forward, grabbing a hand to haul me up to a seat. Then, with more gentleness than I'd expected, he pulled the bralette off my breasts.

"You're perfect." He bent, nuzzling his mouth against my throat. His tongue darted out to taste my skin. "Lie down."

I nodded, my breath coming in shallow pants as I obeyed, resting on the sheets. I hadn't bothered making my bed this morning.

Ronan took my ankles, spreading me wide. "You're soaked."

Drenched.

For that sexy smirk. For that rock-hard body. For those hazel eyes and the man he'd been at dinner.

"You need to come," he murmured, dropping his elbows onto the bed. One stroke of his tongue through my slit and I nearly came off the mattress.

"Yes." I fisted his dark hair as he licked me again.

Ronan Thatcher had a talented tongue.

Thank God.

He devoured me, exactly how I liked it. No toying around. No teasing. I didn't need foreplay because, like he'd said, I needed to come. I needed an orgasm from something other than the vibrator in my nightstand.

Ronan fucked me with his tongue, flicking it against my clit until my limbs began to tremble. Then he added a finger, sliding it inside and curling it into the spot that made my body arch off the bed.

My orgasm came on me so fast I gasped, blanking my mind as stars broke across my vision. Every muscle quaked, my body coming entirely undone as I shattered with bone-rattling pulses.

He hummed, lapping at me while I came down from the heavens. "Fuck, but you taste good."

"Whoa." I covered my face with my hands, my chest heaving as I tried to fill my lungs. That should have taken the edge off, but Ronan was addictive and I needed more. So I reached for him, shoving up on an elbow.

But instead of climbing into the bed, he stood, backing away and wiping his mouth dry. "I don't have a condom."

"Oh." *Shit.* I didn't have a condom because I hadn't been with anyone in years. "It's been a long time. And I'm on birth control."

For the first time, his confidence cracked. His eyes widened, like that was the last thing he'd expected me to say. "You sure?"

"Yes." Without a doubt. Maybe tomorrow I'd regret this. But tonight, I wanted him more than my next breath.

He planted a knee in the bed, straddling one of my legs. Then he gave me that sexy smirk that sent a fresh rush of anticipation through my veins. Ronan stared down at me with a look that spoke volumes. This man knew how to deliver pleasure, and he was about to show me exactly how well he could fuck.

He inched closer, until his knees brushed my ass. Then he took my other leg, lifting it, bending it, until it was curled around his hip.

The position forced me onto my side, so I rested on an elbow, watching him as he put me exactly where he wanted me.

He lifted the leg that he'd curled around my hip, making room for his cock. He dragged the tip through my center, letting it brush my sensitive clit. When I whimpered, he grinned wider. "Grab that pillow."

"Why?" I asked, even though I obeyed.

"Because I'm going to make you scream my name."

Yes, please.

He rocked forward, stealing my breath as he pushed inside, inch by inch, my body stretching around his. This position, with one leg pinned beneath him and the other lifted, put me entirely at his mercy.

Those eyes stayed locked with mine as he went deeper and deeper, that thick cock stretching me until I melted.

"Fuck, you're tight." His jaw clenched when he was rooted. He gave an audible swallow.

"Move," I whimpered. God, it felt good but I needed him to move.

He pulled out, slowing, then thrust forward, this time earning a cry.

My inner walls fluttered, another orgasm building.

Ronan fucked in and out of me three times before he stopped, taking the leg he'd lifted and curling it around his hip again. "Hold it there."

I nodded, knowing it wouldn't last. My body was about to come apart and any control would slip into oblivion.

Ronan moved, faster and faster. The angle meant he hit that spot inside with every single stroke, and my legs trembled. Then he reached for my clit, rubbing it in slow, methodical circles, so light he was barely touching.

I wanted to rock against him, to get more friction and pressure, but I was trapped. So I hugged the pillow, my moans coming with each slap of skin, until the next orgasm hit me like a tidal wave.

And, as promised, I screamed his name.

The pleasure blanked my mind. It stole my senses. All I could do was feel, a head-to-toe explosion. It lasted a minute, an hour, a year. I lost track of all time while my body came apart, then slowly knitted itself back together again.

When I dared crack my eyes, Ronan's bottom lip was pulled between his teeth. His brow was furrowed, his face masked in complete concentration as he thrust in and out, chasing his own release. It hit him on a groan, his eyes squeezing shut as his muscles bunched.

The sight of him coming undone was the most erotic moment of my entire life. He poured inside of me, his body shaking, until his orgasm was spent. Then he eased out before collapsing on the mattress beside me, his chest heaving as he stared up at the ceiling. "Damn, Larke."

I was speechless. That was toe-curling, can't-get-enough-of-each-other, addictive sex.

The orgasm motherload. Ronan had just obliterated the chance for any man on earth to compare.

Oh, damn it.

Ronan Thatcher was going to break my heart, wasn't he?

CHAPTER FOURTEEN

RONAN

I JOLTED AWAKE, squinting as the sun streamed through Larke's bedroom window. Shoving up on an elbow, I searched for a clock, finding one on her nightstand.

Seven eighteen.

"Damn." I rubbed my hands over my face. When was the last time I'd slept past six? Years. Not since before law school. Even on the weekends, my body had been programmed to rise early.

But I'd slept hard last night. Apparently I was the only one. The space beside me was cold. When had Larke slipped out?

I sat up, giving myself a minute to wake up as I took in her bedroom, from the white ceiling to the dark gray walls. The wide, gleaming windows had the same black grid design as the windows at my place. Her cream curtains had been left open, giving me an unobstructed view of her backyard.

But it was the bed that caught my interest. It was a four-poster frame, the same shade of black to match the windows.

Last night, it had been dark enough that I'd noticed the posts, just not their size. They seemed so much bigger, so much more impressive this morning.

The image of Larke tied between them popped into my head and my cock twitched beneath the sheet.

Damn, last night had been amazing. The best sex of my life. The way our bodies had come together was unlike anything I'd felt before. And Larke had been so responsive, so willing.

She'd fallen asleep in my arms, sated and limp. She'd curled into my side and the last thing I remembered was kissing her hair as her breathing evened out.

I didn't cuddle. It wasn't my thing. I hadn't even cuddled with Cora.

But with Larke, I'd cuddled. I dragged a hand through my hair as an arrow of panic shot through my chest. What the hell was happening?

This was too much. Too serious. Larke had crept into every corner of my mind. The last time I'd let a woman have this much headspace, I'd married her.

Whipping the covers off my legs, I searched the cluttered floor for my clothes, strewn alongside hers. Swiping up my boxers, I made my way to the en suite bathroom, washing my face and stealing a swipe of her toothpaste to rub on my teeth.

Then I wandered into the bedroom again, finding my shirt and pulling it on. Next came my pants and socks. Where was my phone? Or my keys?

When I found my keys beside one of my shoes, I groaned.

How many neighbors were wondering why my gleaming, silver Stingray had slept in her driveway? I'd never done a drive of shame before. Today would be a first.

My phone I found beside the door. The battery was nearly drained, and I'd missed a call from Noah. But I tucked it away to deal with later. Then, with my shoes in hand, I headed down the hall.

The smell of coffee and toast drew me toward the kitchen.

Larke was standing at the counter, wearing a pair of magenta silk lounge pants and a simple black tee. Wren was on her hip, still in her unicorn pajamas. Both were staring at whatever Larke was mixing with one hand. Pancake batter maybe.

Larke's hair was up, twisted in a messy knot. A few tendrils trailed down her neck. She smiled at her daughter, oblivious to me watching.

They were perfect together, moving in tandem, encapsulated in their own little world.

Something pinched as I watched them, like the urge to meld my world with theirs, but I forced myself to stay on this side of the room. If I touched Larke, if I caught a whiff of that clean lavender scent and felt the heat of her skin against mine, well . . . the Stingray would be spending another night.

And it was time for us both to go home.

I cleared my throat. "Hi."

Larke turned, her eyes raking down my chest where I hadn't buttoned my shirt. She blushed, ducking her chin. "Morning."

Wren curled into her mother's shoulder, like she was trying to hide. Apparently, our progress from last night had reset completely.

"I, uh . . ." I pointed toward the front of the house. "I forgot to move my car last night. Sorry."

"Oh." She winced. "I'm sure Mrs. Edwards will *love* that. You might have just ruined your chances for another goose casserole."

I snapped my fingers. "Darn."

Larke's eyes sparkled. She leaned her cheek on Wren's head, gently swaying her daughter.

Fuck, but I wanted to kiss her. I wanted to spend the day here, helping her do whatever it was she did on Saturdays, wrapped in their little bubble. Then I wanted to spend another night in Larke's bed, worshiping her body.

"I'd better go." While I could.

She nodded, not stopping me this time. "Okay."

"See ya." I waved to Larke. I winked at Wren. Both felt shallow. Then forced my feet to move, leaving without a backward glance.

The spring air was fresh when I stepped outside, the sky a clear blue. The dew drops on Larke's lawn caught the sunlight and the sound of robins chirping filled the neighborhood.

The windows on the Corvette were wet, the seats cold as I slid behind the wheel. The engine roared to life, too loud for this hour on a weekend morning, so as quickly as I could, I moved it from Larke's driveway to my garage.

Why hadn't I just parked at home last night? *Stupid, Thatcher.*

Probably because I hadn't thought the night with Larke would go that far. I'd gone for dinner, expecting there was a decent chance she'd tell me no. That I'd be eating White

Oak takeout myself for a couple nights. Best-case scenario, I'd simply hoped to share a meal.

I sure as hell hadn't planned to tell her about Cora. Where the fuck had that confession come from? And I hadn't planned to lose myself inside Larke's body.

My limbs felt too loose as I headed inside. My heart beat too hard and my chest felt tight. Taking a deep breath was impossible and my head began to spin. I tossed my shoes onto the tiled floor in the mud room, their clatter echoing like a thunderclap.

Son of a bitch. What was wrong with me?

I rubbed my temples, a headache blooming as I made my way upstairs. Every room I passed was clean. My bed was made from yesterday morning. The bathroom counters were spotless.

Only a handful of boxes hadn't been unpacked, and they'd been neatly stacked in the guest bedroom. I still needed to hang the artwork in the upstairs office. But otherwise, the house was pristine. Some of the furniture I'd brought wasn't quite right for a few spaces, but there were no gaping, empty holes.

Except it felt . . . hollow. It didn't feel like anyone lived here.

What this home needed was a mess of toys on the floor. A cluttered kitchen with unopened mail. Dirty laundry and cheeky cartoons.

No. No, it didn't. This was *my* house. And my house was tidy. My house was new, without broken pieces to fix. Without upgrades to make. Without history in its walls.

My headache throbbed, a dull beat behind my temples.

A shower would probably help, but I didn't want to wash off Larke's scent. Not yet.

I stood in the center of my bedroom, staring out the window to the olive-green house next door. Larke's floor plan was better and entirely different than mine, with the larger bedrooms on the ground level while mine were on the second.

Why did I feel like I was stuck in limbo, not belonging here or there? What was happening to me? Why hadn't I stayed for coffee?

Because she didn't invite me.

Larke had things to do today. She had plans with her family and Wren to take care of. And what did I know about kids? Nothing, clearly, other than to give fist bumps and toss a goddamn pink ball.

Even when Cora and I had been married, we hadn't talked about kids. My career had been my baby. She'd been on the fence about having children. Then after the divorce, I'd been happily single, content to give my all to the firm. To date, to fuck, whoever I wanted.

Larke was a good woman. Wren was the most adorable child I'd ever seen. But that wasn't really the life I'd set out to lead, was it?

If the disaster with Cora had taught me anything, it was that I had an incredible talent for looking out for myself. My priority had always been me.

Everyone around me, well . . . they were on their own.

Hell, I hadn't even realized Dad's eyesight was failing. Not until he'd had to sit me down and spell it out, that he was selling the business and retiring. This was after he'd mistaken his hand for a two-by-four and sent a nail through his flesh with the nail gun. Had I asked *why* the accident had happened? Nope.

Shouldn't a son recognize when his father couldn't see? When he squinted constantly and had to have his wife read a restaurant menu? Shouldn't a husband—or ex-husband—notice that the woman he'd vowed to love and cherish had covered his former coffee table with lines of cocaine?

What kind of partner—or father—did I make?

The fucking shitty kind.

Cora might have tried to slice my heart in half, but she'd taught me something. I had blind spots of my own. They were mine to own and mine to regret.

My phone vibrated in my pocket. When I pulled it out, Noah's name flashed on the screen. "Hey," I answered. "What's up?"

"Just heading to work."

"On a Saturday?"

"You know how it goes."

"Yeah," I muttered. For years, I'd spent most Saturdays at the office. That life seemed like a lifetime ago, not just weeks.

"What are you up to?" he asked.

"Staring at my neighbor's house."

"Um, that's creepy." The sound of traffic rushed in the background. He was probably on the freeway, surrounded by other cars.

"Just admiring the color," I lied, then shook my head, tearing my gaze from the glass and walking to the bathroom. With the phone pinned between my ear and shoulder, I stripped off my shirt. "Can I ask you something?"

"Sure."

"Do you think I could have stopped her?"

"Who? Cora?"

"Yeah." I faced myself in the mirror, taking in the red scar that marred my chest.

This was probably a question I should have asked Dad. But Noah had known Cora for just as long. He'd known her before shit had fallen apart, both in my marriage and after.

"Do you think if I had noticed earlier, I could have gotten her into a treatment program?" A program not tied to a fucking prison cell.

"You guys were divorced."

"So."

"So . . . you can't take her problems as your own."

"Not exactly how marriage works."

"Except you weren't married. Her addiction was her choice."

He was right. My parents had said the same. But I still felt that guilt. That responsibility.

That failure.

"You did the right thing by ending it. You two were miserable. And sometimes you just have to walk away from the crazy-ass woman trying to trap you."

"Nice." I huffed a laugh.

"Yeah. Yeah," he muttered. "Sorry. I sound like a dick. It's just . . . I don't like that you're beating yourself up over this. You can't save everyone, Ronan."

I sighed. "I should have done more."

"You paid for her lawyer. You cleaned up the house. I'd say you did more than enough after she tried to *murder* you."

Maybe he was right. Or maybe not.

I turned from the mirror, walking to the closet. My shirt got tossed on the floor, not in the hamper. "I'll let you get to work. I'm heading out on a run."

"Before you hang up," he said. "Bobbie and I talked about the trip. How about a weekend in May?"

"Sounds good to me." Weekend plans were nonexistent, though Mrs. Edwards had given me a standing invitation for dinner each Sunday. "Just text me the dates."

"Sweet. I'll have my assistant get the details ironed out. See if we can get the same guide from last year for a fishing trip."

"I'm in. Let me know if I can help."

"Will do."

I blew out a long breath after ending the call, leaving my phone on a closet shelf while I stripped off my pants. They got dumped on the floor too. Then I tugged on a pair of running shorts, a T-shirt and my favorite tennis shoes before hitting the road.

The five-mile route I ran should have emptied my head. Organized my thoughts. When it didn't, I kept going, pushing my body to the brink.

Since I'd left my phone behind, I wasn't sure how far I'd gone by the time my legs turned to mush. My body was drenched with sweat. My lungs were on fire. But the unease in my gut seemed ten times worse. And I was fucking thirsty, so I finally turned around and trudged home.

There was no activity at Larke's place. She was probably gone to her sister's. Tomorrow she'd said she had that barbeque with her parents. I'd chased her, relentlessly, but for the first time since I'd moved to Calamity, I was glad we wouldn't bump into each other.

What was I doing?

What did I want?

I didn't have an answer to either question. For Larke, for Wren, I needed answers.

Maybe it would just be better to end this now. We'd had one hell of a night. Sex with Larke wasn't something I'd soon forget.

We could end this amicably, right? Stay civil. Remain neighbors. Larke didn't seem like the scorned-lover type who'd slash my tires or key my Corvette.

Except the idea of saying goodbye, of not touching her again, made me want to punch a hole in the damn wall. Hell, I might lose my license for throwing professional ethics out the window and none of it would matter because I'd be back in California with my tail between my legs.

Maybe I was overthinking this. I'd spent hours agonizing over her feelings and how not to crush them. But she hadn't stopped me from leaving this morning. She hadn't offered me coffee or breakfast. Maybe she'd wanted me out the door too.

Fuck. Another rejection?

This woman had me twisted into a goddamn pretzel. Every instinct screamed for me to cross her lawn. To sit on her front stoop and wait until she came home. To see her, kiss her, make a colossal mess and not give a damn about the repercussions.

But that was how I'd ended up in Calamity. I'd ignored the signs I should have seen. I'd dismissed the chaos and clutter.

Not again.

So I went inside my own house, taking a cold shower to rinse off the sweat, then dressed in a pair of jeans and a T-shirt. With my keys, a bottle of water and an energy bar in hand, I made my way to the garage and climbed in my Corvette. Then I put Calamity in my rearview mirror.

There was a freedom to be found on the open Montana roads. A solitude, just a man surrounded by mountains and meadows. I explored the countryside, only stopping for gas and food.

It should have been peaceful, driving aimlessly with a soundtrack of wheels on pavement. But for every turn of my tires, my head did two. And every spin was around Larke.

I'd just wanted a date. A dinner with the local beauty. A bit of fun with a stunning, unexpected woman.

I'd gotten a lot more than planned, hadn't I?

It was dark by the time I finally returned to Calamity. When I turned onto the cul-de-sac, Larke's house sat dark at the end of the block.

Was that a good thing? Or a bad?

I pulled into my garage and retreated inside. My stomach was too bunched to eat, so I just went to bed. And the next morning, when I woke before dawn, I found myself in the Corvette again.

Another day of driving did nothing to help sort my thoughts, but I drove anyway, forcing myself to stay on the highways until the moon had crested the horizon and I knew Larke would once again be asleep when I finally made it back to town.

Monday morning came too fast. I glanced out my windows as I dressed for work just in time to see her tail-lights disappear down the street.

Any normal Monday, I'd head downtown. Get some coffee. Chat with Gertrude.

Not this one.

I did go to the office, arriving before Gerty. But then I collected my paperwork, leaving a note that I'd be back later. And with my heart in my throat, I walked to the courthouse.

To file Ember's complaint against Larke.

CHAPTER FIFTEEN

LARKE

"I'M PRETTY sure I just got played." I plopped the papers I'd been served today on Kerrigan's counter.

They'd served me at school. Maybe that was standard practice but it felt a lot like an evil power play. And of course, it had been exactly the minute when Asshole Abbott had been passing my classroom.

"Today sucks."

Kerrigan leaned over my shoulder, scanning the legal paperwork. "So Ronan did it. He actually filed the kid's complaint."

"To be fair, I told him to do it." Though I hadn't expected to feel like this. Slimy and criminal.

My sister frowned but stayed quiet.

"Maybe next time, listen to Aiden and don't encourage your next door neighbor to sue you." Nellie, one of my best friends in the entire world, wasn't exactly the stay-quiet type.

"His intentions are pure." Probably.

"There are other ways to help a troubled teenager than by pandering to this asinine idea and using the court system to bully you," Nellie said.

"You're starting to sound like Aiden."

"Neither of them is wrong," Kerrigan muttered, pouring me a glass of white wine.

No, they weren't. "Ronan doesn't want to lose his contact with Ember until he can figure out what's going on." Wait. Why was I defending him?

Oh, right. The orgasms.

"So what happens now?" Nellie asked.

"In a nutshell, wait for a judge to tell me if I have to change this girl's grade." And while I was waiting, I'd be watching Ember.

She'd been in the same outfit today as she had been on Friday. And not just the same shirt and shoes with a different pair of pants. Every single article had been an exact match, down to the pale blue socks peeking out at the hem of her jeans.

But the clothes did look freshly washed. And not once since I'd put her under my microscope had I noticed her skin dirty or her hair in need of some shampoo.

Still, whatever was bothering Ronan about Ember had been contagious. There was something amiss, I just wasn't sure what.

"Did you ever track down her mother?" Nellie took the stool next to mine at the island.

"Nope. I've called over and over. All I get is the answering machine. She hasn't called me back." Either Ashley Scott was ignoring me, like her daughter, or Ember was intercepting my messages and deleting them before Ashley could listen.

"That's strange," Kerrigan said. "Don't you think?"

"Yep." I took the wineglass she handed me, raising it in the air to clink the rim against hers and Nellie's, then swallowed a healthy gulp.

The Saturday get-together I'd told Ronan about had been moved to tonight. Elias hadn't been feeling well this weekend, and we hadn't wanted the kids to share germs. But thankfully it had been a twenty-four-hour bug and from the sounds of the laughter in the playroom, everyone was right as rain.

Mondays were typically the day when I'd stay an extra couple of hours after the last class and hammer through the final details of my lesson plans. But today, the second the kids had been excused, I'd hauled ass to the parking lot, rushed to get Wren from daycare and driven out to Kerrigan's house.

While we'd waited for Nellie and Cal to arrive, Kerrigan and I had watched the kids play. The dads were on patrol at the moment so I could come out here to tell the girls that this lawsuit was, effective today, a very real thing.

"I don't want to go to court," I pouted.

"The judge is not going to side with Ember," Nellie said. "Right?"

I shrugged. "I have no idea. Aiden isn't worried but I don't want to get my hopes up."

A ruling in Ember's favor would mean my complete and total humiliation.

"We could ask Everly to put in a good word with Judge Labb," Kerrigan said. "Dad could call him too."

"Nah." I waved it off. "Besides, we don't know if he'll even be the judge."

"And you probably don't want to shortcut the process and risk stepping on toes," Kerrigan said.

"Exactly."

I had no doubt that Everly would talk to the judge for me. She worked at her husband's art gallery in town and over the years, she and Nelson Labb had become friends. Dad knew him from church and the dealership. But I didn't want any outside interference. Not yet.

Besides, in theory, I had an inside ally. Ronan. He was secretly on my side here, wasn't he?

Or had I gotten screwed? Literally.

"I have to tell you something." I set my wineglass down and hid my face in my palms. "I slept with Ronan." It came out rushed and muffled.

"Huh?" Nellie tugged on my wrist until I dropped my hands.

"I slept with Ronan."

Kerrigan's eyes bugged out.

Nellie's mouth fell open. "Um . . ."

"Not the best decision I've made lately."

"Um . . ." Nellie took a gulp of her wine. "Do you like him?"

"Yes?" Why had that sounded like a question? Yes, I most definitely liked Ronan. Or I had on Friday night. Especially after he'd held me all night long. Every time I'd tried to shift away, he'd just pinned me closer.

Except then he'd been weird on Saturday morning. He'd hovered outside the kitchen like an intruder, scared to step closer. He'd waved goodbye. A goddamn wave. Followed by a wink for Wren. She was one. She didn't understand winking.

Then he'd been a ghost for the rest of the weekend. His place had been pitch black. While all of my other neighbors had been outside on Saturday doing spring yard work, his house had been a tomb.

This was the problem with sleeping with your neighbor. It was too easy to shift into stalker mode.

"Well?" Kerrigan came closer, nudging my elbow.

"Well, what?"

"You haven't been with a man since Hawaii. Years. And now you pick this one? Details, please."

"It was . . . good." A flush crept into my cheeks. "Amazing. Phenomenal." Ugh. I dropped my face into my hands again. "He ruined me. And I really, *really* liked it."

I really, *really* liked Ronan.

"Oh boy." Nellie gave an exaggerated frown. "And he still sued you."

"Again, I gave him permission."

She cocked her head. "This might be the weirdest foreplay I've ever heard of."

I giggled, swatting her shoulder. "Stop. He's trying to help Ember."

Kerrigan studied my face for a long moment. "Then why do you feel like you've been played?"

"I haven't heard from him since Saturday morning. And maybe I'm just being paranoid, but I feel like he's avoiding his house so he can avoid me."

Kerrigan winced. "Ouch."

"He's charming. Clever. And . . . real." That story about Cora couldn't have been easy to tell. And he'd been so brutal about the details. Most men would have sugarcoated it. Or played the victim. Instead, he'd admitted to feeling guilty for not doing more.

"I don't know." I shook my head. "Maybe I'm reading more into it than I should. Maybe I'm just lonely, and he's the most attractive man to move to Calamity in a decade. Maybe the reason I like him is because every other single guy in town is either a relative or someone I watched pick boogers out of his nose in elementary school."

"Ew." Nellie feigned a gag.

Giggles and happy squeals carried from the playroom, followed by laughter from both Pierce and Cal.

Wren was a lucky girl. She might not have a father in her life, but she had good men. She had a loving grandfather and adoring uncles. Except that wasn't the same as having a dad.

She deserved the best. When it came to men, I was exceptionally choosy about who I dated. Probably why I hadn't dated.

I wanted to give her the world. I wanted to protect her from the world. Or was I too busy protecting myself?

These past two years, I'd crawled under a rock. Mostly to avoid the gossip. Partly because Wren had demanded my undivided attention and having a newborn had been hard. But I couldn't live under that rock forever. Either I emerged and stayed. Or I tried somewhere new.

Was it time to make my own *big* change?

"I have another confession." I looked to Kerrigan, knowing that she'd hate this the most. Not that Nellie wouldn't be upset too. My sister tensed, like she could hear the bad news in my tone. "I've been thinking about moving."

Kerrigan's gasp was so loud it filled her massive kitchen. "W-what?"

Nellie shook her head so fast that her white-blond hair was falling out of her bun. "To where? Why? No. You can't move. No."

"It's not a guarantee. There's a teaching job open in Bozeman for fourth grade, and I've applied."

"You applied?" Kerrigan's jaw hit the floor.

"The pay is better." Even to my own ears, it sounded like a lame excuse. "Bozeman is only two hours away." Yep, that one sounded bad too.

But the truth was out there now, and a weight came off my chest. That job in Bozeman had been a secret of mine for months and keeping it had been exhausting. When it came to Kerrigan and Nellie, I'd never been good at secrets. I'd told Nellie I was pregnant before I'd even told my parents.

"Is this because you're in the high school?" Nellie asked. "That's temporary. They know you want your fifth-grade classroom back."

"But I might not get it. And you guys, I don't like the high school. Yeah, most of the kids are fine. This isn't even about Ember Scott. I just . . . I don't wake up excited to go to work. I feel like I'm forcing it. That's not fair to the kids or to me. I feel . . . old. Tired."

"You're thirty-five." Kerrigan gave me a flat stare. "That's not old."

"I know that, but these kids have drained me entirely." The students used to give me this lift. I couldn't wait to see them file into my classroom. Now I found myself faking smiles for hours upon hours.

"Today, I had a girl call me 'bestie.' I can't even articulate why, but I wanted to scream."

Kerrigan waved it off. "Probably because you were the girl who agonized over which friend to give the other half of your best friend necklace to for so long that when you finally decided, everyone had already traded and you had to pick me as your *bestie*."

"Bestie." It was my turn to fake gag. "Who calls their teacher bestie? Or babes? I had that last week."

Nellie's shoulders fell. "You can't move."

I gave her a sad smile. "It's only two hours. It's not like I wouldn't visit."

"It wouldn't be the same."

Nellie worked for Pierce as his assistant, and when he'd moved to town to be with Kerrigan years ago, she'd decided to relocate from Denver too. Since then, I'd claimed her. If adults still did best friend necklaces, she'd have mine.

If I did move, I'd miss her. And Kerrigan. And my family.

"I haven't made any decisions yet. I don't even have the job. It's just an option I thought was worth exploring. Maybe it's time for a fresh start."

Kerrigan crossed her arms over her chest. "You'll be alone."

I was already alone.

It was incredible to have family close to help with Wren. Of course, my parents and siblings made life easier. But I was still alone.

When the dishes needed to be washed, I washed. When the laundry had to be folded, I folded. When the garbage needed to be hauled out, I hauled.

The first time I'd had help at the house in a year, help

without having to beg a family member, had been from Ronan.

Other than college, Calamity had been home my entire life. What would it feel like to walk down a street and have no one recognize me? How great would it be to have some anonymity? Wouldn't it be nice to stop by the grocery store and not face the cashier who had cheered on the gossip that I'd screwed a married man and that was how I'd ended up pregnant?

"You'd really move?" Kerrigan stared at me like my skin had turned purple and antennae had sprouted from my head.

I lifted a shoulder. "Possibly." *Yes.*

A crease formed between her eyebrows, a telltale sign she was mad. Then came the scowl. Without another word, she breezed past me, marching toward some quiet, hidden corner in her enormous house.

Nellie slid off her stood, putting a hand on my shoulder. Then she followed my sister, probably to hug Kerrigan while she angry cried.

"That went well," I told my wineglass, taking a sip.

Better to get this conversation out of the way. My mother's reaction would be disastrous. She'd see this as a personal attack that I was spiriting her grandchild to a faraway land.

I sat alone, sipping my wine, until Pierce came out a few minutes later with Wren on his hip. I took her from him, kissing her cheek before setting her on my lap. "Hi, baby."

"Where's my wife?" Pierce asked.

I pointed over my shoulder. "She's down there somewhere. Be warned, she's mad at me because I told her I was thinking about moving to Bozeman."

Pierce's scowl looked more and more like Kerrigan's every year they were married. "Say that again."

———

SCHOOL NIGHTS. That had always been Mom and Dad's excuse to leave social gatherings early. *It's a school night.*

Even though Wren wasn't in school, I used that excuse to leave Pierce and Kerrigan's the moment we were finished with an awkward and strained dinner.

Maybe I should have waited to tell everyone about the move until I knew if it was actually happening. Maybe I should have mentioned it months ago.

"I feel like every decision I make right now is wrong," I told Wren as we drove home.

Through the mirror in the backseat, I could see her sucking her thumb. Her eyelids were heavy and she'd already kicked off her shoes.

"Bozeman is a nice town," I said. "That's where Mommy went to college."

I'd gotten into the habit of talking to her while we drove in an effort to try and keep her awake. Without fail, she'd fall asleep on the trip into town from Kerrigan's, and it would be just enough of a nap that she'd be hard to get back to sleep after bath time.

But these one-sided conversations had also become a sort of therapy. A way for me to voice my thoughts.

I hoped she wouldn't remember what I told her. I hoped I wasn't scarring her tiny brain with my personal issues.

"Do all mothers feel like they're constantly screwing up?"

Normally, I'd call my sister and ask. But she wasn't speaking to me at the moment so instead, I asked the open road.

By the time we pulled into town, Wren was zonked. Not wanting to fight with her tonight, I parked in the garage, then carefully unbuckled her from her car seat, taking her inside and putting her straight in her crib.

The diaper change was tricky. So was getting her into a pair of pajamas and out of the clothes she'd been wearing at daycare. She stirred, her eyelids fluttering open, but by some miracle, Wren drifted right back to sleep the moment I laid her in the crib.

I was just tossing her clothes in the hamper when movement from the window caught my eye. Ronan's garage door was rolling up. His Corvette's engine rumbled as he eased into the driveway.

It was after seven. Not quite dark.

Good to know he was still alive.

My heart climbed into my throat as I crept toward the window, hovering by the frame and peering out a corner.

He parked his car, unfolded from the driver's seat and stood, dragging a hand through his dark hair. His slacks were wrinkled at the knees. His shirtsleeves were rolled up his forearms per usual and the top button at the collar was undone.

Ronan put one hand on the top of his car, his fingers splayed. He dropped his eyes to the concrete beneath his polished shoes.

He stood so still it was like he'd frozen in place. Then slowly, finger by finger, he formed a fist. He raised it, brought it down hard, like he was going to hammer it on the car. But at the last second, he eased up enough to soften the blow.

Then, with pained movements, like he didn't want to, he turned his gaze my direction. His jaw clenched.

My frame locked. I held my breath, staying hidden as he strode out of the garage and onto his driveway. There was no way he could see me, but the way he walked was like he was aiming straight for me.

I hated how much my heart soared. I hated that I'd been secretly hoping he'd come back. That I hadn't made a huge mistake by taking him to my bed.

Except he stopped. One minute he was coming toward me, the next, he was stuck again.

And my heart crashed, landing beside the basket of stuffed animals at my feet.

Ronan stared at my house for a few long moments. Then he turned away, walking into his garage, his long strides eating up the distance. With a smack on the button, he closed the overhead door.

I waited until it was shut, then I shoved away from the window and retreated to my bedroom.

Okay, so he'd played me. Who cared? At least it wasn't as bad as Hawaii, right?

I got ready for bed and climbed into the clean sheets. Then before I shut down for the night, I sent my lawyer an email.

Please tell me you can kick Ronan Thatcher's ass?

Aiden must have been working because his reply was instant.

I'm sure going to try.

Good enough for me.

CHAPTER SIXTEEN

RONAN

THE SOUND of stomping feet made me grimace.

I knew that stomp. It pounded through the office's front door at approximately three forty-five each afternoon. Coincidentally, my daily headache started at precisely the same time. In ten years, would I think of Ember Scott and get an instant migraine?

I'd been working on a few minor tasks for the past thirty minutes, knowing she was about to storm in for her daily visit. And like every other afternoon this week, she was not going to like what I had to say.

"Hello, Ember," Gertrude said from the reception area. "How are you today?"

"Good."

This kid was nothing if not predictable. Ember was always *good*. Never great, grouchy, grand or grateful. Just good. And I had yet to hear her ask about Gerty's day in return.

Maybe I was the grouchy one. Hell, I'd been in a piss-poor mood all week, mostly because I'd spent too many hours in this exact place, all in an effort to avoid my house. To avoid Larke.

Had this been California, the long workdays would have been a breeze. I could have easily filled fourteen-hour days. Except this was Calamity, and while I was getting new clients, it was a struggle to scrounge up eight hours of work for myself, let alone something for Gertrude to do.

Yesterday, I'd gotten so desperate that I'd read half of Gerty's bodice ripper. It had been surprisingly enjoyable. And it had allowed me to escape reality for a few hours.

To not feel like the coward I was.

This couldn't continue. Tonight. I'd talk to Larke tonight.

It wasn't that I hadn't tried already. Every night this week, I'd tried to cross my driveway. Every night, I'd walked one step closer to Larke's lawn. But then I'd hit this invisible wall that would halt my feet and send me scurrying to my own house like a fucking weakling.

I despised *me* right now.

Larke probably did too.

How mad was she? How badly had I screwed up my chances to fix this?

It had been a week since our night together, and it had taken me that long to realize I wanted more.

More dinners at her cluttered dining room table. More evenings on her living room couch. More nights in her bed.

Chances were, she'd never speak to me again. At this point, I'd settle for friendship. But I was going to chase *more*.

If I could get my feet to cross my goddamn driveway.

"Ronan." Ember waved her hand in front of my face.

I jerked, blinking twice. She was sitting in the guest chair.

If anyone had ever mastered the look of being truly unimpressed, it was Ember Scott.

"Sorry," I muttered.

Ember wasn't the only one who'd had to snap me out of my thoughts of Larke. Gertrude had caught me three times—since lunch—staring off into space.

"Have you heard anything?" she asked.

"Not yet."

"Seriously?" She let out a frustrated groan, then slumped in her chair. "What is taking so long?"

"It's been four days."

"Five, including Monday," she corrected.

"Kid, courthouses have a lot happening." That might be a stretch for Calamity, but I doubted this case was high priority. "Did you ask your mom about a meeting?"

She stared at the corner of my desk. "I told you, she's busy."

The same excuse I'd gotten for days. This busy mom who couldn't be bothered to talk with her daughter's attorney.

It was bullshit. And damn it, I should have called Ember on it weeks ago. I should have stopped this lawsuit before it had even started. But instead, I'd used it as an excuse to gain attention from Larke. What the fuck was wrong with me?

"I'm running out of time," Ember snapped.

"You're eighteen. You have nothing but time."

"The school year ends in a month." She articulated every syllable. It reminded me of a judge slamming a gavel at the end of a long day in court.

"Have you ever thought about becoming a lawyer?"

"What are you talking about?"

"Never mind." I waved it off. "I'm betting we'll hear back next week."

"What if we don't?" She tossed a hand in the air. "I have to get this grade changed. Now."

"It won't be the end of the world."

Those green eyes flared.

When she'd first come into the office, she'd been tight-lipped. I'd had to coax her to tell me her name. But she was sure comfortable with me now. She was a spitfire, this kid. That temper flared and with it, my headache.

If she'd just tell me what was really going on, it sure would make my life easier.

"I won't be valedictorian if this doesn't work," she said. "And my entire future will collapse if I don't get a 4.0."

"Ember, has anyone ever told you you're a tad melo-dramatic?"

No shock this time. Those eyes narrowed and if she could have breathed fire from her nostrils, I would have become a human torch.

The valedictorian tidbit was new. Maybe the person she was competing against was an asshole, and she was desperate to win. "Is there some other student you're trying to beat out?"

"Marie Hawk has perfect grades." Ember rolled her eyes. "She's a princess."

"Ah. So you need a better grade to beat Marie."

"Well, I guess. But that's not really the point. Why are you bringing up Marie?"

"You brought her up."

"No, I didn't."

"Yes, you did."

"No. I. Did. Not."

Lord, save me. I closed my eyes, summoning every ounce of patience. "Is the valedictorian thing a stipulation to the scholarship you're trying to get?" That wasn't something I'd heard of before, but it had been a long time since I'd applied for college scholarships.

"No."

"What are the stipulations? Besides a 4.0?"

Ember frowned, sitting up straight. "Why does it matter? I need to be perfect and that means Ms. Hale has to change my grade."

If deflection was an Olympic sport, this kid could win gold. A budding lawyer if I'd ever met one.

"Where are you going to college?"

"I, um, haven't decided yet." She averted her gaze, talking to my bookshelf.

"Where did you apply?"

"Montana State and University of Montana."

This morning, bored and in desperate need of anything to do besides think about Larke, I'd called both in-state schools. They each had solid financial aid programs and a plethora of scholarship opportunities that didn't require perfect GPAs.

"Did you look at any schools out of state?" If I asked enough questions, would I eventually get to the root of the problem here? Doubtful. But I asked anyway.

"No."

"Why not?"

"They're expensive." She gritted her teeth.

"You can always take out student loans."

She huffed, standing from her chair and lifting her backpack. It hadn't gotten any lighter since yesterday. What food had she stuffed into the pockets today?

"You don't need to rush out," I said, opening a drawer to take out a Rice Krispie treat in a shiny, blue foil wrapper. "Want one?"

Ember shrugged.

Good enough. I tossed her the treat, then took another out of my drawer, eating mine while she shoved hers in a pocket of the same jeans she'd worn on Wednesday. The shirt was the same too.

From what I could tell, Ember had a total of four outfits. They were worn on rotation. Sometimes she'd swap jeans and shirts to mix it up. But the shoes were always the same. So was her backpack. So was her coat. Today, it was tied around her waist.

"Any plans for the weekend?" I asked as I chewed.

"Homework."

"What about fun?"

She lifted a shoulder.

I pinched the bridge of my nose, my headache blooming with every one of her unanswered questions.

"Do you think we'll hear from the judge next week?" she asked.

"Maybe."

"Fine. Then I guess I have to come back on Monday."

"Or you could give me your cell phone number and I could call you."

She dropped her gaze to the floor. "I'd rather just come in person."

"Whatever." I sighed. "Then I'll see you Monday. Have a good weekend."

She walked out the door. That stomp sounded the same going as it did coming.

"Have a good weekend too, Ronan," I called after her. "Thanks for the Rice Krispie treat."

Nothing. I couldn't see her but it wouldn't have surprised me if she'd flipped me off.

I waited until the swoosh of the door closed, then went to the waiting area, watching out the window as Ember looked both ways before crossing First.

She had her hands braced on the straps of her backpack, like she was preparing for a hike.

"Still nothing on her mother?" I asked Gertrude.

"Nothing. It's the strangest thing." Gertrude was getting frustrated that her most trusted source of information, the Calamity rumor mill, had run dry.

Ember reached the sidewalk on the opposite side of the street. She bounced her backpack, adjusting it on her shoulders, then she lengthened her strides and marched.

She was eighteen, without a car or cell phone that I'd seen. There were plenty of kids that age in the city who didn't have their own vehicles, but they could ride a bus or take the Muni trains. Calamity had no public transportation. Had she been walking through the winter too? What about at night?

"This is frustrating." I raked a hand through my hair, watching until she disappeared from sight.

"I wish I knew where her mother worked. I'd just show up one day and get to the bottom of this."

I stood taller. "That's not a bad idea."

"Do you know where she works?"

"Nope." I spun and jogged for my office, swiping the keys off my desk. Then I hurried for the door. "Would you lock up tonight?"

"Uh, sure. Where are you going?" Gertrude's eyes were wide behind her fuchsia frames, but I didn't have time to stop and explain.

Every moment I wasted, Ember was walking.

I jumped in the Stingray, shoving the key into the ignition. Then I reversed out of my space, speeding in Ember's direction.

She'd made it three blocks already, reaching a corner to turn. If I had waited a minute longer, I would have lost her.

I followed her down the side street, keeping my distance and staying as inconspicuous as possible. Every few minutes, I'd pull up to the curb, hiding behind a parked car or truck. Then I'd ease onto the road again, tailing Ember's path.

A sleuth, I was not. If she'd been paying a lick of attention to her surroundings, she would have spotted me. My car was the epitome of ostentatious.

But she kept on trucking, oblivious to me tailing her.

What if I were a pedophile or rapist? What if I were a kidnapper or human trafficker? In four blocks, she hadn't looked over her shoulder once.

And I'd let her walk home alone for weeks. Well, come Monday, that stopped. I wasn't sure what excuse I'd make, but from here on out, I'd be giving her a ride home. Whether she liked it or not.

We weaved through a quaint neighborhood, the homes older but well maintained. Then we passed a park with a baseball diamond on one side and a play structure on the other, the two separated by a lawn so green it was practically neon.

Was she going home? To a friend's house? I checked the odometer. We'd already gone about a mile. This was a long-ass walk and Ember showed no signs of stopping.

Past the park was another neighborhood, this one not quaint or well maintained. Two blocks later we reached a trailer park. The homes formed a line along the street, their yards mostly cluttered with vehicles and the few occasional chain-link fences.

The Stingray was too loud. The engine purred, but this seemed like the kind of block where people expected clanks and roars, not the smooth hum of a pristine machine.

Yet despite the noise from my Corvette, Ember still didn't turn. Was she wearing earbuds? How could she not notice me following or hear my car? At any moment, I expected her to whirl around and flip me off, like she'd led me on a wild goose chase.

But she kept on walking. So I kept on following, this time unable to hide because there was no easy place for me to park.

We reached the end of the trailer park, and when Ember still hadn't stopped at one of the homes, a rock settled in my gut. There was a grove of trees ahead. The street's cracked pavement ended, turning to gravel.

Ember kept going, bypassing the trees for a worn path between their trunks.

"Shit."

The road curved, moving in the opposite direction. I hung back, waiting for her to get deeper into the trees, then I sped forward. There had to be a house back there and this had to be the road. She must be taking a shortcut, right?

The gravel veered around the trees. Out the passenger window was a field full of tiny shoots, the crops just barely beginning to peek through the soil.

Dust clouded behind me as I hit the gas, not wanting to lose Ember. Then, as I'd hoped, the road swung back in the other direction. There were more trailers, these exponentially dingier than the last. And there were only three in total.

A broken-down Chevy truck sat beside the first. I parked next to it, hoping the dust would settle or that Ember wouldn't notice.

In addition to giving her rides from now on, come Monday, we'd also be having a conversation about staying more alert to your surroundings. Or we could talk about it today, if I could find her.

Where'd she gone? While I'd looped around those trees, she'd disappeared. I scanned each trailer, but she was nowhere in sight.

"Fuck." I pounded a fist on the steering wheel. I rolled down the window, listening for noise. A dog barked in the distance, but otherwise, it was still. Almost too still.

She had to be around here somewhere. I guess since there were only three trailers, I could just go door to door—and pray I didn't get shot for trespassing. So I rolled up my window and shut off the Corvette, tucking the keys in my pocket. Then I got out, taking another glance around.

The scent of damp earth and trees filled my nose. The smell was laced with an undercurrent of rust, probably from the Chevy. The trailers had looked bad from behind my windshield, but they were worse now. The closest one had holes in the siding and a handful had been patched with duct tape. Two of the windows were boarded shut. Shrubs were attempting to swallow the trailer at the end of the row. Did anyone live here?

Or was this some abandoned area where Ember came to hang out? Maybe she was meeting up with a boyfriend or something? Oh, God, I hoped she wasn't doing drugs.

Unless one of these trailers was her home.

Well, if I had to pick, I hoped she lived in the middle one. Its windows still had all of their glass and the tin exterior looked to be in the best shape. Not that it didn't have its fair share of rusty spots, but there were no obvious holes.

I took a step, about to start my search, when a voice filled the air, nearly scaring me to death.

"You could have at least given her a ride."

I whirled around, my hand slapping against my chest, as Larke walked up. "Fuck."

She didn't apologize for scaring me. She wasn't the person here who needed to say sorry.

"What are you doing here?" I asked, my heart climbing down from my throat.

"I've been following you for the past mile. Maybe check your rearview mirror every once in a while." Behind her, about twenty yards away and tucked next to the trees where it was mostly hidden, was the 4Runner.

Damn, but she was beautiful.

Her hair was down, those silky chestnut strands curled in waves that cascaded over her shoulders. She was wearing a dark teal shirtdress with white buttons that matched her clean tennis shoes. Her eyes were shielded by a pair of sunglasses, and I could see myself practically drooling in their reflection.

It had been a shitty week without her. I hadn't been in Calamity long, but at some point in the past month, I'd started measuring days in Larke.

Larke was glaring. I didn't need to see her eyes to know she was glaring. Her jaw was clenched, her arms crossed over her chest.

Perfect. Because when I surged, wrapping her in my arms and sealing my mouth over hers, she couldn't push me away.

CHAPTER SEVENTEEN

LARKE

OH, damn it. I should have seen the kiss coming. I should have stopped it before it started. But the moment Ronan's soft lips slanted over mine, it was like my brain went *blip*. Off.

I moaned or he moaned or we both moaned. His tongue swirled against mine and my knees buckled. If not for his arms wrapped around me, I would have dropped. He had to bend to kiss me, like he was folding himself around me, hauling me into his orbit.

Why did he have to kiss like this? Why did it get better every time?

Even mad, I was helpless to resist. Except I was mad. Seriously freaking mad.

Blip.

Brain reengaged.

I squirmed until he loosened his hold enough for me to uncross my arms. Then, with a hand flat against his sternum, I pushed. Hard.

Our mouths unfused and Ronan stood tall, shaking his head like he was waking up from a dream.

"Nope." I held up a finger, my chest heaving as I panted. "You're currently on my Shithead List."

Ronan sighed, holding up his hands. "I'm sorry."

Sorry wasn't enough. Not after the past week. I deserved an explanation, but this was not the time or the place. "What are you doing here?"

He turned, planting his hands on his hips as he examined the trailers. "She won't tell me anything. So I followed her today."

That was how I'd landed here too. I'd been driving downtown, headed to the bank to deposit a check, when I'd spotted Ember walking. Then the flash of a silver car not far behind.

So instead of going to the bank, I'd followed Ronan, keeping my distance because I hadn't wanted him to stop. He should have spotted me a mile ago. I hadn't bothered hiding like he had, unnecessarily parking every two minutes like he was a super spy.

Ember hadn't been paying a lick of attention.

That was something I was somehow going to address. Maybe I'd give a lecture in class one day about awareness and safety, even in Calamity. We didn't have much crime, but that didn't mean it was nonexistent. All the girls could use a reminder to look around when they were walking alone. Check behind them for a classic sports car and nosy attorney.

Maybe I should invite Ronan to sit in because he could use the reminder too.

"Isn't stalking frowned upon?" I asked, shoving past him to walk down the dirty lane.

"I could ask you the same question." His hand wrapped around my elbow, halting my steps. "Just . . . hold up a minute. What are you doing?"

"I want to talk to Ember's mother. I've called about a thousand times with no answer, and she hasn't returned my messages."

"You can't talk to her mother."

"Why not?" I glanced at his hand, the look enough to make him let go. "Afraid I'll ruin your court case by interfering?"

"This has nothing to do with that fucking case." His jaw clenched as he frowned. "I just . . . I don't want to spook Ember."

"Then climb back in your shiny car and disappear. You've been rather good at that this week." I shooed him away like a fly, and damn, it felt good to let a bit of that frustration out.

"Larke." His hazel eyes were full of apology. He looked like he was about to dive into an explanation, but I held up my hand.

"Later."

He sighed. "Fine."

"I asked around about Ember this week. Her family is new to town but no one seems to know where Ashley works."

"Gertrude is having trouble learning anything about Ashley too."

No surprise. It was like Ashley had intentionally avoided any interaction with people around Calamity.

"I, um, took a photo of Ember in class on Tuesday." Admitting it made me feel smarmy, but it wasn't like I could go to last year's yearbook and pull up her school picture. "I took it to a few places. The grocery store. Gas stations. Hardware store. People recognized Ember but they couldn't recall ever seeing her with an adult."

Ronan rubbed his jaw. "Maybe Ashley works nights or something."

"Maybe. How about we find out?" I headed for the middle trailer, bypassing the first with its boarded-up windows. Mostly because it gave me the creeps.

Ronan fell into step beside me.

The hairs on my arms stood on end as we approached the trailer, and though I hadn't planned to come here today, I couldn't regret it. Was she really living here? Or was this just an abandoned teen hangout spot? Whatever the answer, I was glad Ronan was with me. Something about this neighborhood, this trailer, wasn't right.

"She has two brothers. They're in second grade," I said, keeping my voice low.

"Who? Ember?"

I nodded. "I had lunch with a couple teachers in the elementary school today. They asked me about the lawsuit and how I was dealing with Ember."

"How are you dealing with Ember? This, uh, can't be easy. To see her every day."

"It's not." Every time I turned around, I swear I heard snickering. I saw Wilder's stare as he sat in on my class. People failed to hide looks full of pity or condemnation. It was like certain students and staff members had already decided that I was guilty. That I'd set out to ruin this girl's life with a C plus. "I'm just trying to ignore all of it."

Ronan hung his head. "This got out of control."

"What did you expect?"

"I don't know. I just . . . I fucked up. I should have started here." He pointed to the ground. "After that first day when she came into my office, I should have insisted on talking to her mother."

"Why didn't you?"

He swallowed hard, our steps slowing. "Because I wanted your attention."

"Well, you got it."

That confession should have evoked rage. This mess, the gossip, was all because he'd wanted my attention. But the sad fact was I liked his attention. And last Friday night had been incredible. As much as I wanted to deny it, I couldn't. Ronan had shown me enough of himself that I knew he had a good heart. His tactics were flawed, but he was doing this for a good reason.

"For what it's worth, I regret this," he said.

"I know." I sighed. "Anyway, at lunch, one of the second-grade teachers said he had Ember's little brothers in his class. I had no idea she even had brothers."

"Neither did I."

"Eric and Elijah. Twins." Their last name was Scott. It was strange that I hadn't heard of Ember's brothers, but again, not being in the elementary school this year, I hadn't figured out the family connection until today.

"I asked the teacher about the boys. He said they come to school in the same clothes a lot too. But they're always clean."

That wasn't neglect. That was just being poor.

"And the food?"

I shrugged. "He said he didn't notice anything. The boys eat school meals, breakfast and lunch, but a lot of kids do."

Ronan stopped, staring at the trailer about ten feet away. "I don't like this."

I hated it. "Do you think she's even told her mother about the lawsuit?"

"Doubtful," he said. "I'm not charging her, so it's not like she's spending money. And if Ashley hides from the world, then I doubt she's heard the news around town."

No, but news was flying.

It was better than the other gossip tied to my name. Substantially better. But I loathed it all the same.

"Well, I guess now is as good a time as any to catch her up." I strode away from Ronan's side, walking to the trailer.

The faded wooden steps that led to the front door wobbled and creaked beneath my weight. There was no doorbell, so I steeled my spine, raised a hand and knocked on the flimsy screen door.

Behind its rattle, I thought I could hear a cartoon playing. But the moment I dropped my hand from the door, the noise was gone.

A thud echoed from inside, muted and quiet. Then . . . silence.

"Hello?" I raised my hand, knocking again.

Still nothing.

Ronan was standing at the base of the stairs. Our gazes locked as I glanced back.

He peered down the trailer's length, toward the path through the trees where Ember had walked. Then he pointed to the number beside the door: 204. "Is this the address listed on her school records?"

"Yes."

"This is the address we used in the court filing."

That I knew too since I had a copy of the complaint at home on my kitchen counter.

Ronan stepped up beside me on the stairs, raising his hand to knock. "Ember?"

Silence.

"What the hell?" He knocked again.

Oh, she was in there. And she was not coming out. *Awesome.*

When the door stayed closed, I turned and trudged down the stairs. "She's not going to answer." And I had a feeling she knew exactly who was standing outside the trailer.

"Shit." Ronan planted his hands on his hips, then descended the stairs.

"Has she been coming to see you every afternoon?"

He nodded. "Yep. We'll see if she comes Monday though."

"Well, you can talk to her then. I need to get Wren." I walked past him, ready to get in my car and put some distance between us.

But Ronan's long legs made it easy for him to catch up. "Larke, wait."

Once more, his hand wrapped around my elbow, the touch gentle, but he might as well have hit me with a taser. Like the man himself, it was impossible for me to ignore, no matter how hard I tried.

Too bad he seemed to have no problem ignoring me.

"What?" I tugged my arm loose.

"About the other night."

"I'm not talking about this here." Not with Ember's house behind us. Not when I didn't trust myself to stop it if he kissed me again. "Bye, Ronan."

This time when I walked away, he let me go.

When I reached the 4Runner, I refused to look back at Ronan. I kept my eyes on the road and headed to town.

He'd had a week to talk to me about the other night. He'd had a week to cross the driveway and show his face.

Damn it. Why had I let him kiss me? Why had I kissed him back? *Gah!* What was wrong with me these days?

Ronan Thatcher. That was my problem. He'd snuck past my defenses with that gorgeous face and arrogant allure. Now I couldn't get rid of him. And this mess with Ember only made it worse.

Why hadn't she answered the door? Was she scared of me?

Ouch. My chest pinched. The idea that she was scared of me hurt.

Maybe she'd felt betrayed because Ronan had gone to talk to her and instead, she'd seen me with him. Had I just completely screwed up our chances of finding out the truth?

"Shit." I should have stayed away.

From them both.

When I got to daycare, Wren's smile was a balm to my aching heart. She erased some of my anxiety. Not all, but some.

I went through the motions, taking her home and cooking dinner. We did a load of laundry together, folding it on the dining room table, before playing with a new toy my parents had given her last weekend. And when it was time for bed, I held her in my arms in the rocking chair long after she'd fallen asleep.

This morning, the school in Bozeman had called to schedule an interview. It was slated for the third week of June, after school was out for the summer.

What if they offered me the job? Should I take it? Could I really leave Calamity?

I traced a finger over Wren's smooth cheek as she slept. Where would she be the happiest?

In my heart, I knew the answer. I knew a move would be for me, not her. But that didn't mean she couldn't be happy in a new town. Life would just be . . . different.

A yawn tugged at my mouth, so I forced myself out of the chair, carrying Wren to her crib. Then I slipped from her room, making my way toward my bedroom. Except before I could wash my face and put on a pair of pajamas, a knock came at the door.

My heart flipped.

It could be any number of people. Kerrigan, here to scold me for considering a move. Nellie, here to do the same. My mother or father. My brother.

Or a neighbor.

I held my breath as I walked to the entryway, knowing it wasn't Mrs. Edwards with a goose casserole outside. Then the air rushed from my lungs. Ronan's face looked back at me from beyond the decorative glass window.

Turning the lock, I opened the door and stood in its frame, not waving him inside. Considering my sheer lack of self-control with this man, I didn't trust myself to let him cross the threshold. *Do not let him in the house. Do not.*

Ronan's shoulders sagged as he stared down at me. His hair was a mess and he'd changed out of his work clothes into a T-shirt and jeans. His Adam's apple bobbed as he swallowed. "You terrify me."

"Me." I barked a laugh. "I'm the least terrifying person on the planet."

"You have no idea how wrong you are." He gave me a sad smile. "I can't stop thinking about you. From the day we met, you've been a constant on my mind."

I hated the tone in his voice. Wasn't that the dream? To be wholly consumed by a person? I'd seen it happen with Kerrigan and Pierce. Then again with Nellie and Cal. How many hours had I longed for the same? Just a sliver of their happiness. "Why does that sound like a bad thing?"

"It's a bad thing if you get hurt."

"By you."

He nodded. "I'm a selfish man. I get wrapped up in my own life and develop these blind spots."

"What do you mean?"

"Cora."

A name, spoken with so much guilt he didn't need to explain anything else. He blamed himself for every one of her problems, didn't he?

"I didn't realize my dad was going blind and should have," he said. "But I was busy with work. My own life. I missed signs I shouldn't have missed."

"So you're worried that you'll, what? Ignore me? Haven't you been doing that for the past week anyway?"

"No." He dragged a hand through his hair, shaking his head. "It means I don't trust myself not to let you down. Or Wren."

Any other man and I would have told him that was the biggest load of bullshit I'd ever heard in my life. But there was a raw look in Ronan's eyes, like he'd just cracked open his chest to admit his flaws. Like he'd just opened up a piece of his soul. That look made me want to wrap my arms around him and never let go.

"Ronan, you followed a teenage girl home today."

He cringed. "When you say it like that, it sounds awful."

"Probably shouldn't make that a habit," I teased. "I've seen Ember Scott nearly every day since school started. You've known her for how long? Weeks?"

His forehead furrowed. "Uh, yeah. So?"

"So you followed a girl home you've known for just weeks because you're worried about her. Between the two of us, who has the bigger blind spot?"

Ronan's eyes closed. "That's different."

"Why? Because she was a stranger and Cora was your ex-wife?"

"Well . . . yeah."

"Then by your logic, I should send you away too. Ember is my student. And I failed her. Entirely."

She'd gotten so desperate for this grade that she'd hired Ronan to help her. Because when she'd come to me, I hadn't listened. Not truly. He'd heard something in her plea for help that I'd ignored.

"It's not the same. You were doing your job, Larke."

"And you weren't married to Cora when she stalked you and developed a drug addiction."

He held my stare for a few long moments, his mind visibly whirling over what I'd said. "I don't know what will happen."

"Neither do I. Hell, I don't even know what I want, Ronan. But I don't like how I've felt this week. I don't like being played."

"I never played you." Ronan inched closer, his toes nearly touching mine. His fingers threaded into my hair, and even though I knew I should have sent him back to his own house, I was frozen, rooted in place. "You terrify me."

"You said that already." *Don't let him inside. Do not.*

"It's worth repeating." He bent, his mouth nearly touching mine. "I can't stop thinking about you."

"You said that already too."

He hummed, that low rumble vibrating between us. "Fuck, but I missed you."

Hell. I was so going to cave. All it took was one lick of his tongue across my bottom lip. And I let Ronan carry me inside.

CHAPTER EIGHTEEN

RONAN

THIS WAS A MIRACLE. Not just that I'd made it across my driveway to her front stoop. But that she'd actually let me inside.

"Larke," I murmured, peppering kisses along her jaw.

Her fingers threaded into my hair, a breathy sigh escaping her lips.

The door was still open behind us. I hadn't closed it yet because I still wasn't certain I deserved to be standing here.

This wasn't why I'd come over tonight. All I'd wanted was to clear the air, be honest. But now that my mouth was on her skin, my hands roaming her lithe body, I regretted every night that invisible wall had kept me away.

Damn if I shouldn't have been here all week.

Plenty of women would have thrown my fears in my face. They would have called bullshit or called me a coward. Larke would have been right to call me a chickenshit bastard. Instead, she'd offered a different perspective.

Ember.

So I wasn't entirely blind. Though I had made some mistakes, undoubtedly. With Dad. With Cora.

Except Larke wasn't anything like Cora, was she? Larke had fortitude. She had grace and tenacity. The only addict here was me.

I breathed her in, burying my nose in the crook of her neck, then let my hands wander down that steel spine, appreciating every inch.

"Ronan." She rose on her toes to whisper in my ear. "Close the door."

Thank fuck. I stretched a foot and kicked it closed. Then I hoisted her into my arms, waiting until her legs wrapped around my hips before striding through the house.

There were toys scattered on the living room floor, per usual. The dining room table was crowded with Wren's diaper bag, a purse and a stack of papers. As I strode down the hallway, I stepped on a doll.

"Sorry," Larke said. "It's—"

"Friday. I know."

Tomorrow morning, I'd help her put the house back to rights. Or we could just live with the clutter. I didn't give a damn as long as she didn't send me home, to a house that was entirely too clean.

"God, I missed you." I latched my mouth on to her throat as I carried her into the bedroom, once again kicking the door closed behind us.

She took my face in her hands, tilting it up before fusing her mouth to mine, letting her tongue drag across my lips and teeth. Then she dove in, tasting every inch of my mouth. I let her.

It was unhurried. An exploration. A kiss to savor.

She sighed against my mouth, like she was breathing for the first time in a week. Or maybe that was me. Without her, it had been hard to find air.

After tonight, there'd be no walking away. For a man who'd stuck to casual relationships for the past five years, in my bones, I felt the shift. So much for that simple life I'd hoped to find in Calamity. Things were about to get complicated.

And fuck, but I was excited.

"You're smiling." Larke pulled away, her eyes glued to my mouth.

"Yeah, mama. I'm smiling."

Her eyes lifted to mine. Then a smile to match mine spread across her lips, illuminating her face. In the dark bedroom, this woman glowed. Like a ray of pure starlight breaking through a storm.

Complicated, all right. So beautifully complicated.

The bed was unmade, like it had been last week. I sealed my lips over Larke's and carried her to the mattress, laying her down. At some point, we'd have some fun. We'd use those bedposts to play. But tonight, I wanted to sink inside her body and worship.

With a tug, I yanked the tie from her hair, freeing those silky strands to splay across the white sheets.

Larke was still in the blue dress she'd been wearing earlier, buttons from top to bottom. They called my name, begging to be undone. So one by one, starting at the hem, I worked them loose. Each time one popped open, I shoved the material aside, opening the dress like it was gift wrap and she was the present waiting inside.

When I reached her panties, I grazed my knuckles across

the smooth skin of her thighs. Her breath hitched. Her legs parted.

So responsive. So willing. Yeah, playing with Larke was going to be a damn good time. Just not tonight.

I kept working the buttons, up her torso to her breasts. And finally, when they were each undone, I trailed a line of kisses along her skin, exactly where the buttons had been.

She shifted, sinking deeper into the mattress as I gave her my weight. Her arms looped around my shoulders, her fingers bunching up the cotton of my shirt at my nape. "Off."

I nipped at her collarbone, leaving an open-mouthed kiss at the hollow of her throat. Then I reached behind my head, yanking the shirt away to toss aside.

Larke pushed up to a seat as I stood from the bed, stripping the dress from her arms. But when she moved to unclasp her bra, I took her elbow, shaking my head.

"Roll over."

She gave me a wary glance but obeyed, turning to her stomach. Her arms were raised, propping up her chin.

Desire raced through my veins, a pounding instinct to claim. To keep. But I leashed it, wanting to drag this out for as long as possible.

My fingers skimmed across her shoulder blades, leaving goose bumps in their trail. With a flick, her bra was undone, loose around her ribs. My cock throbbed as I took in that smooth skin. The perfect globes of her ass.

Fuck, but she had a great body. Lean and long but with the most delicious curves. Her lace panties were the same color as the dress. I slipped my hands beneath the hem, palming and kneading her flesh.

She hummed, turning over a shoulder to look at me. "Ronan."

"Be patient."

Slowly, I removed my palms, dragging them down the backs of her thighs to the sensitive skin behind her knees. Then I moved up to her hips, carefully peeling her panties off her legs until they were a puddle on the floor.

My jeans came next, the zipper's click mingling with my ragged breaths. The pants and boxer briefs beneath shoved to the floor, I fisted my aching shaft, giving it a few solid strokes.

Another night, I was going to have Larke just like this and instead of coming inside her tight heat, I was going to erupt on her skin. I'd paint her as mine.

She shifted, rolling to her side, but I shook my head, surging forward so that she was forced back to her stomach.

My cock rested in the crack of her ass. *Another night.*

Propped on one arm, I trailed my fingers up her ribs and over a shoulder blade, carefully shifting her hair out of the way. Then I reached around her ribs, beneath the bra and cupped a breast. I rolled her nipple while my mouth latched on to her neck.

"No pillow tonight," I murmured. "I want to hear you when you come apart."

"Yes." She hissed as I pinched her nipple. She lifted her ass, pressing it against my arousal.

"If you keep doing that, you'll get in trouble."

She glanced back, enough for me to see the smirk on her mouth. Then she tilted those hips once more.

I tugged her nipple, letting it go. Then I moved back to her bare ass, smacking it hard enough that the crack filled the room along with her whimper. I massaged the place I'd hit her, licking at her pulse. "You like that?"

She hummed.

"Later," I promised. "We'll play later."

Larke arched against me, then twisted, fast enough that I couldn't stop her from spinning beneath me. Fast enough to remind me that when I pushed, she pushed right back.

I dipped a hand between her legs. "Drenched."

"For you." Her hands threaded through my hair, hauling my mouth to hers.

Her tongue slid against mine, hot and slow. Her lips moved, lulling me under her spell. And while I toyed with her slit, she matched the strokes of my finger with her tongue.

We moved in tandem, like old lovers, until my cock throbbed.

I tore my mouth away, meeting her dark eyes. We stared at each other, a million unspoken words hanging in the air. We had time. We had all the damn time in the world to say it all. Whatever happened. Whatever came at us.

We'd complicate the fuck out of our lives and see how fun it could be.

I settled into the cradle of her hips and, with my gaze locked on hers, slid home.

Her eyelids drifted closed. She threw her head back, her throat arching as her body adjusted to my size. Her nails dug into the flesh of my shoulders.

"Fuck, Larke." I clenched my teeth, summoning my control. Being inside her was a dream.

I eased out, thrusting inside again, her body melting around mine as I planted deep.

"Ronan." She moaned as I rocked against her clit.

Our breaths mingled as I brought us together, over and over. The world around us became a blur.

Stroke after stroke, I kept diving, deeper and deeper, until this woman became the air in my lungs. My fingers got lost in her hair. My heart thundered against her own. I pistoned faster, driving us both toward the edge.

When we fell over the edge, I wanted to go together.

"Don't stop." Larke's inner walls fluttered around me.

"Never."

"More."

I captured a nipple between my teeth. She detonated, her entire body quaking. She clenched, pulse after pulse, as a string of incoherent cries escaped her throat.

Pressure built at the base of my spine. My body tightened. And as she shattered, her orgasm triggered my own.

"Fuck, Larke." On a roar, I poured inside her. My mind blanked, consumed with nothing but pleasure as I exploded. Then I was floating, reality creeping in as I came down from the clouds.

"Oh my God," she panted, wrapping her arms and legs around me.

"Yeah." I collapsed, trying to catch my breath. Without a doubt, that was the most intimate, most electric, fuck of my damn life.

I wrapped her tight, our skin sticky with sweat as I twisted to my back, bringing her with me. "Damn."

Larke sagged against my chest. "This is . . ."

"I know."

This was life changing. Exactly what would change, well . . . we'd figure it out later. Together.

I eased out, bending to snag the covers. And with Larke in my arms, I sank into a pillow. For the first time in a week, I fell asleep with a smile on my face.

———

MY ARMS WERE EMPTY. On that thought, I woke up to a dark bedroom. The only light came from the moonbeams streaming through Larke's windows. I shoved up to a seat, glancing around the room and to the empty space at my side.

I threw the covers from my legs, climbing off the bed. The bathroom was dark. There were no lights coming from the hallway.

Snagging my boxers from the floor, I tugged them on, then padded out of the room, checking the living room first. It was as empty as the kitchen.

"Larke." I kept my voice low, listening for a reply. But the house was still. Asleep.

So where the hell was my woman, and when had she gotten out of bed?

I retreated down the hallway, bypassing her bedroom for the closed door beyond the guest bathroom. Carefully turning the knob, I peered into Wren's room.

Stars and a moon swirled along the walls and ceiling from a star light on a dresser. A sound machine whooshed ocean waves. In the crib was a precious, sleeping girl.

And on the floor, curled beneath a pink blanket, was her mother.

Larke was sound asleep on the carpet.

My hand came to my chest, rubbing against the sudden

twinge. Was she okay? Had Wren woken up? Or was she here because she couldn't sleep with me in her bed?

I eased away, about to close the door, but stopped.

Something had happened tonight. Something had shifted. There was a tether between us now, and damn it, if she was upset, if she was scared or worried, well . . .

Those were my worries too.

So I tiptoed inside the room, silently crossing the floor to kneel beside Larke. Then I spread out on the carpet, lying by her side before lifting the blanket to cover us both as I curled around her.

She didn't so much as stir.

So I held her, closing my eyes.

And this time when I woke, Larke's cheek was on my chest, her arm draped over my stomach.

A pair of happy brown eyes met mine. Wren was standing at the railing of her crib, her hair a mess and her thumb in her mouth.

"Good morning, firefly."

Wren gave me that shy smile.

Larke didn't move, but there was an alertness to her body that told me she was awake.

"Morning, mama."

"Morning."

"You okay?"

She blew out a long breath. "You terrify me too."

"Good." I kissed her hair. "Then we'll just scare the hell out of each other for a while until we figure this out. Sound okay?"

She nodded. "Sounds great."

CHAPTER NINETEEN

RONAN

"DO YOU HAVE PLANS TODAY?" I asked Larke as I stood at her stove, pushing a spatula through scrambled eggs. The bacon in the oven had three minutes left.

"No." She took out plates, setting them on the counter beside me. "I have a to-do list for the house today."

" 'Kay." I nodded. "Cheese?"

She walked to the fridge, taking out a bag of shredded cheddar and handing it over. "I'm expecting you to disappear."

"What if I didn't?"

"I'd like that." She blushed.

I grinned, then sprinkled cheese on our eggs. "Me too."

"Thank you for cooking," she said. "I can't remember the last time someone made me breakfast."

"My pleasure."

This morning, after we'd woken up in Wren's room, we'd taken turns in the shower. Then I'd come to the kitchen, dressed in yesterday's clothes, to find Larke pulling food from the fridge. I wasn't a chef by any means, but break-fast . . . I could handle breakfast. So I'd taken over to give her a break. "What's on this to-do list?"

"Laundry, for starters." She frowned at the laundry room. "Dust. Vacuum."

Fair enough. I'd help her tackle the chores. Then, we'd take a few steps toward complicated.

"We don't know each other very well," I said.

"No, we don't."

"Feel like changing that?"

She smiled. "Yes."

My Saturday was already looking good.

The timer on the oven dinged, so I took out the bacon, removing it from the sheet pan to cool. Then I dished us up some eggs while she put Wren in her high chair.

Breakfast was a lot like dinner had been last week. Relaxed. Comfortable. Wren was the star of the show, happy and noisy as she inhaled her eggs and a pouch of *see see*. When she was finished, Larke wiped her face and let her chase around the house with her empty applesauce while we did the dishes together.

Laundry came next. While the washing machine ran with her sheets, I hefted the clean clothes basket to the dining room table, where we stood side by side and started folding.

"This is weird." She shook her head as I snagged a towel from the heap.

"What's weird?"

"You." She nodded to the basket. "Helping."

"Why is it weird?"

She folded a pair of Wren's tiny pants. "I don't really have help."

"You do today. And I'm awesome help. Just wait until you see me with the vacuum."

She shook her head. "I think after laundry we'll call it good. My pride won't let me let you vacuum."

Oh, hell no. There was nothing waiting for me at home and if cleaning meant I got time to relax and do nothing with her later, then I'd vacuum and dust. "Ditch the pride, babe. Just go with it."

"Fine." She sighed. "Thank you."

"You're welcome, mama." I bent to kiss her head, then plucked a pair of panties from the basket, shooting her a wink before stuffing them in my pocket.

"Ronan." She swatted my chest, trying to steal them back, but I shifted so she couldn't reach.

"What? I can't keep these?" I teased.

"Definitely not."

I chuckled, returning them to the pile on the table. "One of my first cases, years ago, was a divorce settlement. The guy had stupid money, but he was . . . odd. His wife decided to divorce him when she learned he was paying thousands and thousands of dollars each month to have women send him their worn panties."

Her nose scrunched up. "Seriously?"

"No lie. He liked to smell them."

"Ew." She giggled, the sound filling my heart. "What other strange cases have you had?"

"I once represented a woman in a contract dispute with her lover. They were out at a bar one night, drinking. The lover agreed to sell my client a condo for five million dollars. So they wrote the terms on a napkin. The next day, after sobering up, the lover said it was bogus. So my client sued him."

"Who won?"

"Me. Obviously." I smirked.

"Is your ego going to recover when Aiden kicks your ass in this suit with Ember?"

"Normally, I'd say no." The few cases I'd lost had usually resulted in me sulking for a few weeks. I plucked the towel from her hand. But this one . . .

"I want you to win." I sighed. "I think the grade you gave her was the grade she earned. Except I'm *her* lawyer. There's no gray area on the ethics of legal representation here. What I'm doing is wrong."

"Even if it's because you're trying to help a teenage girl? Your heart is in the right place, Ronan."

"This wasn't the way to go about it." I tossed the towel aside, pulling her into my arms. "I should have stayed away from you until the case is over."

"Why didn't you?" She pressed her cheek against my heart.

"Maybe because most people think this case is a joke and therefore, the rules don't really apply. Maybe because I've convinced myself Ember is in trouble and this is my way to rescue her." I kissed Larke's hair. "Or maybe because I just couldn't stay away from you."

"I'm glad," she whispered. "Will you lose your license?"

"Hope not."

"I'll gladly lose if it means we help Ember with whatever is going on."

"I know." I hugged her closer. "You're a good teacher."

"Am I?" She scoffed. "I'm being sued by a student."

"Ember is desperate. That's a reflection on her, not you."

Larke tipped up her chin, resting it against my sternum. "She didn't answer the door yesterday. Do you think she's scared of me?"

"I think she's hiding something. And she's scared that anyone, you or me, will figure it out."

"I hate this."

"So do I."

She sagged against me, giving me her weight. We fit together. She was meant to be in my arms.

It took me off guard for a split second. Larke had a knack for shifting the ground beneath my feet. But instead of running away, I leaned into it. I leaned into her.

"Ember probably saw us together," she said.

"Yep." And depending on all that Ember had seen, she knew I was playing both sides. "I'm expecting her to stomp into my office on Monday afternoon and fire me." Then, if Ember did her research, would come an official grievance and subsequent investigation.

"What will you say?"

"No." Ember could try to fire me, and I'd simply tell her no. The kid was stuck with me. Until this was done.

"What if—"

"Ro." Wren crashed into my leg, holding up a green cup.

Larke's arms loosened, staring down at her daughter. "Did she just call you Ro?"

I let Larke go and bent, hoisting up Wren to my side. "We worked on that while you were in the shower."

"Wee oh wa me." Wren's forehead furrowed as she thrust the cup in my face.

"Sorry, firefly. I don't know what *wee oh wa me* means. Do you want a drink?"

"No no no." She shook her head, kicking her legs to be put down.

I chuckled, kissing her cheek, then set her on her feet and gave her booty a pat as she ran back to the toys in the living room. Then I picked up a towel, folding it into a neat square. Larke was staring at the floor.

I hooked a finger beneath her chin. "What?"

Her eyes were full of unshed tears when she looked up.

"Whoa, whoa, whoa. What just happened?"

She swallowed hard. "Please don't hurt her."

Fuck, my heart. I should kick my own ass for avoiding her last week. "Her? Or you?"

"Both," she whispered.

I tucked a lock of hair behind her ear. "I can't predict the future, but I promise . . . if we walk away from this, I'll still be there for her."

She closed her eyes and nodded.

Chances were, if this did fizzle, the person who'd walk away bruised and bloody would be me.

It took another load of laundry for the heaviness to leave the room. For us to find the ease we'd had over breakfast. Then, as Larke picked up toys and dusted, I followed her through the house with the vacuum until her to-do list was done. All before lunch.

"How about we take Wren for a walk?" she asked, staring out the living room window. The sun was shining, the sky bright and blue.

Summer was coming, the promise of warm days and bright flowers clinging to the fresh mountain air.

"Unless you don't want anyone to see us together," she said.

"Why would I not want people to see us together?"

She shrugged. "Because of the lawsuit." The lawsuit? Or was she worried about the rumors?

"Lawsuit or no, I'm not pretending like you aren't in my life. But would you rather not be seen together for a while?" It would sting, no lie. But if it would make things easier on Larke to keep this under wraps for a bit, then we'd stay behind closed doors.

"No." She raised her chin. "I don't want to hide."

"Good answer." I hauled her into my arms and slammed my mouth on hers, kissing her until she was breathless. My hands shifted, about to slip under her shirt, but then a little girl came walking over to stand on my bare feet.

"Up, Ro."

Larke smiled against my mouth. "She's bossy."

I laughed, letting Larke go to sweep Wren up. "You are bossy. And I like it."

Whatever shyness she'd had for me was gone. She'd been totally fine with me all morning. Maybe all it had taken was waking up on her bedroom floor with her mom.

"Want to go for a walk, firefly?"

"No no no."

"Too bad." I blew a raspberry on her neck, earning a squeal.

Going for a walk with a toddler involved more than I'd expected. A diaper change. Wardrobe adjustments. Sunscreen. Stroller.

Larke did it all quickly, with practiced ease. She did it all alone, wearing a smile.

"What's that look for?" she asked when we were in the garage and Wren was in the stroller, wearing a sun hat and a pair of heart-shaped shades.

"You're rather incredible."

"Yes, I am." She scrunched up her nose. "Ooof. Your arrogance is rubbing off."

I wagged my eyebrows. "It's sexy as hell. I'll rub more on you later."

"Promise?" She smirked.

"Babe, you have no idea. Hope you're ready for a long night. I've got plans."

"Oh yeah?" She stood on her toes, her mouth stretching for mine. "Want to clue me in?"

"Nope." I kissed the corner of her mouth, lingering there for a moment, drawing in her sweet scent. Then I sealed my lips over hers, sweeping inside for a quick taste.

Her hands roamed my chest. My palms cupped her ass. This was the beginning. The fun stage, when you couldn't keep your hands off each other and every touch was a thrill. Except that pull, that tie between us, felt different than simple attraction. It was different than anything I'd felt with Cora.

This felt permanent. Like a tattoo. An undying spark. Like no matter how many times I had Larke, I'd want a hundred more. For every kiss, I'd need a thousand.

I broke the kiss, drowning in those pretty brown eyes. "Still scared?"

"Yes," she whispered. "You?"

"Yeah." I took her hand, lacing our fingers together, then brought her knuckles to my lips.

We hadn't talked about what had driven her to Wren's

floor late last night. I guess I hadn't asked because I already knew the answer.

We were getting serious. Fast. A few more days, a few more hours, and we'd be beyond the point of return.

Terrifying. Exciting. The thrill of my lifetime.

Larke gripped the stroller's bar, leading the way out of the garage. She followed the sidewalk that led us out of the cul-de-sac and toward the neighborhood park. Larke walked with purpose, the pace more than just a lazy midmorning stroll. She went straight through our neighborhood and into the next, like she'd done this walk a hundred times on her way downtown to run an errand. Like she wanted to get in and get out.

"Switch me," I said as we reached First.

"Huh?"

"It's my turn to push."

She opened her mouth, probably to protest, but I just set my hands beside hers on the handlebar, then guided her out of the way.

It was my turn to set the pace. So I slowed us down, way down. Every time she walked faster, I paused, taking in the window of the business we were outside.

"I didn't take you for a window shopper," she said.

"You're rushing this."

"What do you mean? No, I'm not."

I grinned, loving that she'd simultaneously played dumb and argued with me in a single breath. "Mama, you're practically jogging. What's the rush?"

"There isn't one."

"Good." I took her hand. "Then slow down."

She sighed, her shoulders sagging.

"When was the last time you just meandered along First?" I kept her hand as I continued walking, our pace practically glacial. "No agenda. No destination."

"I don't know. It's been a while."

Then today was our day. We'd walk. We'd talk.

"About two years ago, Dad called me up. Said he needed a favor," I told her. "Figured he was working on a project at home and needed an extra set of hands. So I went over to help. It was a Sunday. And instead of finding him neck deep in a project, he was waiting in his car. The Stingray."

"That was your dad's car?"

I nodded. "He gave it to me that day. But first, he told me he wanted to spend a day with the city and his son. I knew something was wrong the minute I got in the passenger seat. But it seemed important to him that he set the pace, so we just explored. We hit Fisherman's Wharf. We walked out on the Golden Gate. Drove around Nob Hill. Then we got home and just sat in the driveway."

I'd never forget the tears in Dad's eyes when he finally shut off the car. The ache in my chest when he handed over the keys. By that point in the day, I'd convinced myself he was dying.

Not dying.

Just going blind.

"His vision kept getting worse and worse. He's a stubborn man, and by the time he actually went to the doctor, the macular degeneration was already serious."

"I'm sorry," Larke said, her fingers flexing against mine.

"Me too. He'll likely be able to always see some things, but the tunnel on his vision gets worse and worse."

"That's why he gave you the car."

"Yeah. It's not safe for him to drive, and he wanted me to enjoy it if he couldn't. The trip around the city was to appreciate it too. While he could."

She looked up, a smile on her mouth. "So you're making me appreciate Calamity."

"It's not such a bad place."

Larke stared ahead, her gaze sweeping around First. "No, it's not."

We fell into step, this time at my pace, crossing the street at the corner. And when she finally relaxed, settling into the stroll, I let go of her hand.

A woman passed by, stopping to give Larke a quick hug before continuing on.

"That was my cousin. You've probably heard this already, but there are Hales everywhere," she said.

"Is that my warning?"

"Probably." She laughed. "My dad runs the car dealership. It was founded by my granddad. Zach, my brother, works there, along with a bunch of other relatives."

"So if I need a new car, don't shop out of town."

"Not unless you want to be ostracized at the next family function. And I'll warn you, there are plenty. Someone is always having a birthday or celebration of some sort."

That sounded a lot like a standing invitation to these future family functions. I'd take it. "How was school this week?"

"Good." Except there was something in her tone that suggested it was anything but good.

I gave her another block before I nudged her elbow with mine. "What's wrong?"

"It's been a long year."

"Because of the kids? Because of Ember?"

"Partly. High school is a lot different than fifth grade. I miss kids who still look at their teachers like heroes. And since this is my first year in the high school, everything has to be built from scratch. It's a lot, and all year, I've just felt behind. I can't leverage a previous year to build upon."

So she was stressed at work, then covering everything at home alone. *Damn.* I should have done more vacuuming today.

"On top of it all, there's this teacher I hate." Larke's lip curled. "His classroom is across from mine, the grumpy bastard. I have no idea what his problem is, but he hasn't liked me since the day he moved to town. We've sort of settled into this mutual hatred. When I was at the elementary school, I could avoid him. Now I can't escape. Especially because he's been sitting in on my class with Ember. He just sets me on edge."

This motherfucker. "Want me to stop by the school Monday?"

Larke snorted. "And do what?"

"Tell him to fuck off."

"Nah." She leaned her head against my arm. "But thanks for offering. One of these days, I'll tell him to fuck off myself."

"Get it on camera for me if you can." I bent to kiss her hair as we passed a couple walking the opposite direction.

Larke held up her free hand to wave. "Hi, Mr. and Mrs. Nanby."

"Hello, Larke." Mrs. Nanby smiled but it didn't reach her eyes. I knew because those eyes were on me. Wary, like she wouldn't be afraid to take that quilted bag looped over her arm and slam it into my face if I hurt Larke or Wren Hale.

I liked Mrs. Nanby immediately.

"Should we get lunch?" I asked.

"Sure. Have you been to the brewery? My sister and her husband own it."

"I have. It's good." Hold up. Had I met her family and hadn't even realized it?

"They don't go often," Larke said, like she could read my thoughts. "And Kerrigan is mad at me right now, otherwise I'd call her."

"Why's she mad?"

"Oh, it's nothing." Larke's pace instantly sped up.

The liar. I'd find out more about this fight with her sister later.

We made it to the brewery and found a table. It was busy and a steady stream of people stopped by to say hello to Larke and get an introduction. The brewery had been designed with families and gatherings in mind, so Wren had plenty of space to play and chase around until our food arrived.

Once our baskets were empty, we lingered, in no rush to leave. We had two beers before setting out to explore the opposite side of First. And because I wanted to soak up my time with Larke, I came up with every excuse possible to keep from going home.

We hit a park to play on the swings and slide. We strolled past the house Larke had lived in before she'd moved to the cul-de-sac. And when Wren fell asleep in the stroller, we just kept on walking. Until it was time to get dinner at the White Oak, then finally head home.

"This was fun," Larke said as we walked through the door, dropping the diaper bag in the laundry room off the garage. "I haven't spent a day downtown like that in ages. Thank you."

"Welcome. But it was just a walk, mama."

"No." Larke wrapped her arms around my waist. "It was a lot more."

"I had fun too." I kissed her hair, breathing in her scent. Much like this morning, the moment I wrapped my arms around Larke, a little girl came crashing into my legs.

"Up, Ro."

"So demanding." I bent to grab Wren, then tossed her in the air, just a foot, but enough that she giggled.

This girl had a fantastic laugh. So I threw her again, just to hear it once more.

As soon as I caught her, Wren launched herself at Larke. "Mama."

I thought I'd see a smile on Larke's face. Instead, she had this pained expression, like she'd gotten the wind knocked out of her.

"What?"

"Nothing." She forced a smile, then kissed Wren on the cheek.

"I told you, I won't hurt her."

"No, it's not that. I just . . . you said you wanted to get to know each other."

More than anything. "I do."

She gave her daughter a sad smile. "Then I think maybe it's time you knew about Wren's father."

CHAPTER TWENTY

LARKE

THE KNOT in my stomach was tight enough to turn dust into a diamond. It took me a while to get Wren in the bath and settle her down for bed. I rocked her to sleep, and when she was finally in her crib, darkness had fallen outside the window.

Ronan was waiting for me in the living room. He'd run home during Wren's bath to grab new clothes and was wearing a pair of sweats and a fresh T-shirt.

"She asleep?" he asked as I sat on the opposite end of the couch, sinking into the smooth leather.

"Yeah." Could he hear my pulse roaring? I sat on my hands to hide the shaking. Why had I thought this conversation was a good idea?

"Hey." He shifted, stretching across the middle cushion to snag my hand. Then he lay on his back, dragging me on top of him.

My ear was pressed to his chest, listening to his own heartbeat. It settled the nerves, just a bit.

His fingers reached for the tie in my hair, setting my ponytail free. Then he threaded a hand through my hair, toying with the strands and massaging my scalp. "This can wait."

"No, it can't," I whispered. "I want you to know." The real truth. The ugly truth. Just like he'd shared his with me.

"Okay, mama."

Every time he called me mama I swooned. Even now, with my nerves ratcheted to the max, I melted.

Today had been a good day. Exploring Calamity had been . . . refreshing.

Ronan had shown me my hometown through different eyes. His eyes. He'd reminded me of what I loved about this community. What I'd taken for granted.

The charm. The serenity. The solace.

"I grew up trusting people. Automatically. You can trust people in Calamity. I can leave my doors unlocked. I can keep my car running at the grocery store in the winter with the keys in the ignition while I run in to grab a gallon of milk. I can go for a walk in the middle of the night and feel safe."

"Please don't go walking in the middle of the night."

I smiled. "I won't."

And though I didn't want Ember walking around alone either, if she was forced to travel on foot, at least it was in Calamity.

"Gossip has always been a part of my life. I guess it's natural to talk about other people. And it wasn't like I hadn't been talked about before, but when I got pregnant with Wren, it was different. It was . . . mean. It went beyond curiosity. These people, who had known me my entire life, threw away everything they knew. They forgot who I was as a person. And they said these awful, horrible things."

Ronan's fingers stroked up and down my spine, his voice a low rumble against my cheek. "They broke your trust."

"Yes." I shifted to prop my chin on my hands so I could look at his face. "I didn't tell anyone outside my family and closest friends that I was pregnant. At first, it was because I was having a hard time coming to terms with it myself. Motherhood. Single motherhood. Not exactly how I'd planned to have children. Then people found out and the rumors began to spread. People made their assumptions. No one ever asked me or gave me the benefit of the doubt. So I decided they hadn't earned the truth."

"Good for you, babe. You don't owe them anything." He tucked a lock of hair behind my ear. "You don't owe me anything either."

He did deserve to know. Our stories had to go both ways.

"I've been thinking about moving," I said.

His entire body tensed. "What?"

"There's a job in Bozeman teaching fourth grade. The idea of a fresh start is appealing. Where the last name Hale doesn't mean much and if someone wants to know me, they'll introduce themselves."

A flicker of guilt marred his handsome face. "I never should have talked to Gertrude about you."

"It's not you." I gave him a sad smile. "I get why you asked. That's just . . . Calamity. It has its good and bad. Today, you helped remind me of the good."

"That's why you're fighting with your sister, isn't it? Because you're thinking of moving?"

I nodded. "Deep down, I think she understands. But she doesn't want me to go."

"Neither do I." He lifted a hand to trace the line of my cheek, his fingers memorizing the curve. "You can't move. I just got here."

Oh, my heart. He had no idea just how much I wanted to stay. For him. Even though we were brand new, the promise of what this could be was so very tempting.

"It's not a for-sure thing," I said. "It's just an option. I'm trying to do what's right for Wren."

"And you don't think that's Calamity?"

"I don't know." I turned on my cheek again, staring blankly at the living room floor. "I want her to have a close relationship with her grandparents. With her uncles and aunts and friends and family."

"But..."

"But I never want her to hear the rumors about me. Or herself."

Ronan had likely heard those rumors, but just in case, I'd voice them. Something I'd never done before.

"People say that I was having an affair with a married man and got pregnant. That I only kept Wren as a punishment because he wouldn't leave his wife. And that the reason I can live in this house, on a teacher's salary, is because he paid for me to stay quiet."

Ronan tensed, his arms wrapping around me as he listened.

"Other people say I went to a sperm bank because no one would marry me. Then there are those who say it was a one-night stand with a tourist. And then some think I got pregnant on accident and hid it from the father."

"You know I don't give a fuck about what people think."

I was learning this. He might have asked Gerty for the gossip, but I was learning that he didn't put a lot of stock in it. Ronan was a man who formed his own opinions. "It's none of the above, for the record."

When I'd told Kerrigan and Nellie the details about getting pregnant, the words had come out in a rush of word vomit—it had gone well with my awful morning sickness. But it had been such a long time since I'd told anyone that the explanation was stuck in my throat.

Ronan gave me time. His hands resumed their trailing up and down my spine until I sank into him. If only I could burrow deep and save myself the words. He'd just learn them from osmosis.

"A while back, I went to Hawaii with my sister and her husband. My best friend, Nellie, and her husband, Cal, came too."

"Cal Stark? Gerty told me he lived here."

"Yep."

Cal wasn't the asshole he was made out to be on old ESPN highlights from his time in the NFL. Ronan would see that himself. They'd meet sooner or later.

Countless people, including my cousin, had seen us holding hands downtown today. My mother had called twice this afternoon. I'd ignored them, but I was expecting another call first thing in the morning. She'd probably summon us to the house so everyone could meet Ronan.

Mom would fuss over him. Dad and Zach would size him up. And Kerrigan would threaten him with castration if he ever hurt me.

"Everyone did their best to include me but I was on vacation with two couples. I was the fifth wheel. So the next year for spring break, I went back to Hawaii alone. It was . . . lonely. I guess I'd expected it to be more relaxing. A week for me to read and tan and do anything I wanted. But I just felt like that sad woman sitting by herself in a beautiful restaurant coming to terms with the fact that her life was not turning out how she'd planned."

Maybe that was society's pressure to get married young and start a family. Or maybe that was just the natural path for most in Calamity. I was the only person in my graduating class who wasn't married—or divorced.

"I met a guy at the bar on my third night at the resort. He was good looking. Charismatic."

Ronan grunted. "That's enough of that."

I lifted to face him, pushing his dark hair off his forehead. "Not as good looking or charismatic as you."

"Obviously."

I rolled my eyes. "Your ego is showing."

"You like it." He bent to kiss me.

Yeah, I did. A lot. "We hooked up. Spent the rest of the vacation together. But we kept it casual. Not a lot of personal details were shared. Names. Room and phone numbers. Bodily fluids."

Ronan groaned. "You're killing me, babe."

I laughed, thankful that he could make me smile through this. "After the trip, I came home and life was normal. I didn't expect or want to see him again. That's not what it was about."

Sex had been the point. And having a companion for a few nights in Hawaii.

"A few weeks later, I missed my period. Found out I was

pregnant. One of the condoms hadn't worked, so I called him. He was . . . different."

"What do you mean, different? That son of a bitch wasn't married, was he?"

"Not that I know of." Though at this point, I didn't believe a thing that Carter had told me. "He acted like he didn't remember me. It had been weeks, not years. But I was just another woman he'd fucked and forgotten."

The tension in Ronan's body spiked, but he stayed quiet, listening. His arms wrapped around me, holding me like he knew this was just the beginning. That I'd need a hug by the time this was out in the open.

"I've never felt so used in my life," I whispered. "So cheap."

"Motherfucker," he muttered.

"Pretty much. He made me tell him how I knew him. It was ridiculous. He made me recount details of our time together, snippets of conversations. And I know for damn sure he remembered, but it was like a test. Apparently I passed because he finally said, 'Oh yeah. I remember you.' "

Ronan huffed. "Prick."

"He asked me why I was calling. Like how dare I have the audacity to use the phone number he'd given me. Then I told him I was pregnant." My temperature spiked as fury brewed in my veins. Just replaying that conversation in my head sent me into a rage.

The phone call had lasted ten minutes, fifteen tops. But every second of those minutes was branded into my mind. Every word. Every insult.

"He told me I was lying. That it was impossible. And

when I insisted I was telling the truth, he said he wanted nothing to do with *it* until I produced a paternity test."

The idea of Wren being an *it* made my lip curl.

Ronan's arms banded tighter, to the point of pain, but I was so livid that I let him squeeze.

"I hung up. I haven't heard from him or contacted him since. From that moment on, Wren was mine and mine alone. I didn't even list him on her birth certificate."

"Good."

Was it? Or had I made a huge mistake? "I feel like I'm looking over my shoulder. Waiting for him to show up and claim her. Or waiting for the day when she hears rumors about herself." I closed my eyes, my hands fisting his T-shirt. "I don't want her to know that her father didn't want her. That he wouldn't even acknowledge she existed."

"Larke." Ronan released his arms so he could frame my face with his hands. "He's an asshole. And if he ever shows up, we'll go after his rights. He doesn't get her. Never."

"What if he's changed his mind?"

"We fight."

I leaned into his touch. "We?"

"We." He gave me a single nod. "Is that why you sleep in her room?"

"Yeah," I confessed. "When she was a newborn, I'd wake up scared that I'd lost her. It was this irrational, out-of-control fear. Like I couldn't regulate it with reality. I realize now it was the hormones and sleep deprivation, but if I slept in her room, then it wasn't as bad. Now it's sort of a habit. If I wake up in the middle of the night, I can only go back to sleep if it's in her room."

His hazel eyes softened, the gold striations especially bright tonight. "You won't lose her."

"I can't." My voice cracked.

"You won't."

"I hope you're right."

"Of course I'm right. And luckily for you, you're sleeping with an exceptional lawyer."

He was exceptional.

"Tonight, will you do me a favor?" he asked.

"A sexual favor?"

"Yes." He grinned, those beautiful eyes dancing. "But after the sexual favors, plural, I have another request."

I held my breath, hoping that he wasn't going to ask for Carter's phone number. I didn't want anyone poking around, stirring the pot. "What request?"

"If you wake up, take me with you to Wren's room."

Not stay in bed. Not be quiet when I slipped out. Just take him with me.

Damn. If Ronan wasn't careful, I was going to fall in love with him.

That idea wasn't nearly as terrifying as it should have been.

CHAPTER TWENTY-ONE

RONAN

WITH THE STINGRAY parked in the garage, I crossed the driveway for Larke's.

A grin tugged at my mouth, widening with every step. In the past four days, this little walk from my house to hers had become a highlight of my day. And when I opened her front door, it felt like I was . . . home.

More than the building at my back. More than my place in California. More than the house I'd shared with Cora. And I'd loved that damn house.

But not as much as I loved Larke's.

The neighbor on the backside of her house, Hank, was out mowing his lawn. We'd met last night when I'd been on the back patio, grilling burgers for dinner. Tonight I raised a hand when he spotted me, earning a nod. Then I walked to the door, not bothering to ring the bell or knock. I just walked inside and breathed it in.

Lavender. Rain.

Mine.

I toed off my shoes in the entryway, where they'd wait until morning, when I'd head to my house for a shower and change of clothes. I bent to strip off my socks, then tugged the hem of my shirt from the waistband of my slacks.

"Larke," I called.

No answer.

The TV was on when I stepped into the living room, the toys mostly contained to the playpen. Wren came toddling out of the kitchen, and the minute she spotted me, those legs started pumping, racing across the floor as she squealed, giving me that wide, drooly smile that filled my heart.

"There's my firefly." I swept her up and tossed her in the air. Then I kissed her cheek as she giggled. "How was daycare today?"

"Ro." She slapped her palms on my cheeks, squeezing them together. This was her latest party trick, tugging on my face to see how she could pull and stretch it.

"Where's Mama?"

"Mama." Her eyes lit up as she pointed to the kitchen. "Dis."

This way.

Slowly, I was learning her language. With any luck, I'd be around to hear it as it grew. As she grew. God, I hoped so. What kind of asshole would want to miss this?

Wren's hair was in pigtails, the ends curling. She was in a navy shirt with a rainbow on the tiny pocket and a pair of overalls. And she was still wearing the yellow Crocs that she'd picked out from her shoe basket this morning.

I'd spent as many moments in this house as possible in the past four days. That was all it had taken for me to fall for this little girl.

She was as much mine as her mother.

Larke's story about that motherfucker from Hawaii had rolled around my brain on a loop. Every time, I'd get pissed about the way he'd used her. About the way he'd made her feel. How he'd accused her of lying.

I hated the idea of her with another man. I hated that Wren was his, this faceless stranger's. At some point, we'd have to deal with it. Larke might be okay pretending like he didn't exist, but I wanted it locked down. I wanted his rights gone. I wanted it legal.

But that was a conversation for another night.

With Wren on my arm, I walked into the kitchen. Larke had the phone wedged between her shoulder and ear as she put away clean dishes.

"Yes, Mom. You'll get to meet him."

"Him had better be me," I told Wren, drawing Larke's attention.

Those chocolate eyes lit up when she turned. She smiled and the warmth that spread through my bones was the best damn feeling in the world.

"Hi," she mouthed.

I closed the distance between us, bending to kiss her hair. "Hi."

"I'd better let you go, Mom. I need to get started on dinner. Talk to you later." She ended the call, and when I lifted my free arm, she slipped into my side, her body molding to mine. Her mouth pressed a kiss to my chest, to the scar beneath my shirt. "Feel like meeting my parents this weekend?"

"Sure," I said.

"And my sister and brother."

"All right."

"And probably a few aunts, uncles and cousins."

"Bring it." We'd meet families. First, hers. Then Noah when he came to visit later this month.

Larke pressed her nose into my chest, drawing in a long breath. "Aiden called me."

"Yeah." I sighed. "Figured he would."

"Friday."

I nodded. "Friday."

A judge had reviewed Ember's complaint and we were scheduled to see him on Friday afternoon. They'd even accommodated our request to have it later in the day to fit Ember and Larke's school schedule.

"That gives me tonight and tomorrow to mentally prepare for an epic ass chewing," I said. "By a judge. I can't wait."

Larke giggled. "He might tell me to change Ember's grade."

"We both know he won't."

Wren squirmed, kicking her legs to be set down. Once she was on her feet, she headed for the dishwasher, taking out a fork and thrusting it in the air. "Hep." *Help.*

"Oh, thank you, baby." Larke took it from her hand, putting it in the silverware drawer, then did the same as Wren hauled out the rest.

"Ember came to the office today," I said, leaning against the counter.

Larke stopped, facing me. "And?"

"She talked to Gertrude. I came out, said hello. She didn't even look at me. And when I told her the judge had finally gotten back to us, that we needed to be at the courthouse by three thirty on Friday afternoon, she just nodded and left."

Ember hadn't come to the office on Monday or Tuesday. Which confirmed that she'd definitely seen me at her house. And she'd likely seen me with Larke.

I doubted she'd come in tomorrow, but Friday, after the appointment with the judge, Ember and I were having a lengthy discussion. I'd stand outside her house all night if necessary. I'd stay until I saw her mother and could confirm Ember was okay.

This ended Friday, no matter what.

"How was she in class today?" I asked.

Larke gave me a sad smile. "She wouldn't look at me. So . . . nothing new."

"Damn."

"I shouldn't have gone to her house."

"Yeah." I rubbed my jaw. "Me neither."

Since the visit, neither of us had tried to call the mother. It was clear that Ashley Scott wasn't going to take Larke's calls, or anyone's. So we'd just backed off, both of us hoping that maybe Ember would want to talk about why we'd come to visit. But since I didn't know the first thing about teenagers, clearly, that had backfired.

"Ember was wearing yesterday's clothes," Larke said. "She looks exhausted."

"Yeah, I noticed too." I sighed. "We'll figure it out." *Friday.*

"Do you think we've totally concocted this? Like she's fine but we're imagining the worst?"

I shook my head. "Maybe. But we were both at the trailer. We both heard Ember hide, like we were the enemy."

That might mean something or nothing. All I knew for certain was that I didn't like my gut feeling.

The guilt on Larke's face made my heart twist. But the sullen mood didn't last. The moment Wren came to stand on my bare feet with her arms raised in the air, I relaxed.

"Up, Ro."

"How about a please?"

She scrunched up her nose, looking more like Larke than ever. "Up. Up."

"Please."

"Pees."

My eyes widened.

Larke's jaw dropped.

"That's new, right?" I asked.

"Yes." Larke laughed.

For the rest of my days, I'd remember teaching this girl please. I hefted Wren up, giving her that toss that made her giggle. Then I tickled her ribs, her happiness ringing through the kitchen.

This house radiated joy. It came with the cluttered counters and the dishes and the toys and . . . life. That was Wren. That was Larke. That was why this felt like home.

"Want me to cook dinner?" I asked.

"You cooked breakfast."

Every day. I'd volunteered myself to do breakfast so that Larke could just get herself and Wren ready for school.

"I'll tackle dinner." Larke walked to the fridge.

With Wren still on my side, seemingly content to let me hold her for a minute, I watched as Larke moved around the kitchen, graceful and unhurried. Five feet away and it was too much distance. So as she stood at the stove, stirring a pasta sauce, I set Wren down to play and moved in behind her mother.

She was still in the black T-shirt dress she'd worn to school. Her shoes were gone and her feet bare too.

My hands skimmed down her hips. My mouth went to the soft skin beneath her ear. "I have an idea. For later."

Larke hummed, leaning back into my chest. "What kind of idea?"

"The filthy kind."

A shudder rolled over her as my tongue darted out for a taste. "You're distracting me from cooking."

This time, I nipped at her skin after I licked it.

She sighed, that breathy, sexy sigh that usually came after I'd fucked her nearly to sleep.

My cock swelled behind my slacks so I shifted my hips, pressing it against her ass.

"Ronan," she warned.

"What?" I kissed her neck again, desperate for more. Just to have my hands on her. To feel her beneath my palms. To know that she was as needy and desperate as I was, and that no matter how often I was inside her body, it was never enough.

A hiss came from the stove. I tore my mouth away from her skin as the pot of boiling pasta bubbled over.

"Shit." Larke quickly turned down the heat. Then she shook her head, laughing. Her cheeks were beautifully flushed. "Go away."

"Why?"

"Because if you don't, we'll never eat. Then Wren will turn into a monster."

"Fine," I muttered, but not before taking her face in my

hands, moving so fast she couldn't stop me from sealing my lips over hers.

This was the dance we had each night. Push and pull.

It had become my personal mission in life to get her so worked up, so turned on, that by the time Wren was asleep, Larke wanted to tear my clothes off. Last night she'd been in such a hurry to get me out of my shirt that she'd popped a button.

While she cooked, I gave her moments of space. Then I'd crowd close, touching her enough to get in her head. A brush of my knuckles against her ass. A fingertip over the swell of her breast. A kiss on the nape of her neck before I took out her hair tie and tossed it on the counter.

And finally, when Wren was dressed in butterfly pajamas and in her crib, I kissed the firefly goodnight and let Larke rock her to sleep while I retreated to the bedroom, stripping off my shirt to save the buttons and lying on the bed, my arms behind my head on the pillows.

My heart began to race, my cock swelling, as I heard the faint click of a door closing. Footsteps followed. When Larke appeared in the threshold of her room, I was rock hard, straining against my zipper.

She leaned on the door's frame, staring.

"Are you coming over?" I crooked a finger.

"Just appreciating the view."

I grinned. "Want to hear my idea?"

"No." She shoved off the frame, closing the door before sauntering across the room, stopping at the foot of the bed. "Show me instead."

I jackknifed to a seat, swinging my legs over the edge. Then I flicked the clasp on my slacks, quickly shoving them and my boxers to the floor. I prowled to her, my beautiful Larke who made the sexiest fucking noises when I was buried in her tight pussy.

"Dress off." I snapped my fingers.

Pink flushed her face as she bent to take the hem, dragging it up, inch by inch, until she'd tugged it over her head. Then came the bra and panties until she stood before me. Miles of glorious, smooth skin. Rosy nipples pebbled to perfect buds. Chestnut hair as soft as silk.

I towered over her, drowning in those pretty eyes. They were full of lust and desire. Anticipation. Affection.

That tether between us grew every time we were together. Like the threads I'd used to fix that button on my shirt this morning. One loop doubled to two, doubled to four, to eight, to sixteen. Until there was no breaking us apart.

I took her mouth, swallowing a gasp. My hands trailed across her skin, leaving no inch of her torso untouched. Her wandering hands did the same, leaving trails of fire in their wake.

Our tongues tangled, another practiced dance, until our lips were swollen and between us, I throbbed.

Never breaking my mouth from hers, I shuffled us to the bed. Then I sat down on the edge, my legs planted firmly on the floor. It forced our mouths apart and it put me at the perfect height to capture a nipple with my teeth.

"Ronan," Larke moaned, her hands diving into my hair as I nipped and sucked.

Only when she was trembling did I break apart, shifting to take the other breast in my mouth, kissing along its swell.

Night by night, I'd unlocked the secrets of her body. Her nipples were a favorite place of mine. She loved it when I kissed along her neck and toyed with her earlobes. She writhed when I strummed her clit and her second orgasm was always stronger than the first, though harder to earn.

Tonight, I wanted these perfect tits bouncing when she came apart. I wanted the red blush that crept into her chest when she shattered. I wanted my fingerprints permanently marring her skin, like an invisible brand.

With a pop, I let her nipple go and shifted deeper into the bed, maintaining my seat. Then with a hoist of her hips, I hauled her into my lap, her legs parting automatically to straddle my thighs.

She rose up on her knees, that drenched core hovering above my weeping cock.

"Ride me," I ordered, lining up at her entrance. My grip on her hips tightened.

She sank onto me, her head thrown back as a whimper escaped her throat. "Yes."

"Christ." I gritted my teeth, that nightly battle to control my body. It should have gotten easier. Except when it came to Larke, I was like a goddamn teenager, ready to spill with one throb of her inner walls.

When I had it under control, I nudged her hips, helping her to rise and sink down again, coating my cock. "Fuck, that's good."

Her nails dug into my shoulders as I thrust my hips up to meet hers, using the floor for leverage.

She lifted again, my hands on her hips to help, then this time, instead of letting her control the descent, I pulled her down. Hard. We slammed together, the slap of our skin echoing through the bedroom along with her cry.

"Ronan."

"Fuck, yeah, babe." I loved that goddamn sound.

I urged her up again, then pulled her down, meeting her with a thrust of my hips. That was all it took for her to get the rhythm. For sex to get wild.

But that was us, night after night. There were no inhibitions. There hadn't been from the beginning. I was a man who liked to experiment and every time I put Larke in a position, she mastered it. Instantly. Our bodies were so in tune with each other's it was like she'd been made to fit me.

I liked that idea, that there was a woman who'd been destined to be mine.

Mine. All fucking mine.

Her breasts bounced and swayed with every movement. When her legs tired, I made sure to keep her weight with my arms, lifting and letting her drop. Then her hands came to cup her breasts, pinching her nipples.

I loved that this woman wasn't afraid to do whatever felt good. To touch me. To touch herself.

A flutter warned me she was close. Her legs began to shake. So I let go with one hand, reaching between us for that bundle of nerves. Two circles with my finger on her clit was all it took for Larke to detonate.

"Ah." Her head arched, that throat long and begging for my tongue as her body was wracked with an orgasm. Her pussy clenched, hard, while I licked the underside of her jaw, tasting the salty sheen of sweat on her skin.

Her hips rocked almost uncontrollably as she came, pulse after pulse.

"Larke." I closed my eyes and let go, letting my own orgasm barrel through me like a wrecking ball. My groan mingled with her cries. A symphony. Harmony.

The perfect swan dive off a cliff into oblivion.

As soon as I was coherent, I wrapped her in my arms, my cock still twitching inside her. "Damn."

There was a smile on her lips as she nuzzled against my neck. "I liked that."

I loved it.

Four days ago, I'd told Larke how she terrified me. I searched for that fear. It was gone. What the hell was there to be afraid of anyway? The woman of my dreams? Hell no. This was a good thing. This was the best thing to happen in my entire life.

Thank the fucking stars I'd moved to Calamity.

The realization made me laugh, my head falling forward, my face buried in her hair.

Larke started to laugh too, her arms banding tighter around my shoulders.

My cock was still hard inside her, so I shifted us, lying on my back and against the pillows. I kept her pinned to me, our bodies connected. She just sighed, shifting with me until she had her cheek over my heart.

I'd never had a woman lie on me like Larke. Like she was trying to sink inside me. Like I was the very mattress beneath her bones.

We breathed, our heartbeats finally calming. "I want to fall asleep inside you."

"Okay," she murmured, sounding like she was already drifting.

With one hand, I reached for the covers, tugging them over us as best I could. Then I trailed my fingers up and down her spine. "Still scared?"

It took her a moment, a long breath, before she whispered, "A little."

We'd get to the other side of it. Soon.

"Are you?" she asked.

No. Not a damn bit. "Just a little."

CHAPTER TWENTY-TWO

LARKE

THE CLASSROOM EXPLODED when the last bell rang at two forty-five. Most days, I breathed a sigh of relief when the kids shot out of their chairs and rushed for the door. But today, I wouldn't mind if a few lingered. Anything to delay my trip to the courthouse.

"Have a good weekend, Ms. Hale."

I smiled. "You too, John."

Then the room was empty. I closed my eyes and sucked in a long breath.

Worst case, I changed Ember's grade. Or maybe that was best case. At this point, I wasn't sure what to think. And given how quiet Ronan had been this morning over breakfast, I suspected he was just as conflicted.

Regardless, today we'd put this mess behind us. *Fingers crossed.*

"Knock. Knock." Emily walked through the door wearing a kind smile. "How are you holding up?"

I shrugged. "Ask me at five."

"Would you mind if I came down to the courthouse?" she asked.

"No, not at all." I'd appreciate the support from the school's principal, no matter the outcome.

"Then I'll be there." She nodded. "I don't want to keep you since I know you need to get going. But I just wanted to say that I really appreciate you, Larke. Giving up your fifth-grade classroom. Tackling high school. Handling this situation with Ember Scott with such grace and dignity. I know you're ready to get back to the elementary school, but if you change your mind, personally, I'd be thrilled to have you stick with us."

"Thank you." When the dust settled, maybe I would be in this exact spot in the fall. Even though I wasn't sure I was doing a good job, it was a relief to hear she would have me back.

"You're welcome." She waved, then slipped out of the room.

It wasn't that this year had been awful. It had just been . . . different. Draining.

Thankfully, this year's challenge was nearly over. Summer was approaching fast, and I couldn't wait for the relaxed pace. Lazy mornings. Long afternoon walks with Wren. Evenings on the patio.

And nights with Ronan.

I opened my desk drawer and pulled out my purse, lifting out my phone to send him a text, but he'd beaten me to it.

Just got to the courthouse.

I typed out a quick reply.

On my way.

I scanned the classroom, making sure there wasn't anything I needed to take care of before the weekend. I went down the rows of desks, straightening a few, then I pushed in my own chair, slung my purse over a shoulder and headed for the hallway.

My heart climbed into my throat. *It'll be fine. Just get it over with.* By five, I'd be on my way to get Wren and this would be over. Tonight, this lawsuit wouldn't be hanging over our heads.

The jitters manifested in my fingers first, making them shake. My footsteps felt a bit wobbly. I was just rounding a corner for the rear exit door when I nearly collided with a solid wall of man chest.

"Oh, sorry." I regretted the apology the moment I found Wilder Abbott's scowl waiting.

He grunted.

This asshole. Apparently he'd never heard of polite apologies before. My hands fisted at my sides as he side-stepped me without a word. How many days had he sat in my classroom without so much as a hello? *What a dick.*

I was about to head for the door, but a whiff of his cologne caught my nose. It was nice. Not as intoxicating as Ronan's woodsy scent, but Wilder smelled nice. He looked nice.

Maybe that was what pissed me off so much, beyond the rude attitude and undeserved disdain. The first day we'd met, my first thought had been *Oh, wow. He's hot.* The beard. The tall, muscular physique. And at the time, even that brooding scowl had been attractive—he'd ruined it since. He'd decided to hate me for no reason, so his appeal had taken a major hit.

Wilder Abbott was probably devastating when he laughed. Yet the only time I'd seen even a whisper of a smile was when he was in his classroom, facing his students. For them, he seemed softer.

But for me, cold as ice.

"What is your problem?" The words I'd been holding back for years came spewing out. There was no time for this conversation, but damn it, today, I was done. I'd dealt with his shit for years and enough was enough.

Ronan's lack of a filter must have rubbed off with some of his arrogance.

Wilder stopped walking, letting out a huff as he turned.

I planted my hands on my hips. "Why do you have such a problem with me? It wasn't my idea for you to give up your prep period. And it's not like you were particularly friendly before this whole mess started. I've never done anything but try to stay out of your way." And I'd been nice. In the beginning, I'd been very nice.

His jaw ticked but he didn't answer.

Typical. I tossed out a hand. "Whatever. With any luck, I'll be back in the elementary school next year where I can pretend you don't exist." And if I had to teach high school again, Wilder could skulk all he wanted. Effective immediately, he'd just moved off my *Shithead List* to my *Dead To Me List*.

"Hate me all you want. I'm done." *Fuck you, very much, Mr. Abbott.* I turned, ready to make my escape and get to the courthouse, but he stopped me.

"Larke." That he'd use my first name was as shocking as the hint of kindness in his voice.

I faced him again, arching an eyebrow. "Yes?"

"I'm married. Or . . . I was married."

"Okay," I drawled. *Poor woman.* "Do you want my congratulations or my condolences?"

"My wife died."

"Oh." I winced. *Shit.* Just because he was an asshole didn't mean I had to be one too. "I'm sorry for your loss."

He studied my face, his jaw flexing once more. "You look like her."

Um, what? I looked like his dead wife. *That* was the reason for his hostility?

"I don't hate you," he said, his gaze going to the wall at my side. "It's hard for me to look at you sometimes. She had brown eyes, like yours. Your hair color is similar. And she smiled a lot. You smile a lot."

I opened my mouth but wasn't sure what to say. Did I apologize for my looks? For smiling? *Nope.*

"It's not you," he said. "It's me."

"Well, that's a first. Usually men save that for their breakup line."

His mouth flattened in a thin line at my attempted joke. "She wasn't as snarky as you."

"If you think that was snark, you haven't seen anything yet." That comment would have made Ronan chuckle. Whenever I gave him attitude, he met it full force with wit and sarcasm. Banter was part of our foreplay. Affection.

Wilder, on the other hand, didn't look even slightly amused.

It was doubtful that we'd become friends, but I'd settle for colleagues who didn't harbor a mutual hatred. "I'm sorry about your wife."

He dropped his gaze to the floor, nodding. "Sorry I've been a—"

"Grumpy bastard."

The scowl came back. "Can you say bastard in school?"

I lifted a shoulder. "The kids do, so why not?"

Maybe I imagined it, but I could have sworn there was a hint of a smile on his mouth. If Wilder was going to be pleasant, I'd have to stop calling him Asshole Abbott. That was progress enough for today, so I turned, but he stopped me again.

"Larke."

"Yes?" I arched an eyebrow.

"You're a good teacher. It's been . . . nice, watching you teach the seniors."

I blinked. Was he seriously giving me a compliment?

"Don't leave the high school because of me."

"I won't." Yes, I disliked him, but he didn't have that much influence in my life.

"Then don't leave the high school. There's good to be done within these walls." He circled a finger in the air.

"And you think I'm the person to do it?"

He lifted a shoulder. Then turned and walked away.

With his words replaying in the back of my mind, I headed for the courthouse. The weight of what was about to happen came crashing down like a ton of bricks as I parked my car.

I scanned the sidewalks, searching for Ember, but they were nearly empty, so I hiked up the concrete stairs, my hands still shaking, and made my way through the labyrinth of hallways to the courtroom. Aiden was waiting outside the double doors.

"Hi." He shook my hand, offering a kind smile. "How are you?"

"Ready to get this over with," I breathed.

"It will be fine. I'm not worried in the slightest."

"Great."

His confidence did nothing to soothe my rattled nerves. Aiden opened a door to the courtroom, holding it so I could enter first.

This was my first time in a courtroom, and it was larger than I'd expected. More intimidating. At the front of the room was the judge's bench, elevated to make sure everyone knew who was in charge. It was made of a honey-stained oak that matched the wainscotting on the walls.

Hanging on gold posts on opposite sides of the room, the American flag and a Montana state flag were the only pops of color in the space. Beyond the wood accents, everything else was a plain white.

There were about ten rows of chairs behind the plaintiff and defendant tables. Emily Cain was sitting in the row behind our empty table. As my shoes thumped on the gray, industrial carpet, she turned to offer a smile.

I forced one in return. *Breathe, Larke.*

My gaze tracked to Ronan, hoping it would help settle my nerves. It didn't.

His hair was perfectly styled and his broad shoulders were covered in a tailored black suit jacket. His spine was rigid, and the tension in his frame made my stomach twist. I didn't need to see his face to know there'd be no sexy smirk today.

Ember was seated at his side. When she heard my foot-steps, she turned and gave me a glare that would have made

Wilder Abbott proud. It was the first eye contact she'd made with me in weeks.

Yep, she hated me. Somehow, I was going to have to live with that fact.

Aiden must have seen it because he moved to my side, his hand gentle on my arm as he guided me to our table. Then he took the outside chair, his large frame blocking Ember and Ronan from sight.

We'd had a call last night for about an hour. Ronan had given Wren her bath so I could talk to my lawyer. Aiden had coached me on what to do and what to say. I was to answer questions when asked but otherwise stay quiet. Ronan had given me the same advice.

So I sat with my hands in my lap, counting the seconds until a door beside the bench opened. A bailiff walked out first, followed by a court reporter—she went to yoga at The Refinery.

My pulse raced as the bailiff called, "All rise."

We stood as Nelson Labb walked out, dressed in a black robe. His white hair was unruly, sticking up at all angles. With his bushy, gray beard, he looked more like a vagrant than a district judge. He took the chair at the bench, glancing briefly at me. Then he focused on the other table.

His attention zeroed in on Ronan.

And with his glare, he put Ember Scott and Wilder Abbott to shame.

———

"EMBER, WAIT," Ronan called after her, but she streaked out of the courtroom, her bulging backpack bouncing wildly as she ran.

Ten minutes. That's all this had taken. Ten minutes for Judge Labb to deliver Ronan an epic ass chewing. He'd had some harsh words for Ember too.

It had hurt, listening to Nelson scold Ronan, lecture Ember.

"Thank you, Aiden." I shook his hand, but my focus was on Ronan.

He was quickly collecting his things, probably to chase after Ember.

"You're welcome." Aiden, noticing my attention was on the other man in the room, picked up his briefcase and shifted out of the way. He hadn't even bothered to unpack, like he'd known from the start exactly how this would go. "Call me if you need anything."

"I will." I waited until he walked away, then went to Ronan's side. "Hey."

"Hi, mama." He bent to kiss my forehead. "You okay?"

"Yes. Are you?"

He sighed. "It's what I expected to hear."

For a man who'd just been reprimanded for wasting court time and putting his license at risk with unnecessary antics—a verbal hand slap that would have sent me straight to tears—Ronan looked unrattled.

Though there was concern in his eyes as he jerked his chin to the doors. "I need to catch up to Ember. Talk to her."

"Okay." I nodded, hustling out of the courtroom with Ronan on my heels, his hand on the small of my back.

Our shoes clicked on the marble floors. We checked

every hallway as we hurried to the courthouse's front doors. When we stepped outside, we both searched the sidewalks, but Ember was long gone.

"I'm going to her house," he said, starting down the stairs.

"I'm coming too."

He didn't protest or ask where I'd parked. He simply took my hand and led me to the Corvette parked against the curb, opening my door first before rounding the hood to get behind the wheel.

The car smelled like him. Felt like him. Smooth and sexy. It was strange that this was my first time riding in the Stingray. Hopefully next time it would be under better circumstances.

"If she's walking, maybe we can catch her." He turned the key and revved the engine, racing away from the courthouse so fast it forced me deep into the seat. He turned like he was going toward First, to take the same path he'd taken the day he'd followed her to the trailer park.

"Go this way." I pointed at a side street. It would lead through a different neighborhood, but from the courthouse, it was the faster route to the trailer park.

Ronan hit the brake, taking the turn. Then his foot sank into the gas pedal as the engine roared. But as quickly as he'd floored it, he backed off, the seat belt heavy on my chest as we slowed.

"Wh—" I didn't need to finish my sentence. Ember marched down the sidewalk.

Ronan weaved for the curb. The moment the tires were stopped and the engine was cut, we were both out of the car.

"Ember!" he called, taking off to catch her.

She glanced back, saw him and started walking faster.

"Damn it." He took off jogging.

So did I, though I'd picked heels today to pair with my gray dress. I'd wanted to look nice in court.

Ronan's jacket flew behind him as he ran. The skirt of my dress swished at my calves as I tried to keep up.

Ember didn't stop when he reached her side, so Ronan jogged around her, holding up his hands. "Hold up, kid."

She tried to move around him, but he shifted, blocking her path just as I caught up.

I rushed around her too, standing beside Ronan. "Oh, Ember."

Tears streamed down her face. Her nose was snotty. The heartbreak on her face broke mine.

I reached for her but she dodged my hand, jerking out of reach.

"You ruined everything!" Her voice cracked as she screamed. She flung out her arms, her backpack so heavy it nearly threw her off balance. She teetered but regained her footing, then stripped off the straps of her bag, letting the whole thing crash at her feet.

"Hey." When Ronan reached for her shoulder, she jerked away.

"I need to go to college. I need to get a good job. I need to make *money*." The tears kept streaming as she shouted.

"Ember—"

"You promised you'd help me," she sobbed, her chest wracking. "You're a liar. You're just like *her*."

This girl was about to break, right in front of my eyes.

Oh, God. "I'll change your grade," I blurted.

Screw my integrity and pride. This girl's spirit was worth more.

Ember's entire body jerked. She stared at me, her chin quivering, like she hadn't heard me right.

"I'll change your grade," I repeated.

A single blink. Then she crumpled.

One moment she was standing, the next her knees were buckling. They would have cracked on the sidewalk if Ronan hadn't moved fast enough to catch her, hauling her into his chest as she cried uncontrollably.

"I got you." He held her, looking to me with as much pain on his face as I felt in my heart. "Breathe, kid."

"I-I can't"—the words were interrupted with sobs— "pay."

"Pay for what?" he asked.

"My brothers."

"What?" I gasped. "You're paying for your brothers?"

She nodded against Ronan's chest, her hands clutching the lapels of his suit jacket.

"Where's your mom?" I asked, even though I already knew the answer. There was a reason Ashley Scott hadn't returned my countless phone calls.

"Gone." Ember cried even harder. Her legs gave way, like the weight of the world had come with her confession.

Ronan never faltered. He held her tighter, he kept her standing, as the truth came pouring out.

"She left us." Ember hiccupped. "Sh-she left us."

"When?" Ronan asked.

"On my birthday."

Her eighteenth birthday. When Ashley had probably deemed Ember old enough to care for second-grade twin boys.

"How long ago was that?" Ronan asked.

"About three months."

His expression turned murderous. But he held her, letting her tears soak his shirt and tie, until she finally relaxed her grip on his coat.

She stepped away, searching the ground for her backpack. But when she bent and tried to pick it up, it was like her strength was gone.

"Sit down for a sec," he told her, taking her elbow and leading her to the yard at our side.

She sank down on the grass, swiping furiously at her cheeks. "I have to get home. They walked after school, but I don't like to leave them for too long."

"We'll drive you." Ronan crouched in front of her while I sat on the grass at her side. "How have you been paying for everything?"

"My money. When we lived in Minnesota, I used to babysit for our neighbors and shovel snow and mow and stuff. I was saving to go to college. I kept it hidden from Mom."

So when Ashley left, Ember had no other choice but to use her savings.

Her only chance at college was a scholarship.

She'd been counting on it because she'd need all of her other money to support her brothers. She wanted a degree so she could pay for Eric and Elijah.

This was too much responsibility for an eighteen-year-old kid. This was too heavy.

"I don't want to lose my brothers." Ember started crying again, burying her face in her hands.

I put my arm around her shoulders and this time, she didn't push me away. She collapsed into my side, letting me hug her as she cried. Then when the tears finally ebbed and her breath hitched a few times, she sat up straight and let me help her dry the tears.

"We'll figure this out. Okay?" I promised.

Utter hopelessness made her face look so very young. "How?"

Ronan held out a fist, just like he did with Wren, for a fist bump. "We got you, kid."

CHAPTER TWENTY-THREE

LARKE

A KNOCK CAME at my classroom door. I set aside the paper I'd been grading as my sister walked inside. "Hey."

"Hi." She gave me a small smile, scanning the classroom. "I haven't been in here in ages."

"Weird, right?" We'd both had math in this room during our years at Calamity High. When Emily had first brought me here last fall, I'd thought it was strange too. "It smells the same. Don't you think?"

She drew in a long inhale and laughed. "Yeah. Like Expo markers and old books and floor cleaner."

"Exactly." I smiled at her as she spun in a slow circle, then finally faced me, her shoulders falling.

"How are you?"

"Tired." My shoulders slumped. "Ready for some answers."

As a teacher, I had a basic understanding of the Child and Family Services process. But living through it had been an entirely different education.

The past two weeks had been grueling as we'd tried to get Ember and her brothers the help they needed.

"Any news?" Kerrigan asked.

I shook my head. "No. Ronan was hoping to hear today, but I haven't heard anything."

And considering it was a Friday at three thirty, the chances were slim. Which meant waiting yet another weekend for news.

"It's good of you to help her."

"Ronan gets the credit." He'd seen the signs that the rest of us had missed.

Kerrigan came to sit on the edge of my desk. "Can I do anything to help?"

"No, but thanks. We'll be all right."

She glanced around the classroom again. "I know I didn't react well when you told me you were thinking of moving to Bozeman. But if you decide that's what you need, know that I'll support you however I can."

"I know that." I sank deeper into my chair. "But I'm not moving."

"Oh, thank God." Her entire body sagged. "I'm giving Ronan the credit for that too. The man is a miracle worker."

I giggled. She wasn't wrong.

Last night, after Ronan had fallen asleep, I'd struggled to shut off my mind—that had been the case for two weeks. So I'd snuck out of bed with my phone and sent an email to my contact with the Bozeman School District, canceling my interview in June.

I couldn't move. Ronan had just gotten here.

Calamity was my home. This was where I wanted Wren to grow up. We'd take the good and the bad and make the best of it. If staying meant teaching high school for the next decade, so be it. This experience with Ember had been eye-opening. There was good to be done within these walls. Maybe I was the person to do it.

And Ronan, well . . .

It was too soon to make promises, wasn't it? To say those three little words that bubbled closer and closer to the surface with each passing day.

"What are you doing in town?" I asked Kerrigan. "Did you have to go to The Refinery?"

"No. I came to visit you."

I smiled. "I don't like it when you're mad at me."

"Neither do I. And neither does Pierce. Apparently I've been 'difficult' to live with lately."

I laughed. "Well, we can't have that."

Another knock came at the door, and this time, I stood from my seat to greet my visitor. "Hi."

"Hey, mama." Ronan wrapped me in his arms. "How was your day?"

"Long, but good." I relaxed into his chest, drawing in his cologne as I stared at a particular student's desk.

Now that the truth about Ember was out in the open, the tension from the past few weeks had defused. She was still quiet in class, but she engaged in the discussions. Every time I looked toward her desk, she'd have a small smile waiting.

The whispering and snickering about the lawsuit had ceased. And by some miracle, Wilder Abbott had been . . . cordial. The grunts and glares had stopped. I wasn't sure if we'd ever be friends, but I'd thought a lot about what he'd said, and if I did stay at the high school, maybe we could be colleagues.

"Hey, Kerrigan." Ronan lifted a hand to wave at my sister.

"Hi, Ronan."

My parents had insisted on having us over for a family dinner last weekend, not only to get the scoop on Ember, but to meet Ronan. No surprise, he'd charmed them all.

I leaned back, taking in his jeans and T-shirt. "You didn't come from work?"

"I came from home. I've been unpacking."

"Unpacking what?" His house was already unpacked, wasn't it?

We hadn't spent a lot of time over there, not when it was easier to entertain Wren when she was surrounded by her own toys, but a few days ago we'd gone over to eat dinner there for a change of scenery. I hadn't noticed any boxes.

Though his brother and friend were coming tomorrow morning, so maybe he'd been unpacking for their visit. They were going fishing, so maybe he'd needed to dig out supplies.

"Got some news," he said, framing my face with his hands.

My heart stopped. "What?"

"Nothing is final, but it sounds like that foster family is interested in keeping the twins until Ember gets out of school."

"Oh, thank God." I dropped my forehead to his sternum.

There was no way Ember could raise Eric and Elijah. Not when she had dreams of her own. She wanted to go to college. She'd have a better shot at supporting them in the long run with a degree. And Ember deserved to live her life too.

She'd really wanted to keep them with her, but this was the outcome Ronan and I had hoped for.

The twins wouldn't get split up. I knew the foster family, and those boys were in good hands. The parents had been incredibly accommodating, letting Ember come and visit her brothers any time she wanted while CFSD sorted the legal details. And eventually, once Ember was established with a home and a job, they could live together again.

"So what were you unpacking?" I asked.

"My place."

I stood tall. "Huh?"

"Ember can't stay in that trailer. Not another night."

No, she couldn't. Even though she'd insisted on it these past couple of weeks.

We'd learned a lot about her life in the last two weeks.

Like Ember had told us, the money she'd previously saved for college had been something she'd kept hidden from her mother. Since Ashley had a habit of stealing from her own daughter, Ember had kept her cash in that backpack, never letting it out of her sight. Even at night, she'd slept with the bag under her pillow.

When Ashley had disappeared, that money had gone to pay for electricity and water and food. Since they were new to town and no one lived in the trailers beside theirs, no one had been the wiser. To their landlord, it had just been Ember instead of Ashley dropping off rent.

Ember had made sure the boys went to school. They'd walk into town together every morning and home each afternoon, sometimes stopping at the grocery store. The days when Ember had gone to visit Ronan, the twins had walked home alone, staying inside until she got there.

Ashley had taken their only car. Since Ember couldn't afford the extra cost, she'd gotten rid of her cell phone. And though she could afford food, she hadn't wanted to deplete her funds, knowing it would be harder in the summer, so she'd taken extra lunches from school.

For three months she'd been the parent. She'd carried a burden that should never have been hers.

"She can crash at my place," Ronan said. "Figured it would be easiest if she was next door. And it's close to the foster house."

"Good idea."

"Mind if I move some stuff into your closet?"

"Not at all."

He held me for a moment. Just us standing, locked together. It had been a constant part of every day. We came together and just held tight.

"What did Ember say when you told her?"

"She doesn't know yet."

I laughed. "So you just moved her out?"

"Basically. I didn't feel like dealing with an argument. I went and hauled everything decent out of that fucking trailer." He shook his head. "I was tempted to burn the rest to the ground."

"Then where's Ember?"

"At the office with Gertrude."

"Ah." I nodded. Ronan had given her an after-school job at the office, helping Gertrude with cleaning and filing.

"There wasn't much to save," he said. "Hauled a load with my truck. Everything else is trash. I don't want her going back to that place again."

"Neither do I."

"Any word on Ashley?" Kerrigan asked.

Ronan dragged a hand through his hair. "Nothing. The cops are looking for her but she's long gone."

The authorities had questioned Ember about her mother's disappearance, but she wasn't sure where Ashley had gone either. Ronan had told me that child endangerment meant jail time, a monetary fine or both, so I doubted Ashley was broadcasting her location. *Bitch.*

How could a mother abandon her children? I just couldn't wrap my head around it.

Ashley hadn't left a note. She hadn't told Ember anything. One day, she'd been at the trailer. The next, she'd been gone with the car and all of her belongings. After a month, Ember had realized Ashley wasn't coming back. By that point, she'd already stepped into mother mode for the boys. Then she'd begun concocting her grand plan.

Graduate. Move to a college town so they could all keep going to school. That plan hinged on her getting a scholarship.

Both of the in-state schools had scholarships for incoming freshmen with exemplary academic performance. Except Ember had missed the application window, no doubt because she'd been busy raising twin boys.

So she'd searched for other opportunities. She'd found three private scholarship programs with application deadlines in June. If she could get all three, she'd be able to afford tuition and fees. To pay for their living expenses, Ember had planned to take on a job and rent a cheap apartment for her and her brothers.

She'd budgeted for everything. She'd accounted for every penny, from utilities to food costs to winter coats to new gym shoes for the boys. To Ember, her plan had been flawless. Up until the day I'd given her a C plus.

She'd been so consumed, so laser focused, that a simple grade had sent her into a tailspin. This grade had become her fixation. Her desperation.

Her cry for help.

I was just glad Ronan had heard it.

"Did you change her grade?" Kerrigan asked.

"Nope. I would have but once we got to the bottom of why she was so desperate for it, well . . . it doesn't matter." I patted Ronan's stomach. "She's on the Ronan Thatcher scholarship program from here on out."

Ronan chuckled. "Mark my words. That kid is going to get her law degree and come work for me."

If she wanted to be a lawyer, he'd do everything in his power to make that happen. Including pay for her education.

She'd been over for dinner a few nights ago. We'd tried to keep her close, especially on the nights when she wasn't visiting her brothers.

While Ronan had grilled burgers, Ember had been fretting over one of those scholarship applications, and when he'd told her to chill, that he'd pay for her college, she'd had another emotional breakdown.

He'd led her to a patio chair and simply sat with an arm around her shoulder while she'd cried.

"It's just not fair," Kerrigan said. "No teenager should have that much to worry about."

"Agreed." I blew out a long breath, my gaze going to Ember's desk again.

The guilt was real. Maybe someday it would go away. Maybe someday I wouldn't feel awful for having a child in my classroom for three months who'd been going through hell at home while I'd missed it entirely.

"Hey." Ronan hooked his thumb under my chin to turn my gaze. "It's not on you, babe."

Maybe someday I'd believe him. "I need to go get Wren."

"I'm going to head downtown and pick up Ember. Take her to the house. Then I'll be over."

"Okay." I let him go. "What time does your brother get in tomorrow?"

He glanced at the clock on the wall above a whiteboard. "Their flight gets into Bozeman about nine tonight. I think they're planning on getting up early tomorrow and driving here around ten. With Ember moving in, I snagged them a couple of rooms at the motel."

"They could stay with us."

"Nah." He shook his head. "I like nights with you all to myself."

"No argument."

I'd take the nights. But he'd earned a fun weekend. They planned to go fishing and take a local hike. Probably explore Calamity some too.

"I'd better get out of here." Kerrigan came over for a hug. "Want to do something this weekend since he's busy?"

"Definitely. Call me."

"Bye." She waved, then headed for the door.

"I'd better go too." Ronan hauled me close for a kiss. He swirled his tongue against mine and his hands roved down my back, disappearing into the back pockets of my jeans to squeeze my ass.

I was breathless by the time he tore his lips away. "Tease."

He chuckled. "That was probably indecent for school."

"That was PG. You should see how the kids grope each other at their lockers." I grimaced. Just this morning I'd witnessed a sloppy attempt at a French kiss by two freshmen. "See you at home?"

Those hazel eyes softened. "Yeah, mama. I'll see you at home."

Mama. I swooned. Every time.

I was so in love with this man.

As Ronan left the classroom, I hurried to collect my things, then left the school to pick up Wren. We'd just parked in the garage when Ronan came driving in with his Corvette, Ember riding shotgun.

"Ro!" Wren took off across the lawn when she spotted the Stingray.

I smiled, keeping pace behind her as she raced for her Ro.

He unfolded from the car, not bothering to close the door as he rushed to meet her. "Hey, firefly."

With a sweep, she was up and tossed in the air, giggling as he caught her. "How was daycare?"

"She had a good day," I said. Behind him, Ember climbed out of the car. "Hi."

Ember lifted a hand, tucking a lock of black hair behind her ear. Then she hauled out her backpack, hefting it onto her shoulders. It was still as full as ever. "Hi, Ms. Hale."

"Larke," I corrected. "When we're here, you can call me Larke."

Ronan set Wren on her feet, then bent to take her hand. "Should we go inside?"

Ember nodded, falling into line behind Ronan and Wren

while I took up the rear, closing the Corvette's door before joining them inside the house. While Ronan did a quick tour, showing her around the kitchen and living room, Ember never once dropped the backpack.

"This is your room." Ronan opened the door to the guest bedroom on the first floor, waving her inside.

She walked in, seeing all of her stuff in a corner.

"I brought your brothers' stuff too. What was left. It's down the hall in another bedroom so they can have it when they come to visit."

Ember stared at the bed and its plush green comforter. Her feet stayed rooted in the center of the room and her hands were holding the straps of that backpack so tight that her knuckles were white.

Ronan glanced over, concern etched on his handsome face.

"It's okay," I mouthed.

There'd been a lot of change in Ember's life these past two weeks. It would overwhelm any person, let alone a teenager.

"We'll give you a minute," I said, bending to pick up Wren.

But before we could disappear from the bedroom, Ember blew out a shaky breath. And her hands on that backpack loosened.

Slowly, strap by strap, she took it off her shoulders. Then it dropped to the floor.

She looked at it, like she wasn't sure she could leave it behind. That first step she took seemed painful and stiff. The second wasn't much better. Then the third came and her entire body relaxed. A smile transformed her face.

"Hungry, kid?" Ronan asked.

"Not really," Ember said. "Gertrude made me eat trail mix at the office and two cookies."

He chuckled. "Okay. We're having pizza for dinner at Larke's."

"I can go home if—"

"This is home." He cut her off. "For now, this is home. Got me?"

Her green eyes flooded but she held back the tears as she nodded. "Got you."

"Good." He threw an arm around her shoulders for a sideways hug just as his phone rang in his pocket. He dug it out, then held up a finger. "One minute."

"We'll go over and order pizza," I said, nodding for Ember to follow.

But we'd only gotten to the garage before Ronan caught up. "We're having company for dinner."

"Who?" Was his brother here early?

Ronan didn't need to answer my question.

Car doors slammed in the driveway as Ember's brothers poured out of a sedan.

"Ember!" They raced for her as she ran toward them, the three of them colliding in the center of the driveway.

Wren squirmed, so I set her down to chase the excitement.

Ronan's arms wrapped around me as his chest pressed against my back. "Love you, mama."

Said so casually, so effortlessly, it was like he'd been saying it from the beginning.

That was why it was so special. No elaborate declaration. No hesitation. Just . . . truth. Raw. Real.

"Love you, Ronan."

He leaned down to kiss my temple. "I knew eventually you'd find me irresistible."

"Your ego." I rolled my eyes.

He wasn't wrong.

———

THE SOUND of laughing children echoed from outside. I finished putting away the last of Wren's laundry, then glanced out the window to see Ember and her brothers playing with sidewalk chalk in Ronan's driveway. The garage was open behind them.

The twins had come over again this morning to spend the day with their sister. The sidewalk chalk had been my idea, something Wren was too young to enjoy, so I'd taken it over along with some water balloons for later.

A pair of sinewed arms snaked around my waist. Ronan dropped his chin to my shoulder, staring out the glass, both of us watching for a few minutes.

"Where's Wren?" I asked.

"Who's Wren?"

I scoffed, elbowing him in the ribs.

He chuckled. "She's playing in the living room. I gave her some razor blades to toss around."

"Funny," I deadpanned.

Not two seconds later, a pair of tiny footsteps came rushing down the hallway. "Mama."

Ronan let me go so I could pick up Wren and let her show me the spoon she'd been carrying around since breakfast.

"Spoon," I said.

"Poon."

"Close enough." I kissed her cheek as a car pulled up to Ronan's curb.

Ronan put his hand on my shoulder, grinning toward the window. "Noah and Bobbie are here."

A Tahoe was parking at the mouth of the driveway.

Ember and her brothers watched as two men climbed out, both waving before they glanced around the cul-de-sac, taking it all in. They were both smiling, oblivious to the fact that my heart had stopped beating.

No.

Ronan said something but the blood rushing in my ears was too loud to hear him.

This wasn't happening.

Wren squirmed, but I couldn't move. I didn't breathe. I just stared at the man standing in Ronan's driveway.

This couldn't be real. This wasn't real. I was still asleep, safe in my bed in Ronan's arms. This was just a bad dream. I'd wake up and he'd go away.

"Larke." Ronan shook my shoulder, yanking me out of my head.

My arms started to shake. Wren cried because I was holding her too tight, but I couldn't get my muscles to relax.

"Babe, you're scaring me." He tried to take Wren, but I shook my head, keeping her clutched against my chest.

This was real, wasn't it? This was happening.

Tears flooded my eyes. *No.*

Why? Why now, when everything was going so well? Why, when I'd just found Ronan?

Ronan shifted, standing in front of me. He blocked out

the driveway as his hands came to my face, forcing my gaze to his. "Talk to me, Larke."

I opened my mouth, but nothing came out. So I faced Wren. My beautiful girl. *My* daughter.

We were supposed to have more time. We were supposed to have years before having to deal with this.

He was supposed to be gone.

But if he was Ronan's . . .

Oh, God. The world turned upside down.

He'd see Wren. He'd see how perfect she was, and he'd want her. He couldn't have her.

"Larke." Ronan shook me again, just enough to make the first tear fall.

I squeezed my eyes shut, forcing myself to inhale. Then I opened my eyes and since I still couldn't figure out what to say, I looked to Wren. Then out the window.

To the man in Ronan's driveway.

He followed my gaze, taking a moment. Then his hands fell to his sides as he put it together. "Hawaii."

I nodded.

Wren's father was in Calamity.

CHAPTER TWENTY-FOUR

RONAN

WHAT THE ACTUAL fuck was happening? How? Why?

My head was spinning as I walked out of Wren's bedroom, heading down the hallway.

Larke hadn't needed to explain. There was only one reason she'd look like she'd seen a ghost.

Wren's father.

Fuck. I rubbed a hand over my face, trying to make sense of this. Why hadn't I asked more questions? Why hadn't I gotten his fucking name?

I moved on autopilot, my feet leading the way out of the house and across the yard to my driveway.

Noah and Bobbie were standing beside their SUV rental. When Noah spotted me, he walked over, his arms open for a hug. They fell to his sides when he took in my face.

"Hi. Sorry. I thought this was your place." He pointed toward my house. His brown eyes, the same color as Dad's, studied my face. "You okay?"

No. No, I was not fucking okay.

"Yeah." My voice sounded hoarse. "That is my place. I was just at La—the neighbor's. Had a headache and ran out of Advil."

"Oh." He stared at me, then Larke's house, probably sensing the lie.

"Hey, there he is." Bobbie appeared at my side, pulling me in for a hug and a back slap. "How's it going, Thatch?"

My stomach churned, breakfast about to make a reappearance. "Hey. How was the trip?"

"Good." Bobbie grinned. "It's good to be here. Forgot how much I like Montana. And Bozeman was fun last night."

Noah smirked, ducking his chin. "College towns always have the hottest women."

Yep, I was going to puke.

"Who's that?" Noah nodded to where Ember and the twins were watching us talk. "Mom said you've been dating someone. A little young, don't you think?"

"That's Ember." My teeth gritted together so hard my molars cracked. "She's a client."

"A client?" Bobbie gave me a sideways glance. "How old is she? What case?"

"It doesn't matter." I waved it off. "Look, why don't we head downtown. Tour around or something."

Anything to get them out of this cul-de-sac until I could figure out what the hell I was going to do.

Noah shrugged. "Fine by me. Later, I want to take the Stingray out."

"Sure." I nodded.

He'd always loved that car. If he was upset that Dad had given it to me instead of him, he hadn't let it show.

"Why don't we take my truck? I'll drive." Without another word, I headed for the garage. Adrenaline fueled my every move. My hands were shaking. My heart pounded. I went to the hook beside the door that led inside, snagging my keys. Then I got in my truck, waiting for them to climb inside.

"Too bad the Stingray only has two seats," Bobbie said, hopping in the back. "Forgot how much I loved that car."

I hummed, not sure what to say.

"Your dad could have made a pretty penny on it. I offered to buy it from him, twice. But he was always set on giving it to you."

I forced a smile, swallowing the panic in my throat as Noah got in the passenger side. While they were buckling their seat belts, I backed out of the driveway, glancing over at Larke's.

She was standing in the window of Wren's bedroom, holding her daughter close. How long had it been since I'd been standing beside her? Two minutes? Three? It felt like a lifetime.

It felt like I was about to lose them.

No, fuck that. They were mine. I was going to figure this out. I was going to fix this. Somehow.

An idea popped into my head. It was a long shot. But I didn't have a lot of other options. Maybe, if I had just a little bit of luck left, it would work.

Please, let this work.

I tore my eyes away, lifting a hand to wave at Ember. Then I left them in my rearview mirror.

"Still feel like hiking today?" Noah asked.

"Not really."

"Oh." He studied my profile as I drove toward First. "Headache?"

More like heartache. But if I had to lose someone, it wasn't going to be Larke. "Something like that."

Bobbie and Noah talked, to me, to each other, but I focused on driving downtown and parking in front of Thatcher Law.

"Nice office," Noah said, hopping out of the truck and taking in the surrounding area. "I forgot how much I liked Calamity. How's it been living here?"

"Good." Better than good. Calamity was home, not because of the town, but because of Larke and Wren.

Bobbie did the same inspection of First, then came close, smacking me on the back. "Good to see you."

"You've been pretty scarce since you moved here," Noah said.

"It's been busy." There was a reason I hadn't called either of them often. Two reasons actually, both with the last name Hale.

If I could get through today, sooner rather than later, I'd make it so their last name was Thatcher.

Let this work. God, let this work.

My hand was shaking, making it hard to get the key into the front door's lock. I fumbled it twice until it finally slid into the slot so I could turn it open. Then I stepped inside, tossing an arm out to the sitting area.

"I, uh . . . I need to print something out."

"Always working," Noah teased. "I see that hasn't changed."

"We'll take the self-guided tour," Bobbie said as I disappeared into my office, dragging in a breath. My ribs felt too tight, but I sucked in a breath, sitting and shaking my mouse.

I listened while Noah and Bobbie wandered around, poking their heads into each space. My knees bounced so fast the vibration shook the desk, but I kept clicking and typing, working furiously to draw up a quick document.

The moment the printer spit out the page, I whipped it free and stood, joining my brother and friend in the waiting area.

"I need to talk to you about something." I jerked my chin for them to follow me down the hallway to the conference room.

They shared a look but kept quiet, following me into the room, where I flipped on the lights and took a seat at the head of the table. The page in front of me was turned upside down.

"What's going on, Ronan?" Noah asked. "You're acting strange. The last time you were like this was after Cora stabbed you. Is this about her? Have you heard from her?"

"No." I swallowed the lump in my throat, my eyes glued to the table.

How did I say this? Before a trial, I'd spend hours rehearsing the words in my mind. I'd practice asking questions, figure out how to state them so opposing counsel wouldn't object.

But this, everything was riding on this, and I had no idea what to say.

"There's, uh . . . there's no easy way to do this."

Bobbie sighed, raking a hand through his brown hair. "Fuck. You know, don't you?"

I narrowed my gaze on his face. Know what?

He couldn't know I was with Larke. I quickly replayed the few phone conversations we'd had in the past month and I couldn't recall having mentioned her name. So what was he talking about?

"Shit, I'm sorry." His shoulders slumped. "It was a stupid mistake, and I know I should have come clean a long time ago."

"Come clean about what?" Noah asked, looking between the two of us.

"I slept with her." Bobbie's confession spewed on an exhale.

Noah blinked. "Who?"

"Cora," I said. This wasn't about Larke. It was about Cora.

Bobbie closed his eyes and nodded. "It was just once. About a year after you guys divorced. She called me. Wanted to talk. We had a few drinks and then I took her home."

No apology. Not that I'd needed one. What had happened with Cora was in the past. And what I'd felt for her was nothing compared to how I loved Larke.

This wasn't about Cora. She was in the past. Today I was fighting for my future.

So I shifted my attention.

To my brother.

"I hope you can understand what I'm about to say."

Noah sat up straighter.

"I'm in love with a woman. She has a daughter."

"Okay," he drawled.

"I want them. As my own. Which means you're going to sign this." I flipped over the document.

And slid it to Bobbie.

———

"WELL, THAT WAS QUITE THE MORNING." Noah stood by my side in the driveway, watching as the Stingray's taillights disappeared around a corner.

"It's done." I breathed, a full breath, for the first time in an hour.

The conversation with Bobbie had gone fairly quickly.

Bobbie didn't take many vacations. He was wholly dedicated to work, missing as few days as possible in a calendar year. He took time off for our annual fishing trip to Montana, but otherwise, he stayed close to the office.

The exception? A trip to Hawaii a couple years ago.

I'd planned to go with him but at the last minute had canceled because of my own work conflict.

Bobbie was a great attorney. A good, loyal friend—though I was rethinking his loyalty if he'd had sex with Cora. Not that I'd been entirely surprised. Bobbie used women for sex. Not once had I seen him with a girlfriend. Not once had he mentioned marriage or children. When it came to commitment, he was flippant at best. Hell, just last year he'd gone in for a vasectomy.

Maybe Larke's phone call had been the catalyst.

When I'd confronted him about her, he'd balked at first, pretending like I was full of shit. Then I'd told him the story Larke had shared, how they'd met and hooked up a few times on vacation. Just the thought of them together made my skin crawl, but I'd shoved past it, doing what needed to be done.

I'd handed Bobbie a pen and told him to sign on the last page.

And in exchange, Robert Carter, a man I'd known for over a decade, a man who hadn't even wanted to admit he'd fathered the most precious little girl in the world, drove out of my life with my father's beloved Corvette.

I'd lost a friend today. In a matter of minutes, my oldest friend was nothing more than a memory. Bobbie was another blind spot, a person with faults I'd overlooked. Hopefully, in time, that wouldn't sting so much.

Hopefully, in time, it wouldn't hurt to know I'd given away Dad's car.

"He always loved the Stingray." Noah shook his head.

"I'm sorry. I know that was Dad's. It was special. But—"

"Don't apologize." Noah put his hand on my shoulder. "You must really love her to give up that car."

"Them. I love them." So much that I'd traded the Corvette for Larke. And for a daughter.

After we'd left the office, I'd texted Larke and told her to keep Wren inside while we'd returned to the cul-de-sac to collect Bobbie's things and hand over the car. I hadn't wanted to risk him seeing Wren. Him melting for her sweet face. Him feeling any sort of attachment.

Because she was mine.

"How pissed is Dad going to be?" I asked Noah.

Before he could answer, a little voice carried through the air. "Ro!"

I turned away from the street as Wren walked across the

grass with an applesauce pouch in one hand. Her hair was up in pigtails, and she was wearing her yellow Crocs.

Noah chuckled. "I think Dad will take one look at her and not give a damn about that car."

"Yeah." I sighed. "I think so too."

The stress from this morning evaporated as Wren walked my way, glancing over her shoulder as her mother emerged from the house.

Larke's face was just as pale and full of worry as it had been earlier. She looked down the street, like she was checking that Bobbie wasn't coming back.

He wasn't. He couldn't have gotten out of here fast enough.

It was done.

"Come meet them." I jerked my chin to Noah, grateful he'd been here today. Grateful he'd decided to stay this weekend.

Wren reached us first, launching herself at me when she was two feet away, knowing I'd catch her.

I swung her up, setting her on an arm, then nodded to my brother. "Firefly, this is Uncle Noah. Can you say hi?"

She ducked her face, hiding it in the crook of my neck.

He grinned as Larke walked over, holding out a hand. "Hey, I'm Noah."

"Hi." Her smile didn't reach her eyes. "I'm Larke."

"Let's go inside, mama. Talk."

She nodded, looking like she was about to cry. So I hauled her into my free side, kissing her hair. "He's gone."

"Are you sure?"

"Reach into my back pocket."

She obeyed, fishing out the copy of the document I'd

made before leaving the office. The original would be going to the courthouse first thing Monday morning.

Quickly unfolding it, she scanned the first page, then the next, her jaw dropping when she got to the end. "He told me his name was Carter."

"Last name."

She flipped to the first page, reading it all over again. "It's really over?"

"No." I hauled her close. "It's just the beginning."

It had started the day I'd spotted her walking down a Calamity sidewalk.

Love at first sight? Nah.

Well, maybe.

EPILOGUE

RONAN

SEVEN YEARS LATER...

"Friday. Four o'clock." I took a seat on the couch in the waiting area at the office, kicking an ankle over my knee and spreading my arms across the back.

"What happens on Friday at four o'clock?" Ember asked.

"Happy hour," Gertrude answered, standing from her chair. "I'll get drinks. What do you guys want?"

"I'll take a beer. Thanks, Gerty."

"No problem. Ember?"

"Um . . . I guess I'll have a beer too."

Gertrude nodded, then disappeared to the break room, returning with three bottles from the brewery. She took her usual seat, behind her desk, while Ember sat in the chair across from the couch.

"So? What did you think of your first day?" I asked Ember.

"I liked it." She smiled, glancing toward the window. "It feels good to be home."

After four years of undergrad in Bozeman, then three at law school in Missoula, Ember was back in Calamity and working at Thatcher Law.

We'd met with three clients today. Ember had mostly observed, but based on the questions she'd asked afterward, I had no doubt that she'd take to working here like a fish to water.

She was smart and hard working. She'd sailed through college with nearly perfect grades, and though she could have gone Ivy League for law school, she'd chosen to stay in Montana to be close to her brothers.

Eric and Elijah would be starting their sophomore year in high school this coming fall. Both were active in sports and clubs. They'd opted to stay with their foster parents until they graduated, but even while she'd been away, Ember had been a constant presence. A big sister.

And I couldn't be prouder of the woman she'd become.

Not only was she a role model to her brothers, but she was one to my girls too.

Larke and I had paid for Ember's education on one condition, that whenever she came home to Calamity, she swung by the house to say hello. She would have done it anyway. Most of her visits, she'd stayed with us, not wanting to crowd her brothers and their foster parents. We had the space for it.

Not long after Ember had gone away to start school, I'd moved in with Larke. We'd sold the other house on the cul-de-sac, and the family who lived there now had two girls, like us. Their oldest was Wren's best friend.

"What's your plan for the weekend?" Gertrude asked Ember.

"Unpack." She sighed. "I'm sick of living out of boxes."

"It's been less than a week, kid. Give yourself some grace."

She'd just moved into a studio apartment on First. It was one of Kerrigan's properties, with a great view of downtown. She'd be in the thick of Calamity and close to work.

"Do you think you'll always call me 'kid'?" Ember smirked as she took a sip of her beer, punctuating her question.

"Yep." I grinned, taking my own drink, just as a swish of chestnut hair caught my eye. The front door blew open.

"Daddy!" Wren bolted across the waiting room, launching herself at me before I could stand.

"Hey, firefly." I kissed her cheek, setting my beer aside. "How was your swimming lesson?"

"I jumped off the diving board all by myself." She smiled, those brown eyes sparkling.

"Good job." I held out my hand for a fist bump as Larke stepped inside with Layla.

"Hi, Daddy!" Like her older sister, Layla came running, barreling into my lap. I managed to shift Wren and catch Layla before she could knee me in the groin.

"Hi, peanut. Did you have fun with Mommy today?"

"Yep." She took my face in her hands, squeezing my cheeks together until my lips were smooshed.

Wren had started doing that when she was little and now Layla did it too. With my cheeks still in her hands, she rubbed her nose against mine, back and forth, up and down.

Layla was five and starting kindergarten in the fall. Every day she seemed to change, but the Eskimo kisses had been her thing since she was two.

"Hi, babe." Larke walked over, bending between the girls to give me a kiss.

"Hey, mama. How was your day?"

"Busy but fun." Larke loved her summer vacations with the girls. She packed each day with fun activities, wanting to soak up the time with our daughters before they were off doing their own thing.

This morning, they'd gone to the library before having lunch at her mom's house. Then it was off to swimming lessons before coming downtown. We'd hang out for a bit before meeting Kerrigan, Pierce and their kids for dinner at the brewery.

Life was busy, but it was a different kind of hectic than I'd had in California. A better kind.

The summer after we'd met, Larke and I had gotten married in a quiet ceremony in our backyard. She hadn't wanted the fanfare and, well, I'd already had the elaborate wedding. The only thing that had mattered to me was making her my wife.

Shortly after, I'd adopted Wren, and within months, Larke had gotten pregnant with Layla.

"So? How was the first day?" Larke stole my beer from the end table, giving Gertrude a quick hug before she went to Ember for the same. Then she sank down in the other chair.

"Good." Ember smiled. "Really good."

"She'll be running circles around me in no time," I said.

We'd had a busy few years at Thatcher Law. Ember's graduation from law school couldn't have come at a better time. Between Gertrude and me, we struggled to keep up and were looking forward to having some help.

Sooner rather than later, I'd have to find a bigger office. Ember was using the conference room for the time being, but she'd need something permanent. I might even need space for another attorney.

When my parents and Noah had come up last month to visit, my brother had hinted that he was growing tired of California. If Noah wanted to make his own *big* change, he'd have a spot here.

None of us had heard from Bobbie again after the day he'd driven away in Dad's Corvette. And my dad, as expected, had taken one look at Wren and told me he was proud that I'd made the right choice.

"Do you girls want a juice?" Gertrude asked, already standing from her chair.

Wren and Layla shot off my lap, chasing after Gerty to the break room. No doubt she'd sneak them cookies.

"Do you want to come over for dinner tomorrow?" Larke asked Ember.

"Sure. Can I bring something?"

"Just yourself."

Flowers. Ember would bring flowers.

She always brought Larke flowers when she came to visit. Even in the beginning, when she'd been a broke freshman in college, she'd come to the house with that old backpack in one hand and a bundle of carnations from the grocery store in the other.

Ember admired me.

But she loved Larke.

During her junior year of college, she'd come home for Christmas, staying with us for the holiday. One early morning, the two of us had congregated at the coffee pot while the rest of the house had been asleep. We'd talked about her brothers. We'd talked about school. And she'd told me that she'd framed the paper she'd written in Larke's class. That C plus had been hanging on her apartment wall.

Larke gave me credit for saving Ember.

But Ember gave that credit to Larke.

That C plus had saved her life. That C plus had given her a future. Her brothers too.

We'd learned a lot about Ember's past in the years that had followed the lawsuit. Ashley Scott had been a shit mother from the start. Ember hadn't known better at the time. I liked to think Larke had shown her how a real mother operated.

Ember wasn't sure who her father was. Ashley hadn't mentioned his name. But Ember remembered the man who'd fathered the twins. He'd been a loser—Ember's word—and the minute Ashley had told him she was pregnant, he'd ghosted them all.

Ashley had bounced her children around from town to town, mostly through the Midwest. She'd struggled to keep a job and every time she'd gotten fired, she'd packed up the kids and moved. Calamity had been Ashley's idea of an adventure.

Through it all, Ember had been the primary caregiver for the boys. While Ashley would flitter around, spending what little money they had at the bar or on her nails, Ember would be home with Eric and Elijah.

Until Ashley had had enough and left on Ember's birthday.

Bitch.

About a year after she'd abandoned them, the authorities

had arrested Ashley in New Mexico. She'd gotten pulled over for driving under the influence, and coupled with an outstanding warrant, she'd gotten her ass hauled into custody.

I hoped that the three months she'd spent in a county jail cell for child endangerment had taught her a lesson, but I wasn't holding my breath. Ashley hadn't set foot in Calamity again, and as long as it stayed that way, I did my best not to give her much thought.

"Oh, is that Mr. Abbott?" Ember sat straighter, pointing out the window as Wilder Abbott walked by.

"Asshole," I muttered.

"Ronan." Larke shot me a frown. "Be nice."

"Nope."

She rolled those beautiful eyes, shaking her head before she said, "I love you."

"Love you too." For Larke, I'd hold a grudge for eternity.

Wilder Abbott had been a prick to Larke, even if it had been years ago and the two worked peacefully alongside each other these days. I didn't give a shit how polite he was now. Every time I was at a school function, I made sure to cast him a glare.

Larke had changed her mind about teaching high school and when the principal had begged her to stay permanently, she'd agreed. That first year had been the hardest, but for Ember, she hadn't regretted a minute.

Ember wasn't the only person grateful for that C plus.

The girls came skipping back to the waiting room, each with a popsicle. Gertrude had a smile on her face as she gave me a beer to replace the one my wife was currently drinking.

We settled into easy conversation, laughing and chatting as people passed by the window.

I was just about to suggest we head for the brewery when a man, probably late twenties with short, brown hair, walked by outside.

Ember's eyes widened. She sat up straighter.

"Do you know him?" Larke asked.

"No. Who is he?"

Larke shook her head. "I don't know. Gerty?"

"No clue."

Ember's eyes tracked his every step. Her cheeks flushed. "He's cute."

Cute? I wasn't ready for this, not yet. A sour taste spread through my mouth. It was the same taste I got whenever I thought about the girls having boyfriends someday.

"Go talk to him," Gerty said.

"No, that would be weird." Ember's shoulders fell when he disappeared from view.

Hell. I shifted, digging into my pocket for my money clip.

And handed her a twenty-dollar bill.

———

The Calamity Montana series continues with *The Brood*.

THE BROOD

The last thing Wilder Abbott needs is a houseguest. Solitude has been his stoic companion for nearly a decade. He prefers to brood over his mistakes in seclusion. Besides, he gets enough social interaction as a high school science teacher in Calamity, Montana.

But when his oldest friend calls, begging for a favor, Wilder begrudgingly agrees. For the next two months, he'll give up his guest room to his friend's little sister.

Iris Monroe isn't the girl Wilder remembers. Gone is the shy, quiet mouse ten years his junior who always had her nose in a book. Grown-up Iris talks too much and asks too many questions, especially about his past. And her bright smile and clear blue eyes are hard to ignore.

Two months. He just has to survive two months. Except Iris is as nosy as she is beautiful. And his secrets prove hard to hide when she's living under his roof.

ACKNOWLEDGMENTS

Thank you for reading *The Brawl*! This book came to be all because of its blurb.

The bane of my existence is writing book blurbs. I will spend an entire day agonizing over 150 words. But it's always the first step in my process. Before anything else, I write the blurb. So I sat down one day to write said blurb and spent a solid hour staring at a blank Word document. I knew it was going to be a single parent romance. Obviously we've got a small town. But beyond that? Nothing. My brain shut off. And what do I do when I get stuck? Spend hours wasting my time on Instagram and TikTok. So I turned to the internet to help me avoid blurb writing and randomly started researching odd lawsuits. That's when I stumbled on an article about a student who was suing his teacher over a bad grade. Boom. Inspiration. Off I scrambled to write my blurb. That's how the premise for this book was born.

A huge thank you to my amazing team for all the work they do on each of my books. My editing and proofreading team: Elizabeth Nover, Julie Deaton and Judy Zweifel. My cover designer: Sarah Hansen. To my publicist Nina and agent Kimberly, thanks for all you do!

Thank you to all the influencers and readers who take the time to read and post about my books. I am forever grateful for your support. And thank you to my friends and family. I am so very blessed.

ABOUT THE AUTHOR

Devney Perry is a *Wall Street Journal* and *USA Today* bestselling author of over forty romance novels. After working in the technology industry for a decade, she abandoned conference calls and project schedules to pursue her passion for writing. She was born and raised in Montana and now lives in Washington with her husband and two sons.

Don't miss out on the latest book news.
Subscribe to her newsletter!
www.devneyperry.com

Printed in the USA
CPSIA information can be obtained
at www.ICGtesting.com
LVHW090326120923
757848LV00037B/624